Humble Fumble

stories

Libby Belle

Pure Luck
Press

Humble Fumble
Stories by Libby Belle

Published by Pure Luck Press
LibbyBelle.com
Austin, Texas

ISBN02: 978-0-9985165-3-0 (eBook)
ISBN: 978-0-9985165-2-3 (print)
Printed in the United States of America

Library of Congress Registration Number:
TXu 1-889-816, TXu 1-805-949 and TXu 2-092-284

This book is a work of fiction. Names, characters, places, and incidents
either are products of the author's imagination or are used fictitiously. Any
resemblance to actual events or locales or persons, living or dead, aliens or
zombies included, is entirely coincidental. She apologizes in advance.

*To Betty White
and all the Golden Girls of the world*

CONTENTS

Energy is like a boomerang
Whatever you put out there
comes right back to you

—Asiya Javed,
Better Than Seven Sons

The secret to enjoying these stories is to release the kite string to your wonderful imagination. It wants to fly untethered. Let it go!

Within these pages, you will meet all kinds of people including a muse, a Bible salesman, a pervert, and a couple of dogs who somehow get caught up in strange, zany, and unpredictable situations. Even though this is fiction, their struggles are real, and things can get a bit dicey. But don't worry, I rarely send you out there without a parachute.

Although they will make you cry, laugh, angry, sad, and sometimes a bit irritated, please be kind to my characters. You may find there's a little bit of all of us in them.

If you enjoy exploring Libby Belle's world of fiction, there's nothing sweeter than hearing from you by email or through a kind review online.

Fly high, my friends!

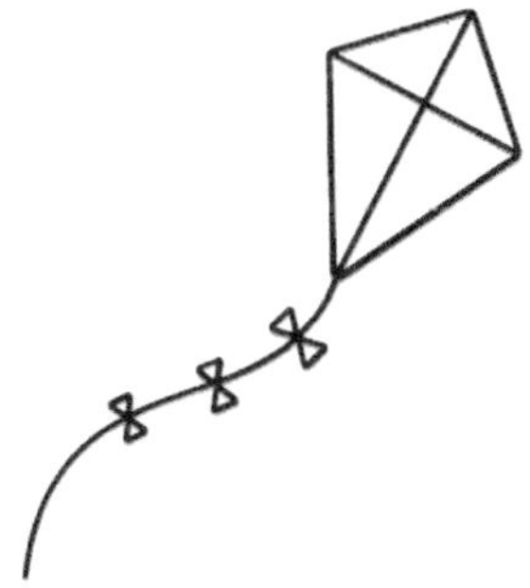

Libby Belle

GO HOME, MEL!

It is well known that by the third day, visitors, like fish, start to stink. And it's also been known that it usually takes three good flushes to finally get your child's dead goldfish down the toilet. So it was with Mel.

Marion stood on aisle three of the Piggly Wiggly tapping her foot to the music overhead while casually studying the label on a jar of Hollandaise sauce. Now an empty nester, she found herself lingering in places she used to blindly rush through.

James, Marion's husband of twenty-one years, and the father of their twins – a college mishap that turned out to be twice the blessing – was in Tokyo on a two-week business trip. Marion elected to stay home, having no interest in wading through thirty million short people, or the dreadfully long plane ride it took to get there. The day before James left, their fourteen-year-old Golden Retriever was found dead in the laundry room. And since the girls left for college, no longer buzzing around the house making lively noises, Tweety, their parakeet, stopped whistling. So, when Marion entered the house, arms full of groceries, the eerie silence made her shiver. This was not only a new sensation, but a strange one. One that she was told in time she'd learn to appreciate. She turned on the radio while she unpacked the bags, hoping Tweety would sing along with the music.

The sun was setting outside the kitchen window, and it was comforting watching it slowly move behind the trees in her suburban backyard. It felt as if her worries had decided to take a nap. She poured herself a glass of wine and stood at the sink thinking about the wonderful meal she was about to prepare for only one. Accustomed to buying groceries for a family of four, she looked back over her shoulder at the excessive items covering the countertop and let out a soft chuckle.

Just when the sun disappeared, a man's head popped up from below the window. Marion jumped back so quickly, she nearly dropped the wine glass, and her sudden movement and shrill yelp startled the parakeet, causing it to beat itself against the metal cage in a futile attempt to fly away.

The man tapped wildly on the window. "Marion, Marion, it's me, Mel, your neighbor! Can I come in for a minute?" he yelled, offering his biggest grin with the request.

"Oh, dear God, Mel!" Marion inhaled deeply, followed by a sigh of relief. "You scared the bejesus out of me! Of course, come in." Patting her chest, she said something soothing to Tweety as she passed the poor, trembling creature to unlock the back door.

When she opened it, Mel wasn't there. "Mel, come on

in," she said, leaning out in the direction of the kitchen window.

"I'm over here," Mel whispered hoarsely from behind the thick lilac bush. "Is anyone home at your house?"

"No, just me. Why? What's wrong?" Marion asked, feeling strange talking to a plant. "Come on in, silly. What are you doing in the bushes?" she chuckled through the question.

Stepping back so that Mel could enter, he dashed wildly past her, knocking the glass of wine out of her hand.

"What the…!" she shrieked, gawking at the broken pieces of glass and the wine splashes on her jeans. When she looked over at Mel for an explanation or even an apology, there he stood naked as a jaybird, holding his hands over his crotch, and looking like a scared child.

"MEL!" she bellowed, quickly turning away. "Why are you naked!?"

"Please close the door, Marion. I can explain. I know this is weird, but I have a good excuse."

"I certainly hope so." Grumbling, she slammed the door. "Is your house on fire, should I call the police? Where's your wife?" The questions blurted rapidly from the side of her mouth as she stood uncomfortably talking to the wall.

"No, no, no, no," Mel objected, emphatically shaking his head, but keeping his hands cupped in place. "Nothing bad like that. There's no emergency, I promise!"

"Alright, then, just stay where you are," Marion ordered, pressing her palm in the air, averting her eyes from the embarrassing scene. "I'll get you a robe."

While Marion went upstairs, Mel grabbed a roll of paper towels and began picking up the broken glass and wiping up the spilled wine. He then wrapped his lower extremity in the towels and sat down, nervously slapping his beefy thighs together.

"Here!" Marion held out her fluffy white cotton bathrobe. She couldn't help but laugh when she peeked through her fingers and saw her neighbor wrapped in paper towels, cowering in her kitchen. "This better be good, Mel. I don't know too many people who would have let you in like this," she lightly scolded, turning her back again to the panicky neighbor.

"I don't know too many either, Marion. That's why I came here. You're one of the nicest people on the block, and I guess I thought you'd be the most sympathetic."

"Depends," she groaned, slowly turning around to face him.

"I cleaned up the mess. See?" He pointed to the floor, his fake grin expecting praise.

"Thank you. Glad it was only white wine."

"I could use a glass myself. Something to calm my nerves would be great," he said, as he straddled the barstool, repositioning his genitals with one hand while the other hand anxiously drummed on the countertop in anticipation.

"Alright, don't keep me in suspense." Marion poured them both a fresh glass. "What in the world happened?"

Mel sighed after first taking a long swallow. "I made a mistake. Let me make that clear. But before I tell you, will you promise not to judge me harshly?"

"Hmmm," Marion paused and leaned in, looking for a sign of malice in his eyes. None there, just a poor attempt at trying to appear remorseful, she thought. "I'll try not to judge, unless you're going to tell me you hurt someone, then that's a different story."

"Well, not physically…I mean, I haven't knocked any teeth out or killed anyone if that's what you mean. Let me just get this over with. And remember, this is the seventies. It's not like this sort of thing doesn't happen these days."

Marion looked sideways at Mel's cheesy smile and frowned. Avoiding her scolding eyes, he pointed at the groceries spread out before him on the olive-green vinyl countertop. "Yum, that all looks so good. Do you have enough for me? I'm starving."

"Don't push your luck, Mel," Marion chided, reaching for a knife to cut the piece of fish in half. "Hope you like flounder," she said resignedly, yet somehow oddly pleased to have a dinner companion – even if it was her quirky, naked neighbor. "Now, quit stalling, and tell me what happened."

"Well, OK. Here it is in a nutshell." He gulped down the wine as if it were a glass of water. "Liquid courage," he announced. "So, you see, Deborah's been traveling a lot ever since she went back to work as a stewardess, and I've been on the road a lot with my business. We haven't really seen much of each other lately, and I guess we've grown kind of distant." Mel frowned at his empty glass and handing it to Marion, he pleaded with his eyes for a refill.

"Don't tell me you're getting a divorce," she sighed, avoiding the pathetic look on his face. Having more than once seen him drunk at the community picnics, she handed him a glass of water instead. "Haven't you been married something like fifteen years now?"

"Just about, and no talk of a divorce, yet."

"Well, that's good. Get on with the story," Marion urged.

"You know Cynthia, our neighbor at the end of the street, don't you?"

"Well, I don't know her, know her. I mean, I've said hello, and maybe once or twice we've chatted on the sidewalk. What has she got to do with this?"

"Everything. We've been having an affair for several

months now," Mel confessed, throwing his hands up in surrender. "Don't hate me, please don't hate me! It just happened. With Deborah gone most of the time, we haven't had sex in, well, a long time!"

"Oh dear," Marion grimaced, hiding her face in her hands. "I guess it's really not right for me to judge you, so I won't…for now. Tell me the rest, and I'll decide afterwards if you should be pardoned or thrown to the wolves."

"Thanks," he smirked, pulling the robe sash tighter and sitting up taller. "Well, Deborah was supposed to be flying to Mexico out of Houston – a seven-day trip. I told her I was heading to Albuquerque and would be away just as long. That wasn't true. I just wanted her to think I was gone while I stayed at Cynthia's. So, here I am having a great time, when all of a sudden Cynthia and I get into a fight. Seems she wants me to leave Deborah and move in with her. Well, that's just ridiculous! Besides the fact that I don't love Cynthia, moving in with her while my wife lives so close is insane!"

Marion jerked back. "Not any crazier than you having an affair with your neighbor!"

"Yeah, well, anyway," Mel stammered, "it gets worse. So, here I am sitting on the edge of the bed, buck-naked, and Cynthia goes to her closet and comes out with a gun. She points it right at me and then tells me to get out of her house. Well, I pleaded with her to let me at least get dressed, but she wouldn't let me. She forced me outside at gunpoint and locked me out!"

"You're kidding!" Marion jumped up to lock the back door. "The idea of an angry mistress with a gun, and right down the street is just too much! It's weird enough that you're sitting in my kitchen completely nude underneath that robe and making a confession. Why aren't you home?"

"Well now, that's a good question. While I was hiding behind two trashcans, waiting for the sun to go down, guess who drives up unexpectedly?"

"Cynthia's husband?" Marion asked, her eyes widening.

"No, she's been separated from him for a while. He doesn't live there anymore. It was Deborah! She drove right up when I was just about to run to our back porch. I guess she got back early, or who knows. Sometimes flights get cancelled, or she changes shifts with another stewardess. Who knows, but there she was, and here I was trying to figure out what to do next." Mel scratched the top of his bald spot and took the opportunity to smell his armpit.

"So, she's bound to know you're back and not in Albuquerque. Your car is in the garage, right?"

"No, it's not. I left it at the airport. I mean, come on, I'm supposed to be out of town. I couldn't leave my car there just in case she did come home early."

"Oh, good heavens! This is crazy! What are you going to do?"

"Heck, if I know. Got any ideas? I'm listening." Mel, suddenly sounding glib, casually reached over to pour himself some more wine.

Marion quickly rescued it from his clutches. "Well, you could walk on over there right now and tell her the truth."

"Yeah, right!" Mel crossed his arms in defiance. "Is that what you'd do?"

"Hmmm," Marion pondered the question before replying. "Probably not. I mean, well, shoot, I hope I never know the answer to that question."

"Marion, please, I don't have any choice but to stay here tonight, and maybe tomorrow I can figure this out." Mel dropped his head and sniffed loudly, pretending to force back tears. "The keys to the house, to my car, they're in my briefcase in Cynthia's living room. I am up a creek without a paddle."

With a sympathetic sigh, Marion walked around the counter to pat her distraught guest on the shoulder. "Well, James would probably throw you out the door, but I guess he's not here, and I guess, like you said, I'm more sympathetic. Yes, of course you can stay, Mel. This kind of decision requires a bit of soul searching after a good night's sleep."

Mel rested his head on Marion's arm, and she politely, but firmly removed it. "You're not off the hook yet, kiddo."

After dinner, Marion showed Mel the guest room and handed him a new toothbrush, one of her husband's t-shirts, and hesitantly tossed in a pair of boxers. "These probably will be a little tight on you," she said. "I think you're a bit larger than James."

"I appreciate anything. It's kind of warm under this robe."

"Goodnight, Mel." Marion turned to go to her bedroom. "I'll throw you in my prayers tonight."

"I can use all the prayers I can get!" Mel yelled after her. "Oh, and what's for breakfast?"

"Crow!"

Marion stood before the bathroom mirror. "What am I doing?" Although Mel and Deborah lived right next door, they were ten years younger, had no children or pets, except a few wild game heads hung sporadically throughout their home. With little in common, the neighbors managed to keep a respectable distance. Sure, Mel was overweight and obnoxious, and Deborah talked through her nose and nervously tapped her teeth with her brightly painted press-on nails, but Marion's trusting nature would never turn her back on anyone that asked for help. Still, she tiptoed across the carpet and locked the bedroom door.

Morning came quickly, and Marion got up with the birds. For a minute she forgot that Mel was sleeping two doors down until she heard him snoring. She hurried back to the bedroom to change out of her nightgown.

The sky was a thick gray, and Marion could smell the rain in the air on her way outside to get the newspaper. Just as she bent down to retrieve it, a man drove into the driveway to Mel's house. He jumped out of the car easily, grabbed a duffle bag from the back seat, and went straight to the front door without acknowledging Marion and entered the house without knocking first. He was a younger man in jogging shorts and a sweatshirt. Marion shrugged and went back inside to prepare breakfast.

Back in Marion's robe, Mel came downstairs just in time to eat. He sniffed the air and beat on his chest like a gorilla. "Can you believe it? I'm starving again. I guess all this craziness is burning up a lot of calories."

"Understandably," Marion said, scrambling eggs and sausage together for her guest's last meal. "So, what did you decide to do?"

"I still don't know. I can't go back to Cynthia's to get my stuff. I can't go home until Deborah leaves. I don't have any clothes to wear. I just don't know. Got any ideas?"

Other than suggesting again that he go home, Marion had nothing new to offer. "I guess the boxers didn't fit, huh?"

"No, I couldn't even get them past my thighs, and the t-shirt was so tight I could barely breathe. Thanks, anyway," he said, chortling and patting his stomach. "I do need to lose a few pounds."

Marion didn't respond, knowing full well that he needed to lose much more than a few pounds. The robe he was wearing was now too big for her, and it stretched tightly across his belly. She had worn it when she was pregnant with the twins and had kept it for sentimental reasons more than anything else. After seeing it on her neighbor, she doubted if she'd ever look at it the same way.

"Mel, I have to run some errands. Enjoy your breakfast and see if you can figure this out before I get back. Oh, and by the way, there's someone at your house…a guy. Maybe a friend or family member of yours?" she questioned. "He let himself in like he's been there before."

"Hmmm." Mel looked puzzled and went to the front window as Marion drove off. He didn't recognize the car in his driveway, and he stood there wondering who it could be. He dashed to the kitchen and piled his plate high. Grabbing a mug of coffee, he returned to the living room and strategically placed himself on a chair near the window to keep the car under surveillance until the driver appeared. He wolfed down the eggs, and when the coffee kicked in, he was forced to the bathroom.

Just when he got back to his chair, he happened to catch Cynthia driving out of the neighborhood. He decided to sneak over to her house, break in, and get his belongings. He found a scarf in Marion's dresser and tied it around his head. On his way out the front door he spotted a pair of sunglasses in a bowl on the coffee table. He felt much braver when he put them on.

The traffic was backed up for miles and Marion, along with hundreds of others, sat anxiously waiting for the wreck to be cleared. By the time she arrived home the sun was setting.

The stranger's car was still in Mel's driveway, and there were no lights on in his house, except for one coming from an upstairs window. Not finding Mel anywhere downstairs, she wondered if he had left, until she went upstairs and caught his shadow in the guest bedroom, kneeling on the floor, peering through the blinds in the dark. "Mel," she spoke softly, "what are you doing?"

"Oh, heck!" he barked, falling backwards, landing awkwardly on his side. "You scared me. I didn't hear you come in. Gosh, I think I fell asleep, and so did my legs!"

Marion stepped back into the hall and kept hidden. "What are you looking at?"

Mel shook out his tingling legs. "Our bedroom window is right across from this room. I was looking to see who's in there. That car has been there all day and hasn't budged."

"How long have you been watching?" she asked, feeling a little creepy at the notion of a peeping tom in her daughter's bedroom.

"Well, I'm kind of embarrassed to say," he hiccupped loudly. "I guess long enough for my legs to fall asleep?"

"That's long enough. Come on down to the kitchen and tell me your plans while I rustle up some dinner. I'm making another new dish. I bet you're hungry."

"Always," Mel said, quickly shoving two empty cola cans under the bed. Not wanting to chance being seen by his wife, he crawled out of the room on all fours. When he got beyond the door he straightened up and pulled the robe back together, not noticing the candy bar wrappers that had stuck to his sweaty knees.

"I'm growing rather fond of your robe," he said, cheekily.

"I hope not too fond, Mel. Don't you think it's time for

you to go home?" she asked, talking into the refrigerator while searching for butter. When she looked back, he was posing like a model, slowly turning around to show her the long, jagged tear in the grass-stained robe, and then bending over to reveal a bare bottom covered with a half-dozen small bandages.

"What happened to you?" Marion shrieked. "Turn back around! Don't show me that again!" she yelled.

"Uh," Mel grumbled. "I did something else stupid. I tried to break into Cynthia's house while you were gone."

"I guess you weren't successful – you're still in my robe, well, what's left of the bloody thing. What did you do this time?" she reluctantly asked.

"It involves a chain-linked fence, your scarf, and an ugly dog with a bad attitude! Oh, and half a box of Band-Aids," he explained indignantly. "I owe you a pair of sunglasses, but really, I don't want to talk about it. I'll just say this…mission aborted!"

Marion clucked her tongue and pleaded again, "Wouldn't it just be easier to go home, Mel?"

"Look, even if I was ready to face Deborah, I couldn't while someone is there. I wonder who that guy could be, and why has he been there all day? Can you describe him to me?" he asked, sliding clumsily onto the bar stool, chewing anxiously on his thumbnail.

"He looked about, maybe, in his early thirties. Blondish-brown hair, about your height, and oh, he had a great pair of legs," she smiled. "I couldn't help but notice. He got out of the car right when I was walking by. I did think it was kind of odd that he didn't even look at me or say hello or anything. He practically sprinted to the front door."

"Really?" Mel squirmed. "That's odd. And you say he let himself in?"

"Yep, he did. And one more thing…he had a duffle bag." Then she stopped what she was doing and biting hard on her bottom lip she looked dead-on at Mel, certain that he was thinking the same thing she was.

"You think?" he said, lifting his eyebrows, holding a dumb expression in place.

"Possibly, I mean, well…you did," she said sheepishly.

"Yeah, yeah, yeah, don't rub it in. Look, I know this is a lot to ask, but do you think you can make up an excuse to call Deborah, and maybe somehow find out who is there?"

"Curiosity killed the cat," Marion cautioned in a singsong manner.

"I'll take that chance." He flashed an artificial grin and got up to hand her the phone. "Meow," he purred.

"Sit down, sit down," she commanded. "I've seen enough of your flesh for a lifetime. No offense, Mel."

"None taken," he gloated, snatching a whole pickle from the opened jar, and waving it in the air.

"Honestly, Mel!" she huffed, "behave yourself."

Marion had recently been asked to sponsor a Mary Kay cosmetic party for one of her friends. An invitation would be a friendly and common request, so she had a good reason to make the call. Without hesitation, Deborah made an excuse not to attend and seemed eager to get off the phone. Just before she said goodbye, Marion asked her, "Oh, by the way, did Mel get a new car? I was admiring it this morning. It's a beauty."

Deborah stalled before answering, "No, no, uh, that's my nephew's car. He's visiting this week. Oh, I've got to run dear, I have something cooking on the stove. Bye bye!"

Mel, not able to take instructions well, nervously hovered over Marion's shoulder, straining to hear what his wife had said. "Did she say that's her nephew's car?"

"Yes, she did. Feel better, now?" Marion smiled, waiting for a sign of relief.

"Yeah, I would…if she had a nephew."

Both neighbors were quiet during dinner. While Marion stood at the sink washing the dishes, Mel excused himself, grabbed a book from a shelf and hurried up to the guest room before she could protest. From the stairs he yelled, "One more night, please, Marion!"

"Yes, Mel. One more night," she forced the words from her tightly squeezed lips. Raising her voice, she yelled, "Then you have to go home!" Remembering that it was the night her husband had planned to call her from overseas, she crawled into bed, relieved that he hadn't, but a little sad that he didn't, and beginning to wish that she had gone with him.

The next morning, Marion found Mel sitting on the couch reading the book, *Love Story*, by Erich Segal. She decided not to say anything, seeing how engrossed he was, with a box of tissue at his fingertips. Instead, she moved cautiously to the kitchen to cook some oatmeal. Just when she sat down at the table, Mel walked in holding the back of the robe with one hand. He plopped down across from her.

"I've been thinking," he started, resting the book on his stomach.

"And so have I," she interrupted. "Before you say anything, I really think you should go home, Mel."

"I know, I know. I can't stay here forever. I'm beginning to feel like a frustrated housewife!"

Marion laughed. "And frankly, I'm getting tired of seeing you in my robe."

Mel dropped his smile. "The car's still out there, you know."

"Yes…I know."

"And last night, I watched through the window, and I'm sure I saw more than one shadow in our bedroom," he lamented, expelling a loud yawn. "I don't think I slept but an hour."

"Oh no, I'm sorry," Marion said and pushed a muffin toward him, thinking something sweet would console him.

"I'm not a fan of blueberries," Mel declared, his bottom lip sagging to show his disappointment.

"Now that the shoe's on the other foot, it doesn't feel very good, does it?" she asked, trying not to sound like a mother reprimanding her child, but finding it hard to resist drawing the comparison.

"No, and I deserve to feel this bad. I think my marriage is in deep trouble."

"Yes, I think so, too, and there's not a lot you can do hiding out here and avoiding the inevitable. You have to go home, Mel."

"I will. I will, after he leaves. Meanwhile, I need to take a shower. I think my skin is sticking to this robe," he complained, pulling the collar away from his neck. "Can't you find something for me to wear?"

Marion went upstairs and found an old mu-mu that was the size of a fullback; one that she used to wear when lounging around the house while her husband was traveling. She wouldn't be caught dead being seen in it and kept it hidden in the back of the closet. When she handed it to Mel and explained that it would be much more comfortable with its elastic sleeves, he laughed and said, "As if things couldn't get any worse, now I'm a cross-dresser!"

While Mel finished reading Love Story, Marion cleaned

the house and followed her regular routine. The day went by quickly.

"When is that guy ever going to leave?" he asked, turning away from the window as Marion switched off the lamp on her way to bed.

I was just thinking the same thing about you, Marion wanted to say, but asked instead, "When were you supposed to be home from your trip?"

"In about three more days," he said, counting the days on his fingers. "We agreed not to call each other with the time difference and the expense of an international long-distance call, so she won't be expecting to hear from me."

With her voice rising, Marion announced, "Well, you certainly can't stay here three more days! James will be home soon. It's going to be hard enough explaining you staying here, period!" Realizing how much she missed her husband and wishing he was home to handle this mess, she lowered her voice, "Goodnight, Mel. Get some sleep. Tomorrow's going to take a lot of energy, and you really must go home."

The rain that had been promised the day before finally came fast and fierce the next morning. Marion lingered in bed a while longer, listening to it beat against the windowpane. She thought long and hard about Mel's dilemma and decided she knew just how to help him.

Over coffee and toast, and three eggs for Mel, Marion told two white lies. "My mother is coming over for lunch, and you just can't be here. I really think the best thing to do is go over there right now in that mu-mu, with your head up high and face this once and for all." She pounded her fist on the table, hoping to cheer her neighbor on. "You're both wrong, and there's no time like right now to move this thing forward!"

"You're right! I need to humble myself, and she needs humbling, too. Will you go with me?" he asked, wrinkling his nose like a little kid.

"What? Why should I go with you?" Marion looked at Mel like he was crazy.

"Support, maybe? Or to keep it civil, kind of like a mediator?" Mel dropped down on one knee, pleading with his hands pressed together in prayer.

"Oh, for heaven sakes," she said, rolling her eyes.

"Please, please! Take pity on me, please," he whined, shuffling toward her on both knees.

"Stop right there!" Marion looked up to the ceiling for some kind of heavenly sign before she answered the miserable creature dressed in her ugly, flowered mu-mu with her husband's black socks on his feet kneeling before her on the kitchen floor. "I may regret this, but OK. We'd better go now before I lose my nerve. I'll get the umbrella and James' garden shoes. They're backless, and probably too small, but at least you can keep your toes from getting wet."

Armed and ready as they'd ever be, Marion stood by the opened front door observing Mel and slowly shaking her head. "You know something? You look better in that dress than I ever did."

They both laughed. Mel leaned over and put his arms around her neck. "Thank you. Thank you for everything," he spoke softly in her ear, staying a little too long for Marion's comfort. She winced and slipped out from under his arms.

"You're welcome. Now, let's go." And as soon as Mel turned his back to her, she shoved him out the door, slammed it shut, and quickly locked it.

"But Marion!" she heard him whimper as she stood there with her ear pressed against the door, waiting anxiously for the flip-flop of the rubber shoes when he walked away. Hearing only his heavy sighing, she yelled with all her might, "GO HOME, MEL!"

NOT ONE IOTA

*H*e had been to many towns in the west, visited lots of major cities and drove through vast farmland, deserts, and mountains along the way. In all those travels as a Bible salesman, Leonard Butts had never met anyone like Iota Inkling – for that matter, not one Iota had ever crossed his path.

Leonard was working his way toward Nacogdoches, Texas after a promise he had made to his terminally ill mother in her final days. In some strange kind of confession, she told him about a mysterious cousin named Jesse who she had abandoned after she married his father. Never hearing about this family member before, Leonard thought his mother might be hallucinating from the heavy sedatives she'd been given. But when she grabbed his nose and pulled him close to her face insisting with her last breath that he find the estranged cousin, Leonard promised his mother that he'd do his best.

The day looked bleak for Bible sales. Overhead, ominous clouds gathered, blanketing the sky, threatening more than just rain for the residents of the sleepy little city of Nacogdoches. Leonard learned at a truck stop that its sister city, Natchitoches, was in nearby Louisiana. Local folks were always supplying him with trivia like that.

Nearing the end of summer, the year was 1964 – a time when neighbors didn't lock their doors, and they waved to complete strangers, and set up lemonade stands in their front yards. A time when children played outside till after dark, as long as the porch lights were left on to guide them home. Hide and seek, hopscotch, and baseball were the favorite outdoor games. When the summer heat became unbearable, Barbie dolls, Monopoly, and various card games kept the children busy inside after running in and out of the sprinkler and up and down the Slip n' Slide, fresh cut grass stuck to their feet and their bottoms as they frantically chased down the musical ice cream truck for that heavenly ice cream sandwich or rainbow pop-up.

All across the country it was also a time of eroding innocence, and the Republicans had chosen as a nominee for president a man known as Mr. Conservative – an anticommunist and Kachina doll collector who was one of the more prominent politicians to openly show an interest in UFOs. But in this small, unpretentious neck of the woods, the most important news to date was that Billy Bob McDufus was staging the First Annual Guitar Championship of Nacogdoches.

Leonard first learned about Billy Bob while at Gertie's bar, just blocks from the hotel where he had booked a room. The hotel manager of the 'oldest hotel in the oldest city in

Texas' claimed that Gertie was his sister and that she made the juiciest hamburgers in the entire county while serving the coldest refrigerated beer known to mankind. Tired of driving and quite hungry, Leonard dropped the hotel key in the pocket of his raincoat and walked to the bar carrying his umbrella along just in case the dark clouds above didn't move on to the next town.

When he entered Gertie's place, Leonard was surprised to see so many people in the tiny one-room establishment. Every table was occupied and all seven stools at the bar were taken, except two. Leonard eased his tall, slender body onto the vinyl-padded seat, still warm from the patron before him. With elbows on the bar, he waited patiently while observing through a glassless window, a stout man with hairy arms and an orange bandana tied around his sweating forehead, flipping burgers. The heavy smell of Angus beef wafted throughout the poorly lit room, and Leonard noticed that there were burgers in front of everyone around him. He sniffed the air with anticipation.

"First time here?" a man to his right asked while wiping his oily lips and chin with a wad of paper towels.

Leonard proudly answered, "Sure is. This place was highly recommended for its burgers by Gertie's brother."

"Oh, I see you met Ed. He's a little biased, of course, being family and all, but you really need to decide for yourself." And then the man leaned over the bar, practically landing his chest into a plate of ketchup, and yelled, "Gertie, you got a live one here!" He winked at Leonard and went back to dragging a handful of fries through the sweet tomato puree and stuffing them into his mouth.

A woman came bursting through a pair of swinging doors, wiping her hands on her heavily soiled apron, and charged toward Leonard like a bull. She put her hand out and said, "Hi, I'm Gertie. Just how hungry are you?"

When Leonard shook her hand, he felt the slippery remains of grease slide across his calloused palm that was rough and dry from driving for hours, his right hand rarely leaving the firm metal steering wheel of his sturdy Pontiac.

"I'm hungry enough," he said after introducing himself. "Could I see a menu, please?"

"Ain't no menu here, sir. I make burgers and fries and the only choice you get is what kind of beer you want, and that shouldn't take you too long because I only have two kinds, Falstaff and Pearl."

Leonard felt all eyes on him as he chose a Falstaff, and when the man next to him grudgingly tossed a quarter to a guy several stools down who pumped his fist up in victory, he knew a regular bet had just been made. He had his order in front of him in a flash. Ed was right, the burger was juicy and probably the best he'd ever had – besides his own home-made version – and the beer was so cold he had to gulp it fast, putting it down as quickly as possible to keep from numbing the tips of his fingers, which he licked often, because the juice from whatever secret sauce Gertie made dripped out of the bun like melted butter.

Shiny painted nails at the end of slender white fingers reached in front of his plate and snatched two French fries so quickly he thought he had imagined it. Leonard looked to his left and watched the food disappear into a wide opened mouth – lips painted scarlet red that matched her long nails and the ketchup on his plate. The thin fried potatoes disappeared without one smack or chewing motion of any kind, like a magician who ate fire or inhaled an entire cigarette.

The sprightly female gave him an innocent smile and thanked him. In front of her sat the remains of a beer, which she gulped down, and then she put her hand out for more fries. Leonard grabbed a handful and dropped them into her palm, looking at the man to the right for an explanation.

The man glanced over at the woman and back at Leonard and said, "Oh, that's Iota Inkling. She's what we call the town garbage disposal – eats all she wants and never gains a pound. Some of us think it's because she's got some kind of parasite living in her digestive system. I'd love to have that problem." He winked again just before he bit into his second burger.

"Yes, he's right," Iota finally spoke. "Food just flushes right through me. Thanks for the fries." And before he could object, she reached over and took his last one.

Leonard wasn't really up for small talk, so he paid his bill and thanked Gertie for the hamburger experience, congratulating her on her culinary talent. When he reached the door, he turned to take one last look at Iota who caught his eye and raised her eyebrows flirtatiously. There was something about her that intrigued him.

Outside the wind was restless, ready to bring on the rain. Leonard got a block away when it started to sprinkle. He turned around abruptly, remembering he had left his umbrella at the bar, and just as he did, there stood Iota Inkling directly in front of him with the umbrella opened over her head. She was much shorter than he imagined while sitting at the bar, and now she glowed with excitement to be delivering the item he had left behind.

"Why, thank you," Leonard said, and the rain came down harder. She handed him the umbrella but held on to it to keep from getting wet. Huddling together, they ran clumsily back to the restaurant. They got through the door just when lightning struck the roof of the historic downtown Main Theatre only one block away.

Back on the same stool, Leonard waited out the storm and bought another beer for himself and one for Iota. There was a lot of talk about Billy Bob McDufus, and Leonard was glad that no one questioned him about his line of work while visiting their fair city. Sitting at a bar indulging in alcohol was not the best time to introduce himself as a Bible salesman. Iota, however, managed to pry out of him his age of thirty-four, where he was from, and a short synopsis of his ugly divorce. At that point, she moved in closer and eased him into talking about how he missed playing the guitar and how he regretted selling it after his wife told him she was in love with an airline pilot. Playing it made him too sad, he explained.

An hour later, it was as still as a dead tree outside, and Leonard excused himself once again from Gertie's bar. Iota followed him.

Thinking that she must live nearby, he dismissed her light footsteps as her high heels tapped the wet sidewalk behind him. When he walked into the small hotel lobby, and she followed him down the hall, he knew something was not right. He turned around quickly and startled Iota. "Are you staying at the same hotel?" he nearly demanded.

"I might be." She produced a sincere smile and looked straight into his serious brown eyes.

"Oh, well, goodnight then." Feeling a little embarrassed, Leonard turned away and decided not to look back at the petite blonde who had claimed earlier that she was once the winner in a hot dog eating contest at the county fair.

Patting his pants, and digging into the pockets of his jacket, Leonard could not find the key to his room. He panicked for a second trying to remember if he had seen the front desk clerk on his way in and made a mad dash to the lobby to find out.

Meanwhile, Iota had slipped behind a tall artificial Cypress tree in the hall corner and was watching Leonard all along. She giggled when she was certain that he was out of sight, took the key from her purse and casually let herself into his room, locking the door behind her.

Leonard pressed gently on the hotel desk bell, hoping that the clerk was somewhere in the back and would come out ready to solve his dilemma. He waited a full minute before tapping the bell again. Fifteen minutes later, after practically pounding it into the counter, Leonard gave up and went to his car.

Back in Leonard's hotel room, Iota kicked off her heels, brushed her teeth, slipped under the sheets, and fell fast asleep.

Leonard drove to the nearest phone booth and called the hotel. A woman answered, yawning in his ear. He explained his problem, and she promised to send her husband with a key within the hour. As soon as she hung up, she fell back to sleep.

Grabbing a fresh new Gideon Bible, bound in fine imitation leather with nine carat gold embossing, from the trunk of his sedan, Leonard pulled his car under the bright, blinking vacancy sign and waited while reading the book of James. If it weren't for the inspiring words from the New Testament, he was certain he'd still be sitting in his father's recliner mourning his life away. What an awful year it had been losing a wife and both parents in such a short span of time. He felt like he had been ambushed. He hoped that getting back on the road with a trunk full of Bibles was the cure for what ailed him.

By midnight, Leonard was asleep at the wheel, the Bible resting peacefully on his chest. Six hours later, he was awakened by the popping sound of the hotel's fluorescent light turning off and on; its elements gradually burning out as the sun began to rise.

Leonard entered the lobby and saw that Iota was standing at the counter talking to Ed.

"Good morning," they cheerily greeted.

"Oh yeah, good morning to you, too," Leonard half-heartedly mumbled. He asked Ed for another key, while eyeing Iota who was wearing the same dress and heels from the night before – only her hairdo was different, now long and flowing down her back instead of twirled up in a French twist.

"I slept great," she reported with a grin. "How about you?"

Leonard rolled his eyes and said under his breath, "Could've slept better, but I will tonight," he yawned, snatching the key from Ed's hand.

"Iota here found your key on the floor," Ed said. "Lucky for you or I would have had to charge you for a new one."

"And I would have gladly paid for it, if…" he cut short his complaint and turned to Iota. "Thank you, miss. If you'll excuse me, I've got a long day ahead of me."

Resisting the temptation to dive face first into the nicely made full-sized bed, Leonard showered instead, eager to get on to selling his precious Bibles, as the meager amount of money he had inherited from his mother was dwindling fast. He looked in the nightstand, as he always did in each establishment where he stayed while traveling, only to find that there was no Bible. In its place was a business card that read, An Amusing Muse. He stuffed it in his front pocket to consider later.

Out in the parking lot, Iota was leaning over his car, her breasts pressed against the hard metal hood peeking out from the neckline of her dress. "I would be happy to buy you breakfast since you shared your fries and bought me a beer last night."

When Leonard's eyes landed on her cleavage, his words got stuck in his throat. Iota took that as a clear affirmation, slid seductively off the hood, and hopped into the front seat. A look of sheer delight stretched across her lively face.

Leonard scratched his head and couldn't come up with any reason to disagree. "Why not?"

In the car, they casually chatted in between Iota's directions to what she called 'the oldest diner in the oldest city in Texas with the oldest waitress in Nacogdoches.'

While seated in the diner, Leonard observed a more vibrant woman from across the table in the bright morning sun instead of side by side at a dim lit bar. He considered her quite pretty and was enjoying her company so much he told her all about his Bible selling business.

After a full breakfast consisting of a stack of pancakes each, with eggs, bacon, sausage and grits, and the extra cup of coffee Iota had ordered to wash down her third biscuit, she rummaged through her purse and claimed that she had left her wallet. Expressing her regrets and offering to buy him dinner that evening, Leonard gladly paid the bill. Back in the car, he asked Iota if she wanted to be dropped off at the hotel.

"Would you mind terribly if I accompany you today? My grandfather was a Bible salesman, and I used to go with him on short trips. He said I was an inspiration. Besides, I know just where to go."

Leonard tilted his head and studied the attractive lady for a few seconds and surprisingly heard himself answer again, "Why not?"

Iota described the perfect subdivision for Bible sales where the minister of the Beacon Baptist Church resided, and before he knew it, Leonard was driving to the outskirts of the city. He parked his car where Iota suggested, and the two of them walked down neatly paved sidewalks with a stack of Bibles on a cart rolling behind them.

The residents of nearly every other house bought the books without hesitation, and after the money exchanged hands, several commented sweetly that the two made a great couple. Each time Leonard started to correct them, Iota would grab his chin, squeeze his lips together and say, "Yes, the angels brought us together, and he is one lucky fella!"

Driving back to town, Leonard's spirit was lifted, and not just because he had sold twenty-four Bibles, but thanks to Iota, he felt a kind of happiness he had sorely missed. They spent the rest of the trip recalling the people they had encountered and the interesting things they noticed – like the little boy standing behind his mother with a colander on his head and an entire finger stuck up his nose. And most intriguing was the elderly lady dressed in a glittery evening gown, wearing heavy false eyelashes, and toking on an Audrey Hepburn style cigarette holder. Surprisingly enough, the eccentric old gal bought two bibles. One for the mailman and one for her deceased husband who she just happened to be entertaining at that moment. Leonard felt certain that this was a day he'd never forget. Iota laughed it off. "All in a day's work!"

Back at the hotel, Ed flagged down Leonard. "Hey, Mr. Butts," he yelled, covering up his snicker with a cough. People always looked like they were stifling a laugh when they said his name out loud. "Iota tells me that you sell Bibles and customers don't feel right in an unfamiliar room without a Bible in the drawer next to their heads. She said they are comforted by it being there. So, my wife and I decided that we should put one in every room. I'd like to buy sixteen of them today. Do they come in burgundy?"

Leonard was beaming when Ed placed a stack of crisp bills in his hand as Ed's wife proceeded to place the Bibles in their prospective rooms. This had been the biggest sales day of his entire career. After writing up a detailed receipt, he turned to thank Iota again and invite her to dinner, but she was nowhere to be seen.

He asked Ed, "What room number is Iota in? I really would like to thank her for her help. She was instrumental in making today a great sales day."

"She's not in any room," Ed answered. "What made you think that?"

"Well, I…" Quickly changing his answer to another question, he asked, "Do you know where I can find her?"

"Nope, never have known and doubt if my wife wants me to either. She's an interesting little thing, kind of pops in and out, but everyone around here thinks she's nice, just kind of strange…you know, but in a good way."

Leonard left that last remark hanging in the air and went to his room. He promptly stripped down to his socks and threw himself onto the bed. Stuffing one pillow under his head, he reached for the other only to find that it was missing. He searched the floor and giving up he rolled over to open the nightstand to find a shiny burgundy Bible beaming from the bottom of the wooden drawer. A smile of gratitude crossed his face, and when he closed his weary eyes, he inhaled a strong scent of perfume on the pillow– a scent he had recently caught while walking with Iota under his umbrella, her head pressed against his shoulder. Exhausted, he drifted off to sleep, not thinking of dinner or his ex-wife, but of a five-foot-two wisp of a woman who could eat a side of beef in one sitting.

The grumbling from his stomach woke him up around eight o'clock, and Leonard felt as hungry as a teenage boy after football practice. Putting on jeans and a light cotton plaid shirt, he left the hotel excited about sitting down to a fine meal. When he got into his car, he didn't notice the small figure hidden under a blanket in the back seat resting on the missing pillow from his hotel room.

He drove around the city, looking for an Italian restaurant – the kind that's small and quaint with dripping candles and Dean Martin singing "That's Amore." Where clanking pots and pans could be heard from the kitchen while the staff barked orders at each other and passed steaming hot pasta to the waiters who balanced trays of wine through the slim aisles between a scattering of red-clothed tables filled with happy customers toasting everything from a successful gall bladder removal to the arrival of a new pair of Italian leather shoes.

He found just the place, and minutes later was settled at the bar because the tables were all full, which was quite fine with him as he liked sitting high above the room, so he could survey the crowd. People amused him, and he decided long ago that he'd rather watch than talk to them. Bible selling tends to wear out the need for conversation. Although, at that very moment, he wished that Iota had joined him for dinner. Talk with her came easily. He liked that she didn't say too much, or too little.

The bartender served him a glass of Chianti from a large bottle wrapped in a traditional fiasco basket that was being passed around the bar. Leonard drank heartily while dunking hunks of bread in olive oil. As it happened before, a familiar hand with brightly painted nails snatched a piece of bread from his plate. Leonard turned to his right, pleased to see the woman who had made his day so marvelous. The bread, like the fries the night before, passed magically from her hand to her mouth.

"Welcome," he said, so glad to see her he dismissed asking her how she had found him. "I'm really glad you're here. I can't thank you enough for today."

Iota gently patted his back while they ordered huge plates of pasta and more wine to celebrate. When they finished dinner, Leonard asked her to join him for another day of selling. She agreed to meet him in the lobby the following morning, kissed him on the cheek, wished him a good night's sleep, and walked briskly into the night. Leonard stayed behind to pay the bill.

The next day was identical to the day before, and Leonard was overjoyed with the result of their sales. He was so excited to be with Iota, he hadn't noticed that underneath her light jacket, her clothes were the same, yet slightly wrinkled. He did, however, notice that her lips were as shiny as the red ribbon wrapped around her ponytail. He offered her a portion of his proceeds, and she gratefully took it in the form of twenty-dollar bills. When he invited her to dinner again, she asked for a raincheck and excused herself for the night. Leonard picked up another burger from Gertie's and ate it in his room before falling fast asleep, leaving the crisp pages of the new Bible in the nightstand unturned.

Dressed in new slacks with blue flats and a yellow, flowered shirt, Iota arrived rested and eager to make their sales day another success story. Topping the day before, Leonard counted out another pile of twenties and placed six of them in Iota's hand. They ended the day at a Chinese restaurant where they sat contentedly playing with chopsticks and with very little talking. When they finished eating Iota said that she had some shopping to do and hurried out the door, leaving Leonard at the table once again waiting for the bill.

After a quick stop at Gertie's place where the topic of the night varied between the guitar festival, a new high school football coach, interrupted by an argument about Caddo Indians founding the town, Leonard bought a soda pop and drank it slowly in the hotel room. He slept long and hard, without one single dream.

On the fourth day of his stay in Nacogdoches, Leonard was having such a good time he had forgotten all about trying to find his mother's cousin that supposedly lived in the area. It was a Sunday morning and folks frowned at solicitors on a holy day, so he lounged in bed and decided this would be a good day to search for Jesse.

Iota surprisingly showed up at his door just before noon looking pretty as a peach in a new orange summer dress with a bright purple belt. Leonard, now familiar with her sudden appearances, was happy to see her.

He told Iota about his mother's last dying request and how he had not found the relative's name in the White Pages. Updating her on his latest thoughts on the matter, he wondered if Jesse, too, had died.

"Jesse Croton?" she asked. "I've seen that name before.

It's written on a sign over the door of an old historic home just a few blocks from here."

Leonard agreed that was a good place to start and asked Iota to join him. With no dark clouds gathering overhead, the day was nice enough to walk. On their way, Leonard took the liberty to ask Iota some personal questions. "I understand you're not staying at the hotel. Where are you staying?"

"Not far from here, actually." And that was the end of that topic.

"I told you I was once married. How about you?" Leonard asked.

Iota looked down at her feet as they strolled along. "No, I'm not sure that's my style."

In a strange way, Leonard was charmed by her vague answers and decided he liked Iota remaining a mystery.

Approaching 208 Cherry Street, they stopped and stood before an ancient house, adorned with two gargoyles looking fiercely down at their visitors. Four steps up they landed on a tiled porch, in the corner a marble statue of a naked woman curling a long piece of cloth between her legs. Above the door, surrounded in English ivy was a sign with gold carved letters: Inspiring Creative Endeavors – Jesse Croton.

Iota stood behind Leonard when he knocked on the door. He felt her cowering behind him and started to say something when suddenly the door burst open.

"I was expecting you," the woman dressed in blue chiffon announced, stepping back, and giving him a formal curtsey. "Please come in."

"I, uh, I'm Leonard Butts, and I, uh, I'm looking for Jesse Croton?" he stammered, confused by the abrupt greeting.

"I'm Jesse, and you are the son of Harold Butts, one of my favorite subjects. Do come in and bring your lady friend with you," she coaxed, peeking around Leonard, and smiling sweetly at Iota.

"Follow me to the terrace where we'll have a lovely Sunday afternoon lunch." Jesse waltzed ahead, waving her arms about in excitement. Iota nudged Leonard forward – his feet glued so firmly to the floor, he nearly tripped on the threshold.

The terrace was fashioned after a European restaurant: a round table formally dressed in white linen and matching pressed napkins, a placing of china and silverware sparkling in the diffused sunlight. In the center sat a large bowl with carvings of nine Greek women dancing. Inside it held a bunch of grapes surrounded by small clusters of various fruit. Beautiful strands of ivy hung delicately overhead and trickled down the fluted pillars.

"Please have a seat," Jesse encouraged. "I've been looking forward to meeting you, Leonard." Stretching her long white neck toward Iota, she asked, "And darling Ms. Inkling, you are full of surprises."

"You know each other?" Already flummoxed by everything else that was happening, this one really threw Leonard for a loop. His jaw dropped open.

"Of course, we do. How else would you have found me?" Jesse looked at him as if his head had been in the sand too long. "Close your mouth, Leonard…that's not your best look."

Leonard snapped his mouth shut. Iota giggled.

While the ladies chatted, Leonard studied Jesse's face, trying to remember where he'd seen it before. "Jesse, how well did you know my mother?" he interjected.

"Well enough, though it's been many years since then. It was your father that I knew best. I was his muse back in the day when he was a young artist. Unfortunately, he was distracted by my cousin, your mother, and I could no longer assist him. We are not always as successful as the ancient Greek goddesses were." She pointed to the dancing women carved on the centerpiece. "Modern men do not grasp the concept well, and very few are trustworthy." Jesse furrowed her brow. "I recall the moment I lost the stubborn artist to my imprudent cousin, but that's another story for another time."

"That may explain why my father didn't pursue his art career. His work is quite amazing, but he kept it hidden in a storage room because mother wouldn't let him display it in the house." Leonard bowed his head. "Sadly, he died…over a year ago."

"Yes, I know. Again, unfortunate." Jesse frowned, taking a moment of silence for the deceased, then clearing her throat, she said, "Thank goodness your mother had enough sense in the end to instruct you to seek me out. Now, I highly recommend that you gather up your father's art and have it appraised. He should have enough pieces to make you financially comfortable." She directed her eyes over Leonard's head and pointed to an exquisitely framed painting of a voluptuous beauty, a thin opaque scarf draped across her nude body. "Your father painted that one of me."

Leonard nearly dropped his tea when he saw the likeness of his father's style and his familiar inscription. Suddenly, he remembered where he'd seen Jesse's face – in many of his father's paintings. No wonder his mother objected. She must have been terribly jealous of her gorgeous cousin. The thought of selling the precious collection swirled through his brain, recounting over one hundred pieces of art in his possession, thirteen of which he had hung throughout the house after his mother died.

Jesse patted Leonard's arm. "I've had many offers, as

high as five thousand dollars for that piece," she said, followed by a sly wink, and then she looked over at Iota. "As for you, my dear, are you ready for your journey?"

"Yes, I think I am. My mother was a muse, and I am certain I am one, as well. Albeit not especially a good one," she admitted, biting back a nervous smile, "but I think, well, I'm sure I can learn."

Leonard chimed in, "Oh no, she is good, I can vouch for that. I have had three successful days like no others since I met Iota. I have never felt so rejuvenated." Iota blushed.

"You have not had the good fortune I have had, but you passed my test with flying colors," Jesse said and reached out for the young woman's hand, placing a small book in her slightly sweating palm. "This will help you learn while you are staying in my home. I expect you to do exactly as I say, and above all, I expect nothing but the truth, and of course, your trust in me."

Tears came to Iota's eyes as she caressed the lettering on the cover of the book titled, The Muse in You. "I will be that and more." She squeezed Jesse's outreached hand and looked at Leonard with adoring eyes. "Because you placed your trust in me, I now will become who I truly am with Jesse's guidance. Thank you, Leonard."

Leonard wasn't exactly sure what was happening, but he knew for certain that he would not spoil the moment with more questions, followed by answers he would most likely never comprehend. Instead, he ate to his delight.

The following day, fully renewed, Leonard packed his bags and drove back to Tallulah, Louisiana where he aired out his mother's home and began taking inventory of his father's art. Consulting with the best in the art industry, as Jesse advised, he hitched an enclosed trailer to his Pontiac, and in mid-September, when the days began to cool, he towed the paintings to New York City, keeping six of his favorites.

During his long trip, Leonard sold with ease the remaining stock of the holy books, keeping one on the front seat for himself and thus ending his Bible selling career. While in Nashville, he stopped at Sears and Roebuck and bought a Silvertone Model 621 acoustic guitar which he would play while at rest stops along the way.

Driving across country gives a man time to think, and out of the blue, the name Billy Bob McDufus came into his head, and he wondered if the First Annual Guitar Championship of Nacogdoches ever took place. He hadn't read about it anywhere in the newspapers. And then he started wondering if that little town was real at all – being that it changed his life so dramatically. Iota, Jesse, his good fortune, it all seemed almost like a dream.

When he arrived in the Big Apple, Leonard stood on the balcony of the hotel room and counted his blessings while overlooking the opulence of the city. Spotting a huge American flag, he instinctively put his hand to his heart and proudly quoted the "Pledge of Allegiance." He felt something in his front pocket and fished out a business card. On the front it read, An Amusing Muse. He recalled how he had found it in the hotel drawer in Nacogdoches, the morning after he slept in his car, and he remembered fondly the scent of perfume on his pillow. Flipping the card over, in the tiniest print was a name he recognized: Iota Inkling. Resting assured that it wasn't just a dream, he kissed the card and went downstairs for a drink.

While savoring an expensive snifter of Cognac, his very first, he carried on a casual conversation with the bartender who asked him, "How in the world did you end up in New York City all the way from Louisiana?"

A whimsical smile parted Leonard's lips when he said, "Not really sure…but I might have an inkling."

The beach is a wonderful place to enjoy your imagination.
The continuous sound of the ocean makes every thought
seem real.
The endless grains of sand remind us we are not alone.
The limitless sky gives hope, and the everlasting water
greeting the sun calms the soul like no other.

DUNKED

$\mathcal{M}$any a night Gwendolyn Gala Garrison sat quietly alone propped up in bed imagining her name on the spine of a brand new book: Gwendolyn Garrison or GG Garrison, or a simple, catchy *GGG*. She was still undecided, but the cover would be shiny and colorful with crème-colored interior pages, not too thick or too thin, exactly two-hundred-seventy-two pages with glossy pictures scattered throughout. Not heavy like those massive, oversized sternum-bruising hardbacks. No, her paperback could be held delicately in the palm of the reader's hand. The dream of completing her first book was becoming real. The hardest part was finding someone to publish it.

Coffee shops were the current obsession. Before that it was small cafes and libraries. Gwen had been determined to visit every java house in the city, and today she was about to enter the last one on her list. The book of stories about these establishments and the people that frequent them would end here. She cheerfully hopped off her bicycle with the extra padded seat and innocent looking fat tires and grabbed a notebook from the metal basket, a red balloon tied to its brackets. To appear friendly and trustworthy, the lanky fifty-nine-year-old typically wore a flowered dress and yellow Converse tennis shoes with a floppy hat on her silver-streaked hair while interviewing people for her book. And sometimes, if the subjects were cooperative, she'd record them with her thrifty little waterproof camera. She was comforted in knowing that if she accidentally dropped it in the toilet or got caught in a monsoon, she could always rely on the bright, yellow recording device to capture the moment.

The day was mousy gray. A blanket of moisture hung over the city, so thick there was no chance the sun could peek through. In the coffee shop, people were different on days like this; shy, more subdued, and they buried their heads in books or laptops, rarely looking up to see who entered or exited the door. They lingered longer, drank more than one cup of coffee, and the cookies were usually all gone by noon. The proprietors must have anticipated this because today Gwen noticed that there were twice as many cookies in the glass case. Relieved, she found a seat by the window and settled in for a morning of writing and socializing.

"Under the Boardwalk" was playing softly overhead and it reminded her of a bizarre incident, an unsolved mystery that happened years back. Gwen stared out the window into the oyster-stained light and let her mind take a stroll down memory lane.

It was nine years or so ago, and she was sitting on a blanket on a beach in the Outer Banks of Nags Head, North Carolina. She and her late husband had spent many summers at the hotel across the highway from the pretty little beach, and because it was friendly and familiar, she found herself still vacationing there.

She had been absorbed in a Stephen King novel, completely unaware of the time. Halfway into the book, she finally looked up to see the tide changing, the sun just inches from the horizon and the shore empty of visitors. This time of day produced eerie shadows and strange sounds that easily spooked Gwendolyn, which is why she was always anxious to leave way before dark. Rattled, she quickly gathered her things and hurried toward the wooden stairs ascending to the hotel. Just when she reached the first step, she heard a scream coming from somewhere behind her. She scanned the area while listening in the wind, and when she heard it again, she dropped her beach bag and walked toward the ocean. Stopping at the water's edge, she watched the waves for any sign of life.

"Hello, anybody out there?" she yelled at the top of her lungs. She waded timidly into the water and stopped when it reached her waist. That was as far as she was willing to go. "Darn you, Stephen King," she said under her breath. No doubt this was her imagination playing tricks, and she blamed it all on the wicked author.

Turning to head back to the hotel, a shadow flickered in the corner of her eye, and she saw movement to her right. Just a few feet away, a man walked out of the water and stopped suddenly at seeing her standing there. He shook his wet hair and before she could question him, he took off running. Confused, Gwen stood watching the man's chiseled body heading toward the stairs, and when he dropped his arm, she caught a glimpse of a big black circle tattooed on his right elbow. She looked back out on the ocean and feeling a little ridiculous, she said in a meek voice, "Is anyone there?"

With the waves getting higher by the second and the wind picking up its pace, Gwen found it hard to find her balance. Bracing herself against the tide, she saw something coming toward her. Thinking it was a shark, she fell backwards into the water. Petrified, she stood up and identified a female floating on her back, her eyes closed and the bottoms of her black bikini clinging tightly to her ankles. Pushing panic aside, Gwen instinctively lunged forward, reached out, wrapped her arm around the victim and tugged her to shore. She immediately turned her on her side and began pounding on her back. Within seconds, the woman let out a stream of coughs.

"Oh, thank God, thank God," Gwen cried, replacing the pounding with gentle rubbing. The woman rolled over and looked up at her. A sudden streak of fear crossed her face.

"It's OK, it's OK. I'm here to help. It's OK," Gwen assured her. "You're alive. Yes, you are, dear girl."

The woman lifted her head and scanned the beach with wide eyes. "Where is he? Did you see him?" she asked breathlessly.

"Yes, I did. Who is he?"

"He's, he's...he…."

"Did he, well, did he hurt you…good heavens, did he try to drown you?"

"I don't know," the woman lowered her head and began to sob.

"Oh, dear Lord!" Gwen gasped, and realizing that the perpetrator may still be nearby, she combed the area in the slow dimming light. "We need to get out of here now. Can you walk?"

The woman stood up too quickly and fell back down; her feet tangled up in the swimsuit. "Give me a second, I just need..." She pulled the bottoms up and snapped at the elastic until it settled in the right places.

Gwen studied her closely and noticed a long, thin, pinkish scar below her navel. It moved up and down as she took three slow methodical breaths. She guessed that the young woman was in her mid-twenties. Her skin was flawless and untouched by the coastal sun. Gwen grabbed her elbow when she stood. She was a tiny little thing, almost the size of a ten-year-old, and Gwen thought, if necessary, she could probably carry her. Before they had reached the top of the stairs, the woman collapsed into her arms, and she was forced to test her own strength.

What a sight they must have been when they were seen coming through the hotel's revolving door – an older disheveled woman struggling to keep from dropping a ninety-pound female on her head. Before she knew it, the bellboy had swept the woman out of her arms and taken her to the nearest empty room. Quite relieved, Gwen followed and stood by as the doctor was called and the maître d' gently placed a heavy guest robe on her back. "How nice, thank you," she said, wrapping her wet body in between the thick folds of cotton fabric.

"What happened?" the maître d' asked, handing her a cup of hot coffee.

"I'm not sure. I was just leaving the beach when I heard screaming. Before I knew it, I was standing in the water, then...."

Gwen was interrupted by the young woman wide awake on the bed. "Please, please, I need to talk to you before you say anything else. May I have a moment alone with you, please?"

The maître d' looked askance at Gwen; one eyebrow raised. "Well, if you need anything, just press zero on the phone."

"Thank you so much for the robe and coffee. I'll be with her until the doctor arrives." Gwen waited for the door to shut before she moved closer to the bed. She looked down at the woman, who was inching up on her elbows. "You must lie back down. You need to rest," she said, patting her arm. "Now, what is it you want to tell me?

"My name is Christina. I am the stepdaughter of a well-known diplomat, and my mother is a famous socialite."

"I'm Gwendolyn Garrison. Pleased to meet you my dear, even under these wretched circumstances. I'm afraid I'm just a vacationer here, no high-ranking credentials to speak of, except soon I'll be retiring from my job as a librarian with plans to become a writer."

"Yes, yes," Christina nodded nervously. "Thank you for saving my life. I owe you a great deal."

"Oh no," Gwen chuckled. "It may not have happened if you had been far from shore. You see, I'm not the best swimmer, and I might have drowned right along with you if I had gone out much further." Pausing to reflect, she added, "I'm very grateful for Stephen King right now."

"Who?"

"Oh, the author. You know the guy who writes horror stories and then later turns them into some ghastly movie. I usually never read things like that. I'm afraid it will get lodged in my imagination and carry over into my daily life. I prefer lighter fiction. Much safer. But anyway, it's because I was engrossed in his book that I was there to help you. I usually don't stay that long. But, oh, listen to me rambling. Now, again, what is it that you need to tell me?"

"I need to ask you to keep what you saw to yourself. The part about the man, that is."

Gwen looked into the young woman's pleading eyes and down at her small hand squeezing her arm. "But what if that man tried to kill you? How can I keep quiet about that? Aren't you afraid that he'll try it again once he finds out that you're alive?"

"He won't know where to find me if you allow me to stay in your room for the night. I can explain everything to you later, after the doctor examines me. It's really not as it seems. Please."

"But surely he'll find out and then what?" Gwen placed her hand, warmed by the coffee cup, over the top of Christina's cold fingers.

"You must trust me, please. There's no time to make you understand."

The door to the room slowly opened and a very tanned man dressed in a pink golf shirt and brown khaki pants peeked around it. "Hello, I'm Dr. Franklin. May I come in?"

"Of course, Doctor." Gwen turned to acknowledge him, but Christina would not let go of her arm until she agreed.

"OK," Gwen mouthed, widening her eyes to assure the frustrated girl that she would comply.

"Well, I understand you nearly drowned, young lady," the doctor said, smiling with his practiced bedside manner.

"Yes, well, not quite. My legs cramped up, and I'm hypoglycemic. I hadn't eaten all day. I guess I fainted."

"I see. I was told that a very brave woman saved your life." Flashing his dazzling, veneer-coated teeth, he winked at Gwen, "Please tell me all about it while I examine the patient."

Gwen told the doctor everything that had happened and reluctantly left out the part about seeing the man. The relieved look on Christina's face made her feel that she had done the right thing. She just hoped that she would feel the same way later.

After explaining to the hotel that Christina would be staying with her, Gwen arranged for another room with two full beds. Afraid to go alone, she asked the bellboy to accompany her to pick up her belongings that she had left lying on the dark beach. He obliged and after a substantial tip, he helped gather her things and her new friend into what appeared to be a much nicer room than the one she had left.

"Compliments of the hotel," the bellboy said, leaving a fresh vase of flowers on the nightstand. After hot showers and room service delivered, the two women sat on the beds opposite each other, cross-legged and dining on fish and chicken; Christina, looking relaxed and even younger in Gwen's baggy green t-shirt.

"This feels like we're having a sleep-over," Christina said, biting down on a chicken leg.

"Be glad I'm not that age now, because I was the one who stayed up all night and played practical jokes on my girl-friends, like putting their bras in the freezer and whipped creme between their toes."

"That's funny. All we did was sneak out and smoke cigarettes on the corner with the boys. And if someone had the nerve to steal a beer out of their dad's stash, we'd all take turns sipping it."

Changing the subject, Gwen asked with a serious tone, "Why did you give the doctor a different name?"

"I guess, well, I suppose it's time to tell you everything."

Gwen nodded and said in between bites, "You talk, I'll eat. I'm famished!"

"OK," Christina chuckled and then quickly dropped her smile. "Well, first of all, I came here to get Desmond back."

"Desmond? Well, I hope he's not the man on the beach that left you to die?" Gwen spoke with a mouth full of corn that spit out and landed on the bedspread. "Oh dear, I know better than to talk with food in my mouth. Carry on."

"Yes, the man on the beach. I love him. You saw him, he's gorgeous, isn't he?"

"Well, I suppose he is. I didn't notice so much his looks as I did those piercing eyes. My goodness, they were incredibly disturbing. I was afraid I'd turn to stone if I looked at them much longer."

"I know, I know. They make me weak in the knees. I suppose I sound like a schoolgirl, don't I?"

"No, I understand. I'm not that old to forget what power men have over us."

"I'm not trying to minimize the fact that Desmond was wrong for leaving me out there in the water the way he did. Believe me, I am very hurt and upset by this. But, on the other hand, I understand why he did it."

Gwen looked confused at the young woman and couldn't begin to imagine what she would say next. Christina was much too calm after the near-death experience. She moved her plate to the desk and resumed her position on the bed. "Go on."

Christina bit her knuckle and hesitated, as if she wasn't sure if she should tell the truth. "I told you earlier that my mother is a socialite, and my stepfather is a diplomat. I'm not at liberty to tell you more than that. But that's why I gave the doctor a different name."

"I'm certain I would not know them anyway. I don't run in those circles, but I do watch Downton Abby." Gwen laughed at her own remark.

"Desmond is an Italian Catholic. My family is Jewish. Because my mother would not accept our plans to marry, everything went wrong. Desmond left me and returned to Italy. He stayed to help his father with their vineyards, and we decided that under the circumstances we'd separate for a while. We were both completely unhappy.

"Perhaps you can imagine what a scandal it would be to get pregnant and not be married. Well, that's what happened to me. But the father of my child wasn't Desmond." She stalled and stared down at the floor.

"It's okey, Christina," Gwen said, reaching over and patting her hand. "You don't have to try and explain."

"But I want to. I was visiting friends from college, and they met me at my hotel. They wanted to go bar hopping, and I was not in the mood. We had a few drinks, they left, and I stayed behind. That's where I met *him*. He was charming and sophisticated, and although much older than me, I was feeling lost without Desmond and desperately wanted the attention. We had a wonderful talk, danced, and of course drank the finest wine. We never told each other our true identities. In my world, it's not necessary, and it's socially understood. It was a one-night fling that should not have happened."

"But they do, so very often, don't they?" Gwen wanted to relieve Christina of the guilt she knew very much about from her own life's experiences. She gave her a sincere look of understanding.

"My mother travels internationally quite often. We rarely see each other and unless I read it in a tabloid, I don't know where she is from one month to the next. She called me several months after that night at the hotel and told me she was getting married again. This is her fourth husband, and this time she knew he was the one. When she returned to the states a married woman, I went to see her. I didn't want to spoil her happiness, so I thought I'd wait a while longer before telling her my situation. When I arrived and saw who my new stepfather was, I nearly threw up right there in front of them. It was him…from the hotel. Like the trained diplomat he is, he held his composure. But I thought I would die."

"Your stepfather is the father of your child? Good heavens," Gwen gasped, "I'm without words." Now, eager to hear the whole story, she said, "I don't mind if you tell me the rest. With my imagination, no telling where this could go."

"Well, I waited as long as I could to tell my mother I was pregnant. When I did, she was terribly upset. She made it easy for me and immediately assumed the child was Desmond's. I didn't deny it."

"And your stepfather?"

"Yes, he knows the truth, and naturally we both want to keep it our secret. Too much is at stake. My reputation is already ruined if Desmond doesn't marry me. It all looks so ugly, I know."

"And what about Desmond?" Gwen held her hand to her heart.

"He came to see me and when I told him, he went nuts, of course. He flew back to Italy, and I had the baby without him. I have a son. About a month old now. He's beautiful."

"Oh, I bet he is." Gwen's eyes softened as she studied Christina's fine features, imagining a boy with her naturally plump red lips.

"This weekend I met Desmond here to decide what to do next. The fight we had in the water while swimming was because Desmond confessed that he's blackmailing my stepfather and receiving large monthly funds to keep his mouth shut."

"Oh dear," Gwen said, shaking her head slowly, trying to digest the whole thing. "How can you have a relationship with a man that is blackmailing your family and leaves you to die in the ocean?"

"He's having trouble getting over what happened between me and my stepfather. This is his way of torturing him. And if it makes you feel any better, Desmond put the money in a savings account for me. It's hard to understand, Gwendolyn, but Desmond didn't want me to die. It wasn't deliberate, it was just a 'in the heat of passion' sort of thing."

"You're kidding? I didn't see much passion in those eyes when he walked out of the water and ran away."

"Believe me, he does love me. I'm not really sure what happened out there. This year has been so hard on us. He was angry, I was angry…"

"OK, well, I suppose there is such a thing. I did see the movie, *I Love You to Death*. Love can make you do things you never thought you were capable of." Gwen looked over at Christina and recognized the innocence of young love in her eyes. "I'm sorry, I'm being over-dramatic. I do hope it all works out for you."

"You saved my life, Gwendolyn, and I'm eternally grateful. I think Desmond will be, too."

Gwen got up and paced the floor. "I suppose there's nothing more to talk about tonight then," she said softly. "I'm glad you're fine now, but honestly, I think we should get some sleep and start the day over tomorrow."

She walked over to Christina and lifted her chin. "You do know, Christina, life always finds a way. It doesn't matter how your son came into this world, he did. He's a gift to cherish forever."

After brushing her teeth, Gwen tiptoed past the sleeping roommate tightly cocooned in the sheet. Under the covers she pulled the blanket up to her chin and reached for the Stephen King novel. What am I doing? This is the last thing I need. Exhausted, she gently placed the book in the night-stand drawer for the next visitor and within seconds she was fast asleep; her usual soft snore floating lazily across the room.

"Goodnight, Gwendolyn," a small voice whispered from the next bed over. "Thank you for not judging me."

The next morning when she awoke, Christina was gone, along with Gwen's favorite yellow sundress.

Gwen wasn't aware how long she had sat there in the coffee shop reliving the bizarre experience. Of all days, why would she decide to think about that now? Never knowing what happened to the couple had left her feeling sad at times. They could have at least sent her an anonymous email or letter. She fluffed her hair and turned her thoughts elsewhere.

Realizing that she hadn't ordered any coffee or even a cookie, she saw that the line had gotten longer, so she waited until it thinned out to approach the counter. She pulled a folded up handmade vest out of her backpack and put it on. She had sewn a small pocket the size of her camcorder and neatly cut out a hole for the camera's eye. The pocket was strategically placed so that it could rest perfectly in the cleavage of her bosom. It was well camouflaged, as Gwen had picked a busy fabric with lots of flowers and playful dogs covering most of the white background. She had managed to catch children saying the cutest things this way, and on occa-sion, she'd film someone walking funny in front of her. Sitting up straight, she aimed her breasts toward the counter where a very odd-looking teenager dressed in Robin Hood attire waited in line. She hoped that she'd get a chance to talk to him before he left.

Watching with anticipation, she scanned the other patrons in their casual dress, and then she spotted a man's elbow – a black circle tattooed around it. Oh dear, it's him! She put her hand on her chest and feeling the hard camera underneath her palm, she continued catching in action the man she believed was Desmond. His thick, dark hair was now flecked with bits of silver, but the rest of his body looked the same as when she saw it nine years earlier. Gwen fished in her bag for sunglasses and discreetly put them on. When Desmond headed toward the condiments counter, she looked down at her journal and pretended to write, watching his every move behind the dark lenses shielded by the brim of her hat.

Stirring cream in his coffee, he ambled toward her area. "Is this seat available?" he asked, pointing to the small table and chair next to her.

His amazing black eyes looked straight through her, and Gwen was so startled the words got stuck in her throat. She let out a modest cough and nodded a yes.

"Good," he said, sitting down to read the paper.

Gwen adjusted her body to make sure that the eye of the camera was completely on him. The longest fifteen minutes went by when finally, Desmond got up to leave. Scrambling to gather up her things she followed him; noticing as she passed the counter that there was only one cookie left. She hoped it would still be there when she returned.

Desmond stayed on foot for nearly five blocks and then slipped into the exclusive Westin Resident Hotel. Gwen stood across the street watching the entrance. Nearly an hour passed, and he didn't come out. This is ridiculous! What am

I doing? She started to walk back to the coffee shop and just when she did, Desmond came out of the building with Christina by his side holding the hand of a young boy. Dressed to the nines, they looked like a family out of a fashion magazine. They stopped to discuss which direction to take, and it was then that Gwen noticed Christina was pregnant. She couldn't stop herself from following closely behind.

They entered a small toy store and browsed for a while, finally coming out with a small package that the boy proudly carried close to his chest. They walked casually on to the next block and entered Sonoma Bistro. Gwen stood nearby window shopping and waited a few minutes before entering the establishment.

She glanced around the small, elegant restaurant and didn't see them. Through a large plate glass window, she spotted them seated in the outside dining area. The hostess led her to a table catty-cornered from the couple. Gwen kept her sunglasses on and watched closely. They seemed to be the average family on a typical outing, smiling, and chatting away. Yes, she was spying, but she felt as though they owed her something – especially after the scare they had put her through. And Christina leaving without a word; knowing that she had planted a seed of doubt that would follow Gwen for the rest of her life. It was a crazy and selfish act on their part and at that moment, she knew just what it was that she needed from them, and it was not the return of her favorite yellow sundress.

Reaching into her vest pocket, she switched on the recorder and walked slowly over to their table. She glanced at Desmond, then smiled at Christina, and winked at the boy.

"May I help you?" Desmond spoke first.

"Yes, you may. I'm hoping you will remember me." Gwen slowly removed her sunglasses and smiled long enough to give the couple a chance to recall her face.

Desmond squinted up at her. Christina said meekly, "Hello, Gwendolyn." Then everyone looked over at the boy all at once.

"Hi, I'm Gwendolyn Gala Garrison, an old friend of your parents," she said, reaching out to shake the boy's hand.

"Hi," he said proudly, chopping the air with his hand. "I'm Dominik."

"Nice handshake," Gwen said, taking the liberty to sit down. "I'm sure you don't mind if I join you. It has been a long time. About nine years, and I bet that's about how old you are Dominik."

"I am, and I'm about to turn ten. This is one of my birthday gifts," he said proudly, holding up the bag he had carried out of the toy store.

"Wow! A decade old. That sounds more important when you say it that way, doesn't it?"

"Yes," he smiled, clearly liking the comparison.

Gwen cleared her throat and turned to address the couple, who looked mildly nervous watching the exchange. "My, you two look wonderful. Been back to Nags Head since I saw you last?"

"No, not really. We're not all that fond of the place," Christina said. "What brings you to Virginia Beach?"

"Oh, I was about to ask you the same. I live here."

"We do, too," Dominik spoke up, pleased to be in the conversation.

"That's wonderful." Wanting his full attention, she turned her body to face the little boy. It was then that she saw his full plump lips identical to his mothers. "Imagine us living in the same town after all these years. Did you know that I saved your mother's life a long time ago?"

"Really?" Dominik's eyes grew wide, and he leaned in anticipating the story. "Mom, did she really?"

Christina glanced at Gwen uneasily and then at her husband and then back at her son. "Yes, she did. I almost drowned in the ocean, and Ms. Gwendolyn saved me."

"Wow!" Dominik exclaimed. "That must have been really scary." Then he looked over at his father and asked, "Were you there, too, dad?"

Desmond's jaw clenched and he looked straight into Gwendolyn's eyes with a deep, dark, ink-filled glare, just as he had when he saw her on the beach. The black edges gradually softened into a muddy brown as a smile slowly formed, revealing a hidden set of dimples that made him look remarkably innocent. "No, I wasn't. I'm very sorry that I wasn't there, but I'm sure glad that Ms. Gwendolyn was."

"So was I," Christina said and reached out for Gwen's hand, her eyes filling with tears.

Silence flooded the scene as everyone looked at each other with awkward smiles.

Dominik crossed his arms, leaned in, and asked the question nobody wanted to answer. "How did it happen, Miss Gwendolyn?"

Gwen picked up a menu and said, "You know, let's let your mother tell you that story later. Right now, I bet you're hungry. Shall we order?" Gwen caught the relief in Christina's eyes, while Desmond heaved a sigh and handed a menu to his wife.

When the orders were taken, and Gwen found a nice glass of white wine in front of her, she spoke with confidence about her book. "I've been to every coffee shop in the city, many cafes, and all the libraries. You wouldn't believe the wonderful stories that I've collected. Oh yes, some are a bit weird, too, but that spices up the book. Meeting *you* today," she stretched her neck toward Dominik, "and your lovely parents, is the perfect way to end my stories."

"You mean we'll be in your book?" Dominik's eyes grew wide with excitement.

Gwen answered with a nod and a smile. "All I need now is a backer." She shifted her eyes over to Christina.

"What's a backer?" the ten-year-old asked.

So pleased that his natural curiosity was moving the conversation in just the right direction, Gwen sat up taller. Now was her chance to drive it home. "Someone that's got your back. Someone that supports your idea and believes in you. That's all I need to get this book out into the world, and once that happens, I plan to write tons of children's books. I have so many ideas."

"I have lots of ideas, too. I can help you. I bet my parents believe in you, since you saved my mother's life." He turned to his parents and asked excitedly, "Will you please be Ms. Gwendolyn's backer?"

Christina let out a laugh, then Desmond joined in, and when Gwen started laughing, Dominik, not knowing why, laughed with them.

CLOSET LOVE

*A*bbey snapped her vinyl briefcase shut, looked around the office and seeing that everyone had left, she stuffed three more company pens and a handful of candy into her purse. Glad to be leaving the stuffy conference room and the arrogant instructor, she glanced at her watch, brushed past her chatty employer, and hurried out the door. She had fifteen minutes to make it to the property where her client would be anxiously waiting to preview the latest luxury rental listing.

At the stoplight she applied new lipstick and pressed down a fake eyelash detaching from her eyelid. She took this opportunity to admire her new hair color, Barbie Babe Blonde, the hairdresser had called it before she squirted it all over Abbey's mousy colored mane. Noticing chocolate caught between her teeth, she grabbed a wadded-up napkin and wiped the top four teeth vigorously. While cramming a square of nicotine gum and a stick of Juicy Fruit in her mouth and applying one more layer of lipstick, she had not noticed the light turn green until the car behind honked several times, startling her so much that she accidentally ran the lipstick tube across her cheek and nearly choked on the wad of gum.

"Alright already!" she yelled, sticking the gum to the steering wheel, and feverishly rubbing out the streak of red. Deliberately stalling, she punched through the yellow light, leaving the woman behind honking in protest and forced to sit through another whole sequence of lights. Abbey thoughtlessly responded by thrusting her middle finger in the air. "And the horse you road in on, too!" she emphatically added.

The same thing happened at the next stoplight while Abbey worked diligently to blend the lipstick stain on her cheek with a layer of foundation make-up. This time when she missed the green light, the man behind her got out of his car and walked determinedly toward her. As soon as he reached her window, she stomped on the gas pedal, ran straight through the red light, and nearly collided with a moving truck. The alarmed driver was gifted with not only the one finger salute, but a long degrading honk of Abbey's horn.

By now you may have gathered that Abbey isn't altogether in charge of her bad temper, her driving ability, or her middle finger.

Upon approaching the house, her pulse quickened when she spotted the old red Ford Taurus parked in the driveway. This happened every time she met this client at a house viewing. He was from Liverpool, both cheeky and charming, but it was the accent she liked the most. She braced herself for what was to come.

Abbey was not surprised to see that Nigel was not sitting in his car waiting. He generally didn't have the patience and was no doubt walking around the property or having a smoke by the pool. Every home in this six-figure neighborhood contained a lanai covered by clay-tiled roofs protecting elaborate Tuscany style outdoor furniture and exotic plants that would otherwise wilt along with their owners under the merciless Texas summer sun.

Slipping out of the sensible flat shoes into a sexy pair of black high heels, Abbey entered the front door cautiously. She remembered to rid of her gum and stuck it on one of the pillars adorning each side of the massive front door. She scoffed at the magnificence of the two-story entry, knowing full well that she'd never own anything as grand as a mini mansion on a rental assistant's measly salary. The foyer alone was the size of her living room. "Rotten rich people!" she grumbled.

Abbey has quite an envy issue and she knows it, which is why she takes the liberty to snatch a fancy bar of soap, a kitchen towel, or anything she thinks won't be missed that will fit in her big purse while showing properties. Matter of fact, she has an impressive collection of washcloths and steak knives, along with a lovely assortment of silk flowers.

I think we can agree that Abbey could be considered a gum chewing kleptomaniac attached to an unhealthy case of envy in sexy high heels. But let's not judge her too harshly…not yet anyway.

From the kitchen window Abbey watched her client draw in a slow stream of smoke from the cigar that he held delicately with his thumb and forefinger. His long, lean figure appeared relaxed on the cushioned lounge chair, his feet resting on an ottoman, and by the size of the smoked cigar, she could tell that he had been there awhile. If he had not been seen arriving in the beat-up used car, he would have been mistaken for one of the many millionaires residing on that street in his white rolled-up sleeves and designer jeans, wearing a tweed flat cap and a smug lackadaisical expression. But the cheap knock-off Birkenstock sandals and the chipped toenails were a dead giveaway. No matter. The evenly stressed syllables that melodically dripped from his words made up for any discrepancies. Rearranging the bangs on her forehead, she stood up straighter and made her grand appearance.

"Ah," the man spoke from his chair, "you have arrived."

"Yes, I hope you haven't waited too long, Nigel. My meeting went a bit longer than I had expected. You know, first time buyers have so many questions, and…."

"It's quite alright," Nigel said. "I understand you're a hard-working real estate agent in the million-dollar sales club. I get it."

Hearing him repeat her lie in that heavenly English accent was like hearing Prince Charming tell Cinderella the shoe fit. But hey, she often told herself, let's get this straight right now, it's not my fault I failed the real estate exam four times. Trickery, the questions are all about tricking the student! Next time, if there is a next time, Abbey is convinced that she won't be so easily tricked.

"Yes, not everyone gets to be a member of that fancy club," she casually repeated the lie.

So, what is more disappointing, that Abbey is a bad tester or a liar with a file full of excuses?

"I thought you might be late because you were farding in the car, like most women do," he said with a straight face.

"Excuse me?" Abbey stepped back and cocked her head in place. She acted like she was repulsed by the word, although at that moment she had to stifle a laugh recalling exactly why she named her cat, Sir Arthur Fart.

"Farding," he said again. "You know, applying make-up while you are driving. Farding always slows a woman down."

Is the man psychic? Abbey wondered. How did he know I was doing just that? Farding, she repeated the word in her head. Farding. Farding. Farding…Farding! That word would attach itself to the forefront of her brain for hours, if not days. She couldn't wait to use it on one of the stuck-up agents in the office.

Seeing Abbey drifting off with her thoughts, Nigel changed the subject. "Can you tell me why Americans have to build such large pools?"

"Everything's big in Texas." She slowly sat down, allowing her skirt to crawl up her thighs.

"It takes a bit getting used to, all this vastness" he said, tapping the cigar on the nearby ash tray, eyeing her legs with interest.

"Hmmm," she purred, delighted when he noticed. Then tilting her head back, she inhaled the spicy smoke and alluring accent – a seamless fit, unlike the men she dated that smelled of cigarettes and beer with their annoying East Texas twang. "Well, as soon as you're finished, let's see what wonders this home has to offer."

Before extinguishing the cigar, Nigel took in a final swirl of smoke and swished it throughout his mouth as if it were the first taste of a fine wine. "Yes, let's see if this is the one."

As they entered the home, out of habit, Abbey turned and guardedly scanned the stone fence surrounding the property. Spotting the handsome crystal ash tray, she picked it up, tossed the cigar remains into a potted plant and stuffed it in her purse, while Nigel with little interest, briefly surveyed the kitchen.

Bypassing the living room and taking two steps at a time, he scaled the wood stairs to the second floor. "Now, this is the best part of the house," he yelled from above, his voice echoing off the bare walls. "Bedrooms with *lots* of closets!"

Abbey stood in front of the hall mirror, sucked in her stomach, and cupped her bosom. She reached inside her bra and carefully lifted each breast to form a fuller cleavage. Raising her skirt, she straightened the candy laced G-string panties that had rolled up in a bunch, pinching her skin. Once again, she admired her new hair color and the way the hair had been cut to shape her round face. She rubbed her finger across her ruffled eyebrows that always seemed to frizz in different directions from the humid weather. The exciting new word popped in her head again. *Farding!* Glancing back at her legs, she walked up the stairs. *Farding, Farding, Farding,* with each step, as tiny heart-shaped pieces of candy fell to the floor. When she reached the top, she stood still, listening for her client to determine which room he was in. She heard cabinets slam to her left, and she slowly advanced toward the owner's suite.

In case you're wondering, Abbey doesn't get invited to many parties, but she does get invited to lingerie parties because she's single and crazy about novelty undergarments. And by the way, did you know the word farding? See the asterisk at the end of the story for more information on this intriguing word. *

"Look at this, will you? A whirlpool tub! As if the hot tub by the pool wasn't enough! Can you explain that?" Nigel scoffed while delicately stroking the smooth gold-plated faucet handles.

"Well, yes, I can," Abbey said, clearing her throat to prepare her explanation. Tossing her hair back she said in a sultry voice, "I've been told that in order to get the full effect from those powerful jets one must be in the privacy of their own bathroom." Even if she wanted to, she couldn't stop from batting her fake eyelashes.

"Ohh?" Leaning casually against the sink, Nigel lifted his eyebrows and slowly scanned Abbey's body starting at her high heels. She posed just long enough to make sure he took her all in, then she turned and proceeded to the next room.

Over her shoulder, she said, "There is a lot more to this house. Come see the cinema room." The Englishman practically tripped over his own feet following her.

"Now step inside." Abbey motioned with a dramatic sweep of her hand, a well-practiced move she learned from Vanna White, the hostess of *Wheel of Fortune*. "I want to demonstrate the effectiveness of a windowless media room. The sofa is built in and conveys with the house. Sit down and get comfortable, please."

While Nigel nestled his body into the corner of the L-shaped sofa, Abbey located the remote control. She shut the double doors and eased toward the sofa. "Oh, it *is* dark in here." A cushion grazed the side of her leg. She patted all around it first and then slid her body into the soft corduroy fabric. "Nigel, are you comfy?"

The room was quiet, and she could smell a tinge of cigar smoke to her left. "Nigel, I asked you, are you comfy?" Silence. She asked again, this time with a hint of fear in a higher, squeakier voice. "Nigel, Nigel?"

When Nigel finally spoke, he was not in the corner of the sofa, but sitting right next to her. "Quite comfy, and you?"

"Oh!" Abbey gasped. "I'm sorry, I didn't realize I had sat so close to you."

"You didn't," he whispered in her ear. "I just felt that you might be afraid of the dark."

"Um, well, uh maybe." She paused to listen and all she could hear was his light breathing and the pounding of her heart. "See, you can't hear a thing. Perfect for sound effects."

"Yes, let's just sit here quietly for a bit," Nigel suggested. "I love the power of a still room. Almost like being in a closet."

Abbey placed the remote control in her lap and sat motionless. *Farding, Farding, Farding* and one more *Farding* pounded in her ears. The word evaporated the second she felt the warmth radiating from Nigel's forearm as it lightly caressed hers; the course black hair tickled her bare skin. She noticed his breathing had quickened. They sat muted for a while longer until Abbey pushed the button to turn on the home theatre. A dull light filled the room. She turned to Nigel and saw that he was watching her. Startled by the creepy grin on his face distorted by the blue light emitting from the screen, she jumped up and ran to the door.

"I really don't know how to use this thing, but I think you get the idea. No windows, no outside noise, a perfect theatre experience..." she rattled on, frantically fumbling around for the doorknob. Finally locating it, she opened the door and let the sunshine enter. "Yes, yes, and look at the sun exposure from these huge windows, but not in the cinnamon room. Ha! Ha! I mean cinema. Anyway, a nice touch, but maybe it's making it too warm. Phew, I'm feeling rather hot," Abbey complained, pulling at her blouse that had clung beneath her heavily padded bra. With a sudden flush of her cheeks came a toneless chuckle, more like an exasperated grunt.

What was that all about? Is Abbey really afraid of the dark, or afraid of blue men? Inquiring minds want to know.

"I am quite warm myself. Perhaps, it's not just the sun," Nigel spoke in a low buttery voice.

Abbey gathered her wits and in her most professional voice – one could only imagine what that sounds like – she said, "Well, let's continue looking at the other rooms, shall we?"

"Of, course. Right behind you."

"I know you have suggested that you need ample closet space, and this home has plenty." Abbey pointed inside the first bedroom closet, while Nigel leaned in closer and stuck his head inside.

"Hmm, nice, but not for me."

"OK, then, let's check out bedroom number two."

Nigel shared his disappointment again with the size of the next closet and followed Abbey to the last bedroom. "Now, this just has to suit you," she said, pressing her body against the closet door. Nigel leaned into the smallest closet of all and when he drew back, he brushed against Abbey's breast. "Oh, forgive me," he said.

"You're forgiven," Abbey assured him. "Is this a good size?" She lifted her chest shamelessly.

"Umm, well," he said, eyeing the perspiration secreting in her cleavage, "let me see, let me see." He stepped into the closet and resting his back against the wall, he slowly slid down to the floor. He removed his cap, revealing a shiny, glistening bald head. "Shall we test it?"

Looking away, she made a sour face, picked up the cap and put it back on his head. For some unknown reason, she was disturbed by bald heads. Smiling down at him, Abbey moaned with pleasure. She stepped out of her heels, and while holding the edge of the skirt with her teeth, she slipped out of her panties. She pulled off a piece of candy, stuck it in Nigel's mouth and then hung the strand of underwear on the doorknob. Seductively, she unbuttoned her blouse, exposing a bright yellow, fluffy, fur halter bra. She stood before him, biting hard on her bottom lip while slowly massaging her breasts in a circular motion. Bits of fuzz floated in the air.

"Oh, I see you brought along your furry friends," he said between chomps on the hard candy, while he hurriedly unzipped his jeans. He pulled them down to his knees.

Abbey leaned in and squinted hard to read the words written on his boxer shorts. "World's Greatest?" she questioned. "We'll see about that." She knelt before him and removed his sandals. They slid easily from his sweaty feet. Wishing she hadn't touched his moist, clammy feet, she concentrated on unbuttoning his shirt. His nipples had hardened and Abbey bit on one, then the other, licking her way toward his lips.

I'm sorry to interrupt this crucial moment, but if you're thinking Abbey is a slut, then pray tell, what is Nigel?

With her thighs straddling his, she chewed on his chin and when their lips met, she sighed into his warm and peppery mouth. The bitter taste of his potent aftershave on her tongue made Nigel gag.

"Blah," Nigel spouted and turned his head away from hers.

"Whhhhaaaat?" Abbey whined. "Doesn't the wittle baby wike the taste of wubble wum? Wah, wah, wah!"

Oh no, to top it off, now we know she's a whiner, too. And the baby talk, yuck! You can stop right here if you're feeling a little uneasy or queasy...well, don't say I didn't warn you.

While Nigel kept his face turned, Abbey began playfully licking around the edges of his ears. Now, *that* got his attention, and everything suddenly sprang into action. But not for long because from downstairs came a robust voice announcing her arrival. "Agent entering! Anyone here? I'm coming in!"

"Oh, how I wish," the frustrated Brit moaned, when Abbey slammed her thighs together, forcing him to retreat. She jumped up so fast she hit her head on the clothes rod and fell clumsily backwards. Landing on her bottom, one foot caught inside his boxers, the other held high in the air, she let out a tinny, "Owww!"

Nigel laughed. Not a simple little chuckle, but an all-out guffaw.

"I bet you like watching pianos fall from six flights up and land on little old ladies, too!" she hissed. Hearing the agent talking to her clients below, she sat up, slapped her legs together and quickly covered his mouth with her hand.

Making sure that she wasn't seen, she crawled on all fours over to the stairwell and yelled, "I'm an agent showing the house. Please wait outside, we're almost finished." She heard a loud "humph!" from downstairs and waited to hear the door shut before returning to the closet; her knees making awful squeaking sounds as she dragged them across the highly polished wood floor.

Nigel was standing up, jeans and underwear pooled at his ankles and clearly disturbed by the interruption. Pleased that he had at least stopped laughing, Abbey stood upright, turned around, lifted her skirt, and holding onto the clothes rod she spread her legs and wiggled her bottom like a duck. Nigel shuffled over, and from behind her he grabbed onto the clothes rod with both hands. Leaning in he pressed his body hard against hers. The weight of the two bodies yanked the brackets right out of the wall, the rod with it, forcing the couple to crash to the floor. Abbey's hard head flew back and slammed into Nigel's sharply beaked nose.

"Bloody closet!" Nigel cursed through clinched teeth, cupping his injured nose with his hands, while Abbey, barely suppressing the giggles, rushed to the bathroom. He pulled up his pants, gathered up their shoes and followed.

The agent opened the front door again and yelled, "We are on a tight schedule, are you about finished?"

"Shut up, you old cunt!" he growled, raising his fist angrily in the air as blood began to spurt from his nose. He watched Abbey cringe, either from the foul language or the dripping blood, he didn't care to ask.

Another "humph!" was uttered from downstairs, and the door was slammed harder this time.

"I'm very sorry, Abbey," Nigel said, stuffing toilet paper up his nostrils, "but this house just doesn't work for me."

"No problemo, sir," she sighed, heavily disappointed. "But there is another one just a few miles away. The owners are out of town. Can we try out their closets tomorrow, por favor?"

"Well, I'm very particular, you know. *Lots* of closets?" he asked with a grin.

"Si, senor," she answered excitedly, but at a safe distance. "And there's mucho more, and I will gladly show you all of them," she assured him. "Todos!"

Well, look at that! Not only is Abbey bilingual, but she is also perfectly willing to waste her day showing homes to this hard-to-please client with bad credit, an ugly car, sweaty feet, nosebleeds, and a foul, stinky cigar mouth.

"Count me in, you little tart," Nigel teased with a flirty wink, leaning in for a kiss. Abbey shrunk back in disgust.

"Yuck, you've got blood on your face *and* your shirt," she said squeamishly, "and besides, we better get going, that agent is probably fuming by now." Abbey pulled away, grabbed the roll of toilet tissue from Nigel's hand, snatched up a fancy soap dish and walked toward the stairs, just as the agent and her clients were heading up. She stepped back, clutching the stolen items to her chest, and let the angry woman pass. The couple with her stared straight ahead, visibly incensed.

"Oh, Abbeeeey," Nigel called out after her, laughing as he playfully pranced down the hallway. "Look what I found hanging on the closet doorknob!" He had her panties stretched over his bald head and his shoes and hat in his hands when he turned the corner and ran smack-dab into the agent.

"Oh, shite!" he shouted, looking over at the couple and managing a fake insincere grin. The agent pressed her back against the wall, dropped her purse and put up her fists, ready to defend herself from the deranged barefoot man with a wad of tissue stuffed up his nose.

Nigel laughed, a kind of one-nostril snorty horse laugh and doubled over in hysterics. When he could finally contain himself, he pulled the underwear from his head and waved it in the air. "What a howler!" he yelled, as candy flew from the strings in all directions. The twisted, blood-saturated tissue fell from his nose to his feet, and his left nostril spewed like a geyser. The agent and her clients huddled together in the corner looking horrified at the dangerously unbalanced man. Abbey, refusing to give up any of the toilet paper for the cause, stood back and stared in revulsion.

It appears that Abbey is not only selfish, she also doesn't like the sight of blood. We can safely rule out that she's a vampire. As for Nigel, he is clearly a walking time bomb or a bad actor with bad timing and a potty mouth.

Nigel, pinching his nose and holding up what was left of the panties stood up stiffly and said with a flat nasally accent, "So, Abbey, do these knickers convey with the house?"

Abbey was painting her last fingernail when she looked up and saw the traffic light turn red just when she was right upon it. Braking hard, the cup of ice coffee held tightly between her thighs sloshed all over her clothing. She put the car in park and blew on her nails. Then she climbed over the back seat and fished out another outfit she had stored in the small tote she kept handy just in case, well, just in case. Disgruntled drivers honked as they drove around her when the light turned green.

Struggling out of the wet skirt, including her panties, a police officer on a motorcycle pulled up next to her. He stood patiently watching her clumsily disrobe in the limited space while yelling obscenities under her breath. "Farding, farding, farding!"

Arching backwards, she shimmied into a dry skirt. Just when she put her leg over the front seat, she saw him.

"Oh, dear…hi, officer," she said with as much humility she could find in her irritated voice.

"Ma'am, please step out of the car and explain yourself," he ordered with a hint of amusement in his tone.

"Si Senor." Abbey pulled herself together, and in her bare feet she exited the car.

"Please, don't give me a ticket. Pleaseeee!" she whined, bowing down at his feet, clutching the sides of his long, shiny boots. While on her knees, she slyly unbuttoned her blouse. Then she slowly stood up, puffed up her chest and went directly into her spiel.

"I'm on my way to an interview, and I spilled coffee all over my clothes…they're on the floorboard if you want proof…and, and, I really need to get there on time…it's a great job opening I want so badly to ace, because you see, I kind of lost my last job, but I have another specialty I want to pursue, and I'm *very* good at it, and I'm certain the company I'm meeting will hire me on the spot because I have so much experience, and it's important that I look the part," she spewed all of this in one breath, expanding her arms so that the officer could get a good view of her latest purchase.

The officer, staring google-eyed behind heavily darkened sunglasses at Abbey's bra made entirely out of beads and feathers, stood erect and speechless.

"And you know what else?" she offered, "the company has the ideal name for the business…*Closet Love*. Isn't that perfect because I *love* closets, and I'm a very efficient men's closet organizer. I bet even *you* could use my expertise…."

So, there you have it! Abbey is a selfish, gum chewing, envious klepto with road rage, often lies, has bad taste in men and underwear, frequently whines and fails tests, hates the sight of blood, is guilty of farding while driving, most likely afraid of the dark and blue men but not police officers, pretends she's bilingual, is more than a tad slutty, and is not a natural blonde, a good driver, or holds a license of any kind. But you can be thankful for one thing…she's merely a fictitious character in a short story.

Or is she?

* Merriam/Webster dictionary defines Farding – to paint the face with cosmetics. Archaic: Gloss over. Fard was borrowed from Anglo-French (from the verb farder) and first appeared in English in the mid-1400s. It is ultimately of Germanic origin and akin to the Old High German word faro, meaning "colored."

There was a time when the train was a romantic symbol,
where lovers met, where mysteries evolved,
and the passengers surrendered to time,
leisurely enjoying the moment as life
rushed past them just beyond the windowpane.
The tracks led them to and from without deviation, and
those aboard were comforted within the moving walls – as if
they were resting in their mother's womb, knowing with
certainty that they would be safely delivered.

FAST TRACK FANTASY

The Dixie Flagler passenger train was over an hour behind schedule. Edwin was worried that by the time he got to Chicago he would lose his nerve and his job, all because of one late train. Frantically pacing up and down the platform he stopped and kicked at a full trash can, disturbing flies that instantly swarmed, buzzing wildly around his head. Violently swatting the air, he backed into a woman, slamming her against the red brick wall. "I beg your pardon, miss!" he exclaimed, stepping awkwardly to the side. She was carrying a satchel that she clutched to her chest and a folder in her hand that was now on the ground; the blustery wind scattering its contents across the platform.

"Oh, no!" she cried. The eyeglasses that had fallen to the tip of her nose flew off as she ran after loose papers, trying anxiously to collect them before they landed on the railroad tracks. Dismissing the flies, Edwin snatched up the glasses, stuffed them in his coat pocket, and on impulse he began collecting the papers that blew the opposite direction. A little boy pulled away from his mother and darted after one that had teasingly grazed his ear and was being tossed in the air like a lost kite. He reached it just before he tumbled off the platform and just when Edwin grabbed his shirt collar and yanked him back to safety.

"Thank God!" the mother shrieked and pulled her son from Edwin's grip, causing him to stumble backwards and knock over an elderly man who was bending down to put a cigarette butt in the cuff of his pants.

"I got it, mama, I got it!" the boy exclaimed triumphantly, proudly stuffing the paper in her face. Clearly upset the dazed mother cried tears of relief when her husband rushed over and took the child from her arms.

Edwin picked up the trembling old man, steadied him, and apologized to the others who had been knocked down like dominoes from his fall. Grumbles and moans were heard from all around as the crowd stepped back to watch the crazed man feverishly gather up the rest of the papers.

Scouring the area for more, Edwin spotted the woman he had bumped into comically chasing the last visible piece of paper at the other end of the platform. Each time she bent down to pick it up, a gust of wind would carry it away. He chuckled when she finally caught it and walked back toward him, appearing quite aggravated, mumbling in frustration, her forehead tightly scrunched as she squinted hard to see in front of her. Waving her glasses and the papers in the air, Edwin guided her toward him.

"Thank goodness you have my glasses. I'm as blind as a bat without them." she declared. "Were you able to get them all?"

"I think so," he said with a twisted smile, while attempting to place the bent glasses back on her nose. "We'd better go inside, out of the wind. Here, let me help you with your satchel."

"Thank you, but I'd prefer to carry it myself."

He followed her through the door to a row of empty seats. When they sat down, Edwin secured the papers on his lap. He took a moment to catch his breath and reached out to shake the woman's hand. "I'm Edwin Dunworthy."

Gripping his hand firmly, she clearly announced, "I'm Frances Wolski, and your hand is shaking."

Edwin kept her hand in his while he studied the woman's intriguing face – captivated by her dramatic eyebrows and large doe eyes grossly magnified behind abnormally thick lenses.

"I believe yours is trembling, as well," Edwin said.

Quite uncomfortable with his staring, she let go of his sweaty palm and leaned down to tend to the papers. She was not accustomed to men looking at her and so closely and in that particular way. As nice as he seemed, he had only added to her frustration, and she wished he would just leave.

While her nimble fingers thumbed efficiently through the stack of papers, Edwin clumsily sorted through the ones in his lap, taking the liberty to scan the words written on them.

Frances sat up abruptly, blowing a loose strand of hair that had fallen out of place. Catching Edwin reading her papers, she thrust her hands out, palms up, and with a severe look she demanded that he hand over the disheveled stack right then and there.

"Oh, of course! I, uh …," stumbling over the words, he placed them in her hands. "I didn't mean to pry. I, well..."

"Hmm," she groaned disapprovingly, shuffling the papers, and stuffing them into the folder. Then reaching around the back of her head, she removed a jeweled clip from her hair to clasp the folder tightly together. "I should have thought of this before," she said, when turning to meet Edwin's eyes.

"Very clever." Edwin smiled at seeing the long, silky locks of hair falling loosely around her face. "I'm very sorry about what happened out there. Are you okay?"

"I'm fine, thank you." Frances shifted restlessly in her seat, wanting to pace the floor as she had been doing earlier, until she decided to go outside for fresh air. She didn't think she could sit still long enough to have a simple conversation, at least not until she was settled on the train gliding fast and furiously toward her destination.

"What in the world is causing this delay?" she asked defiantly, stomping one foot on the floor. "This is utterly ridiculous!"

"Do you travel on trains much?" Edwin asked.

"I may never again!" she spouted, and promptly stood up. "Could we finish this conversation on the train? Right now, I'd like to question someone in charge of this so-called mode of transportation!"

"I'll come with you."

"Oh no, don't bother," she said without looking back.

Edwin ignored her remark and stayed on her heels to the nearest station attendant.

Just as promised, they found themselves fifteen minutes later boarding the sleek all-coach streamliner to Chicago. The trip featured a twenty-nine-hour leisurely ride at an average speed of forty-nine miles per hour. The popular extended route was added in 1940, just a year earlier. Frances had wished her very first trip on a train would be one of relaxation. But not so. As she was led to her seat, Edwin departed to the next car. He turned to say something to her, but she was standing with her hands on her hips, apparently unhappy, frowning down at a man who was sound asleep, his legs loosely spread out in front of her seat.

Behind Edwin, a stout, matronly nun tapped him on the

back with her cane. "Stop dawdling and gawking at that young woman!" she ordered. He knew better than to argue with a sister in full black habit, especially one with a flat face of a bulldog. He clamped his mouth shut and reluctantly moved forward.

Frances left the snoring man undisturbed and went to the ladies' room to freshen up. It took nearly an hour for her to finally escape a group of women who had corralled her into listening to their spiel about the latest Max Factor make-up. They refused to let her leave until she allowed them to apply it to her clean, unadorned face, fussing over her with excitement at the amazing makeover. "You could pass for Ginger Rogers," a small voice stated. "No, more like Betty Grable," another argued. When Frances slipped her glasses back on, the women sighed heavily. "But must you wear the glasses?"

"Well, only if I want to see!" Frances retorted. The silly question had been directed at her more times than she cared to remember. Attempting again to excuse herself, she finally got their full cooperation when she confessed in a white lie that she was meeting a man.

"Why didn't you say so, darling?" the oldest of the flock spoke up. "He will fall madly in love with you the moment he sees your gorgeous new face," another said, dabbing Frances' nose with powder and then shooing her out the door. The second she was no longer in sight, one of the ladies whispered, "I doubt that even Max Factor can help that girl with those ghastly thick glasses. Mercy me!"

As she stood at the entry to the dining car, absentmindedly licking off the freshly applied lipstick, Frances saw that the room was full. She spotted the back of Edwin's head, recognizing the thick jet-black hair that had pressed against her chest when he slammed her into the brick wall earlier. Feeling anxious and hoping to calm down with a nice alcoholic beverage, she realized that she had no choice but to sit with him. She took a deep breath and tapped him lightly on the shoulder.

"Oh, there you are!" His dimpled smile came easily, and the look in his eyes reflected pleasure at seeing her. "Please join me."

Surveying the car once more to make sure that he was her last resort, her eyes stopped at the bottle of wine on the table placed next to a little plate of hors d'oeuvres and an empty wine glass. "I, well, are you expecting someone?"

"Yes…you." Edwin motioned for her to sit down. "You did suggest we continue our conversation on the train, so here we are."

"That's right. I guess I did. Thank you for saving me a seat."

"You look nicely refreshed," he said, pouring wine in her glass. Frances caught herself licking her lips again and bit down hard on her tongue.

"Now, what is a lovely lady like you doing all alone on a train to Chicago?"

She eyed Edwin curiously, as no man had ever called her lovely. *Why, I believe he's flirting with me. It must be the make-up, or he's as blind as I am.* Whatever was transpiring, she felt the need to sit up taller. Requiring a little time to ponder his question, she held up the long-stemmed glass and took a sip. "Oh, this *is* lovely." Although she had wanted to confide in someone, her story was a long and complex one. Until she felt more comfortable with the man sitting in front of her, she decided not to tell him the real reason why she was traveling. Posing, she smiled impishly over her raised shoulder, batting her newly painted eyelashes behind lowered spectacles. "Well, if you must know, I'm on a secret mission that I cannot reveal, lest I suffer the consequences."

"Oh, dear lady, you now have me in suspense," Edwin said, playing along, deciding this was not the time to tell her that she had lipstick on her front tooth.

"And I shall keep you there. So, do you live in Miami?"

"No, I go there to vacation, but also my company has a branch in Miami so I can mix business with pleasure. Only this time my vacation was cut short."

"Ah, a secret mission?"

"Ha!" Edwin rolled his eyes. "I can assure you mine is strictly company business. Matter of fact, if I had missed this train, well…I'll just say thank heavens we left when we did. It was a close call. I guess I appeared quite ridiculous swatting at those silly flies. Again, I'm very sorry I caused all that trouble."

"Oh my, don't be. It was the most exciting thing that's happened today," Frances said, suddenly wishing she could withdraw the bold statement, but seeing the relief on Edwin's face made it worthwhile. "My aunt, Beulah Wolski has stake in several companies in Chicago and Florida. What's the name of your company?"

Edwin appeared to be bothered by her question. "Well, hmm, I'm not at liberty to say. It's currently in a delicate state and like you, I'm sworn to secrecy." With a taut smile, he quickly lifted his glass and changed the subject by making a toast.

Realizing they were struggling through the conversation, both sidetracking the reason for their presence on the train, Frances willingly let down her guard. The trip would be long, and she could use a good conversation in exchange for her worries. Despite the dark rings under his eyes and the unruly cowlick, he had a pleasant face, and thank goodness she wasn't stuck with a cold fish or a teetotaler. Soon they were chatting about everything from the weather to the latest news regarding the impending war before finally getting around to what really mattered.

"So, tell me about yourself, Frances. I assume that you are single since I see no sign of commitment on your finger. Or did you by chance leave your wedding ring on the bathtub this morning?"

Frances chuckled. "I doubt if I would leave such a valuable sentiment anywhere," she paused, looking down at the glass in her hand, swirling the contents and imagining a luxurious bubble bath with wine. As it often happened, she began thinking about how to put that thought in a poem. Then realizing that Edwin was waiting for an answer, she said, "Oh, I'm sorry. Sometimes I get caught up in my imagination. Yes, I mean no, I have never been married and thankfully my heart is still in one piece."

"Well said. Tell me about that imagination of yours. Are you a writer?"

"In a sense. I'm an aspiring poet." Frances took the opportunity to boast. "I've written quite a few poems in my short career, and some have actually been published," sheepishly adding, "in local publications, anyway."

"That's wonderful. I see you have your folder with you. Are those your poems?"

"Well, yes, it's some of my collection I'm editing while on this trip." Shying away, she shoved the folder into the corner of the seat and placed the satchel underneath the table by her feet. "But please don't change the subject. It's only fair that I should ask you the same question."

"Oh, you mean, am I married? No, my heart is not altogether in one piece, but what's left of it is all mine…for the time being."

Frances wasn't sure how to respond. There was obviously a story of lost love behind his comment. She decided not to pursue the subject and made herself busy by scooping up a teaspoon of pâté. "This is marvelous," she said in between bites.

"I'll have some, too. I'm ravenous! I think my pacing up and down that platform added up to nearly three miles. Although I am accustomed to long walks. I find that I release much of my tension that way. What do you enjoy doing outdoors? I suspect by your healthy form, and that peachy complexion, that you do more than write. Do you sail?"

Frances muffled a laugh. *Lovely, now peachy? Oh my, he is flirting with me.* "I have sailed a few times, but mostly I love to walk, especially in the woods and parks. That's where I play my flute. I have this insatiable desire to be a wood nymph. Why, I've been known to spend *hours* playing under the canopies of those tall, enchanting trees." She gazed out the window in deep thought.

Seeing Frances in a different light, Edwin settled back and rested his arm atop the leather seat. "You, as a wood nymph. I can visualize it now," he spoke softly. The honeyed tone of his voice piqued her interest, and she turned to give him her full attention. "You have the wild, wavy, golden hair. You are tall and slender, and what I have seen of your legs, I am betting that they are sturdy, and quite capable of dancing and climbing trees. Your fingers are perfect for the flute, graceful, agile, and I bet with those full luscious lips you have played many enchanting lullabies, and...," he leaned forward meeting Frances' eyes and said in a sultry whisper, "there is a childlike expression that you are wearing right now that tells me you have sat amongst nature, the birds and the bees, and have been one with them all."

Frances had eased forward on her elbow, her chin resting in her hand, imagining herself exactly as Edwin had described, and the look on her face was one of sheer pleasure. She slowly leaned back and placed her hands in her lap, allowing his words and the sweet wine to seduce her. They sat silently smiling at each other until the waiter interrupted. "May I get you something else?"

Frances looked up at him and said with a straight face, "Ah, yes, how quickly can you get me a flute, a forest, and a midsummer night?"

While Edwin laughed and Frances joined in, the waiter stood stiffly rolling his eyes, clearly not amused. From that moment on, the two of them shared easily with one another.

"I'm an only child. I would have loved to have had siblings, but five?" Frances said, sipping on her second glass of wine. "My goodness, you must have had a wonderfully crazy childhood."

"I did. It's also the main reason I must keep this business deal alive." Edwin's smile dropped as he decided to explain. "You see, my family fell on hard times, and I have been helping them. They now depend on me solely. After we lost my mother, my father took ill, and he was responsible for my youngest sister. My other sisters are married, and both are far south, and my older brother is in the Navy, currently on a battleship. So, you can see why it's up to me to make things right. Other than a few vacations a year, I don't need to spend my money on much else. I recently moved my father and sister into my home. I probably don't sound like the perfect catch, do I?"

"On the contrary!" Frances frowned and softly pounded her fist on the table. "What you're doing is quite admirable. I would not want to know anyone who could turn their back on their own family, especially during wartime. As it is, I know of too many people that live in practically palaces that could house several families, and yet they keep it all to themselves.

All those empty rooms wasted, when so many people need shelter. What are they thinking? When they die, will they haunt their own homes, floating mindlessly through each room longing for their furnishings?" Hearing her voice rise and feeling her face redden, she sensed a need to apologize. "I'm sorry, I am a bit passionate about certain things. When I have my way someday, I will do a great deal more to help others."

"I wish more people felt that way. I'd do anything to help my family." Edwin sighed and closed his eyes. "Anything," he murmured.

"I'm so sorry you lost your mother." Frances bowed her head trying not to imagine the unthinkable, and that was not easy to do. Appreciating Edwin's candor along with the wine beginning to loosen her tongue, she decided to share more. "I feel I should explain why I was so irritable earlier. I've been under a lot of pressure lately. The truth is, I am the granddaughter of the late Madam Florence Wolski. She was quite the socialite in her day and had a hand in opening orphanages all over the world. A remarkable woman. The reason I'm on this train is to deliver her Last Will and Testament to her attorney."

"Her will?" Edwin asked, moving the wine from his waiting lips back to the table, appearing quite interested.

"Yes, an original that my grandmother left with her personal nurse. It's dated just a few days before she died. It supersedes the one that the lawyers have now. Matter of fact, it changes everything and has already disturbed several members of my family, especially my aunt."

Frances cleared her throat. "But not my parents. They are currently working in New York with the refugee effort and aren't the least bit interested in monetary gain. Although, they don't realize it yet, their lives will change dramatically if I don't get this will to Chicago." She let out a deep sigh.

"I'm sorry for your loss." Edwin gave a respectful pause for the deceased. "And I would be a bit nervous, too, carrying such a valuable document. I certainly can understand the anticipation of change. My life will also change dramatically if the wrong decision is made tomorrow." Glancing at the empty bottle of wine and his watch, he leaned in closer to Frances. "But, since we are becoming friends, perhaps we could share more later. After all, we do have a long ride ahead to get to know each other better." Edwin smiled, opening his eyes wider.

Becoming friends? Frances liked the idea and fought back another giggle. "This has been nice, Edwin. I'm feeling a lot better than I did earlier, but I could use a little freshening up."

"Would you like to continue at dinner? Say, six o'clock in the formal dining car?" he asked, clasping his hands together as if he were praying.

"Are you certain? I'm so hungry, I might snatch food off your plate, too."

"I'll fight you to the death for the last roll," he said, standing up with his hand on his hip and the other one in the air, pretending to be a Musketeer.

"May the best man win," Frances said, in her deepest voice. When she stood, the wine and the tilted glasses made her a little dizzy. Edwin reached out for her shoulders and guided her to the aisle. He turned her around and pointed. "That way," he said. Giggling, she gripped the back of the seats as she attempted to proceed with dignity toward the women's quarters, completely unaware that she had left the satchel in the booth.

Edwin spotted the satchel. He quickly tucked it under his

arm and turned to walk the opposite direction. When Frances realized she was without it, she yelled from behind him, "Oh, dear God, I almost left my satchel!"

Startled, Edwin turned and teasingly held the satchel up in the air, high above his head. "My goodness dear girl, if you are carrying the will in here, you should hold on to this a lot tighter. They have a safe onboard for valuables. I will gladly see that it's properly stored."

An instant frown and a confused expression fell on Frances' face. Reaching up on her tiptoes, she snatched the satchel from his grip and hurried out of the car, leaving Edwin standing in the middle of the aisle looking more than slightly disappointed.

When Frances did not show for dinner, Edwin became concerned. The woman in the next booth eyed him curiously, and several times in between bites, he caught her kittenish smile. She was a pretty red-head in a smartly styled short haircut with eye-skimming side bangs that made her look mysterious. Edwin knew he could easily engage her, but he thought better of it. Not on this trip. He reluctantly dismissed the lovely passenger and avoiding her alluring eyes on the way out, he walked purposely past her to try and find Frances.

As he thought more about Frances, she didn't seem to him like the kind of person who would scare easily or deliberately break an engagement. Not the least bit shy, she expressed herself with ease, and she was naturally charming. He considered that she would be prettier without the glasses or squinting eyes. He tried to imagine her in something other than the conservative clothing she wore – solid colors without patterns or frills and the skirt ending respectably below her knees. She buttoned her blouse to the top button that rested just inches from her chin. Edwin wondered if she looked as lovely underneath all that fabric as he had described her earlier. Determined to stay focused on his present mission, he would not allow himself to think of her that way.

He was heading toward the lounge when the attractive lady he had seen in the dining car stepped right in his path.

"Oh, excuse me," she said. "I was hoping to run into you."

"Oh?" Edwin looked at her curiously. He didn't know why, but he found it somewhat disconcerting standing so close to her. He politely took a step back.

"Yes, I saw you earlier with a young lady, and I noticed that she wasn't at dinner with you tonight." She took a step forward.

"Well," Edwin replied with an unexpected mouthful of embarrassment, "I suppose she changed her mind."

"Hmm," she tapped her chin. "I wonder. I just saw your friend in the ladies' quarters having a darn good cry."

"Oh, you did? Did you speak with her?"

"No, but I can give her a message if you'd like." She smiled demurely, yet Edwin noticed a puckish gleam in her eye.

"Would you tell her that I am here to help, and I will be in the lounge?"

The woman's smile broadened as she patted Edwin on the arm. "I think I can do that. Well, good luck, handsome. And if it doesn't work out, I hope to see you at breakfast." With a slow wink, she walked away ever so seductively, allowing Edwin to grasp a clear image of what he'd be missing.

"My goodness, women are *very* direct these days, aren't they?" said an older gentleman who had been listening nearby.

"Yes, indeed, they are," Edwin chuckled. "And frankly, I like it that way. Saves a man a lot of unnecessary chit-chat."

Frances strolled into the lounge and sat next to Edwin. Before she said anything to him, she ordered a beer. Edwin pretended to wait patiently as he watched her fidget on the barstool, dabbing at her runny nose with a pretty handkerchief. The makeup she wore earlier had been removed. Her cheeks were blotched. He was surprised to see her without her satchel or her coveted folder, carrying only a small purse.

"I'm very sorry for not showing," she said softly, and reached over to touch Edwin's hand that was neatly wrapped around his drink.

"I accept your apology, and I just want you to know that I wasn't angry, just very disappointed," he reassured her, resting his other hand on top of hers. "Would you like to tell me why you're crying?"

"I'm sure I should, but I really don't want to burden you." She began slowly slipping her hand out from under his.

Edwin gently squeezed it and looked into her eyes. "I am just the person to talk to, Frances. I have broad shoulders, and remember, I still have a great deal of my heart left. I tell you what," he turned on the stool to face her, "I trusted you with my story, I'd like to think that you can trust me with yours. Sound fair?"

Frances nodded and let out a long sigh that she had carried since she discovered what had deeply disturbed her.

"Well, it's about my grandmother's will."

"Yes, I see you are without your satchel and folder. Did you take my advice and have them put in the safe?"

"No."

"Oh? Well, go on then."

"What I didn't tell you earlier, is that my grandmother left me *and* my father the bulk of her estate. It is a significant amount of assets, and more than we need in a lifetime. For years it had been willed to her sister, my Aunt Beulah. They were very close when they were younger. But Grandmother did not tolerate liars and people who spoke ill of others. It seems my aunt excelled in that type of behavior, and as much as Grandmother tried, she could not change her sister's ways. Something dreadful must have happened for her to suddenly revise the will. And then to die shortly after." Frances bowed her head in deep thought remembering things her grandmother had shared with her.

"Hmm," Edwin sat motionless, staring at his nearly empty glass, choosing his words carefully. "I understand the loss of a loved one. I was devastated when my mother died. But think of all the wonderful things you can do and change for the better. Isn't that what you said earlier…if you had your way?"

"That was my very intention, to support what is left of the declining orphanages. I would have even helped my Aunt Beulah with her failing businesses and so much more."

"You would *still* help your aunt after all you know about her? You're a saint!"

"But you don't understand…the will is gone. I discovered that after I left you earlier. That's why I didn't meet you for dinner."

"WHAT? How can that be?" Edwin shot up from his seat. "Where was it last?"

Frances spoke almost in a whisper, shaking her head back and forth in despair. "In my folder."

"In your folder? You mean…" Grasping what she had said, he slumped back on the stool. "Oh, no!"

"It was only one document, the final page with the signatures. I was so nervous about carrying it, at the last minute I sort of panicked. I took it from my luggage to my folder, and then I decided it would be safer locked away in my satchel. I didn't realize I had left that one page in the folder. And then the train was late and that fiasco on the platform, meeting you, well, it must be blown to the high heavens by now."

Seeing the anguish on Edwin's face, she tried to relieve him of his guilt. "It's not your fault, Edwin. I should have…"

"No, I'm afraid it *is* my fault. I am so deeply, deeply sorry." He bowed his head, covering his face with his hand.

"Oh, please Edwin. It could've happened to anyone." Frances brushed away her bad feelings with a wave of her hand. "Anyway, who knows why these things happen. Fate surely has a hand in this. But for now, it will only make me feel worse if you blame yourself." Wiping a tear away, she took a big gulp of the beer that was no longer chilled.

Edwin reached out and lifted Frances' chin. He gently wiped the frothy foam from her top lip and lifted her glasses. Looking into her sad, innocent eyes, he kissed her tenderly on the mouth. "I am so sorry," he whispered. "I will find a way to make it up to you."

The sweet sensation from the trace of warm scotch on his wet lips put her at ease. "That's a very nice start," she expressed in the softest voice, keeping her eyes closed and her lips pursed for another kiss. Seeing her glasses fogging up, Edwin chuckled inwardly.

"My pleasure."

Frances felt her body go limp and realizing another kiss

was not to follow, she straightened up and put on her best face, deciding to focus on what was real – the fine, humble man in front of her.

They talked until the staff dimmed the lights and announced that the lounge was closing. Promising to have breakfast together the next morning, they parted.

The red-headed woman rose from where she had been eavesdropping, hidden in a booth behind Frances and Edwin. She extinguished her cigarette and walked casually out of the lounge.

Although emotionally exhausted, neither Frances or Edwin slept immediately but lay quietly in their berths thinking about each other and a lost will.

Determined to be of good cheer, Frances refused to ruin the morning with regrets. Her job now was to at least convince Aunt Beulah to continue supporting her parents and the refugee cause. Surely her heart was not so cold as to turn away her own brother and sister-in-law. She would remain hopeful.

Edwin awoke feeling lousy, after a restless sleep worrying about the impact the lost will had on Frances. *I'm a fat head, that's what I am. Fat head!*

The lady who had earlier delivered the message to Frances was sitting alone and caught his eye the second he walked into the dining room. Her striking red hair was aglow from the morning sun shining through the window. She smiled, excited to see him. Edwin pointed to Frances, who was seated nearby and mouthed silently, "Sorry." The lady lowered her eyebrows with a look of disappointment, shrugged, and returned to reading the menu.

Frances greeted Edwin warmly and warned him in advance that since she had skipped dinner the night before she would not be sharing and to guard his plate well. He was relieved that she was in a good mood, and they kept the conversation light. "Being over an hour late when we arrive, I'll just barely make my appointment," Edward said.

"As, will I. Although, I don't know what good will come of my attending. But who knows, maybe my grandmother left me her Polish artist painting. I love that piece and have always dreamt of hanging it in my flat." Her smile dwindled and her shoulders shook with a sudden chill. "Oh dear, I just realized I'm going to be in the same room with my wretched aunt and her silly, forty-year-old baby. Lord, please give me strength," she said through a labored chuckle. *But oh, how happy she'll be when she learns that I lost the will.*

When the Dixie Flagler slowly rolled into the Chicago station, the light-hearted mood between them moved toward a more serious one. They exited the train in an awkward silence as if they had just waltzed out of a dream. After they said goodbye, and Edwin kissed Frances on the cheek, they turned and walked opposite directions.

Edwin sulked, believing she must be blaming him for the missing will after all. He tried not to look back.

"Wait, wait Edwin!" Frances yelled. Turning around, he saw her running toward him.

"Here's my address." She handed him a folded-up piece of paper. "Let me know how it all goes! Good luck!"

Caught off guard by her bright-eyed enthusiasm, he blurted, "If all goes well, I will come pounding on your door with flowers!"

"I look forward to it," she said, hugging him tightly around the waist. "Please don't blame yourself anymore, Edwin. I'm a poet, remember? Things happen for reasons we can't explain, and if we're lucky, we'll understand it later."

Watching her dash off, Edwin mumbled despairingly under his breath, "I doubt you will ever understand."

In the cab he unfolded the note. On one side was an address and on the back was a poem that she had signed and dated. He had mixed emotions after reading it, but he couldn't help but read the last few lines again before putting it safely away.

> *The sweet warm breath*
> *A lingering tingle*
> *Anticipating more*
> *Such was the kiss*
> *Alas, I am alone on this train*
> *Gazing far beyond the windowpane*
> *At you chasing rainbows without me*

Scolding himself for letting Frances into his heart, he tried to focus on the more important business at hand. His mission had been accomplished. He knew his employer would be ecstatic with the result.

He paid the taxi and with head bent in shame, Edwin walked into the building where he would report the lost will directly to his boss, Beulah Wolski.

Later that day in the lawyer's office, Frances slipped in unnoticed and sat perfectly still at the very back of the large echoey room. She was trying to see through the small gap between Aunt Beulah and her son who were huddled together in front of the attorney's desk. They were giggling. Why would they be giggling?

The attorney interrupted her thoughts when he asked the loud and giddy heiress, "I have a note here that says Miss Frances Wolski will be attending this hearing and will provide some additional information. Should I be expecting her?"

The aunt lifted her son's head from her shoulder and answered haughtily, "Most likely not. I imagine she's rather upset with my sister's decision. Tell me what my dear sister left her, and I'll be sure that she gets it." She waved off the man peering suspiciously over his spectacles.

"Um, I'm here." Frances cleared her throat and stood up abruptly, knocking the wooden chair behind her on its side, startling her feeble cousin who jerked and let out a whiney squeal.

"Oh, I see." The attorney smiled, and scolded Beulah with his eyes. "Do you wish to submit something regarding this will?"

"No sir, I did, but…no sir." Frances could not find the courage to admit she had lost the will.

"Of course not!" Beulah smirked in a harsh whisper.

"Well then, young lady, your grandmother has bequeathed you with a Boznaska oil painting and two thousand dollars that she has instructed you to use toward publishing your book of poetry. It looks like she's also leaving you her home, once your aunt," he paused to look at Beulah to make sure that she was listening, "passes on."

"What? What did you say?" Beulah grabbed her son and pulled herself up, her substantial weight nearly bringing him to his knees. "This can't be true! It was always supposed to be mine to give to my son. Besides, we're already occupying my sister's home during the summer!"

"It is right here in writing, madam." The attorney read it again, to make perfectly clear that the outraged woman understood. "Furthermore, until the time comes for her to take ownership, Ms. Wolski, your niece has the option to live under the same roof, along with you and your child, uh, excuse me, your…" he paused to look at Beulah's son whose eyes were nearly popping out of their sockets. Sucking in a breath, he continued reading.

When the meeting ended, Frances walked past her aunt sitting on a bench outside the building gloating over her good fortune. Before she rounded the corner, Aunt Beulah yelled at her niece, "I plan to live to one hundred, dearie, so don't get too excited about claiming my home any sooner!"

"I sincerely hope you do. And don't worry dearie, I won't be moving in."

After hearing the hostility in her aunt's voice, she knew in her heart that asking her to support anything would be in vain. She was prepared to give up the rights to her grandmother's home in exchange for keeping at least her parent's livelihood intact. Those poor children without their families. Oh, how she wished she had not lost the will.

The train ride home subdued Frances, and she found herself thinking a great deal about Edwin. She hoped that he had gotten his business in order and was celebrating somewhere with his family; but she mostly hoped that she would be seeing him again. She closed her eyes and fell asleep thinking of his kiss.

When she arrived back in the warmth of the Miami sun, she scoured the platform for the missing paper, checked the Lost and Found, and even questioned a few of the employees. Surrendering again to her fate, she left the station with a little less bounce in her step, until she once again counted her blessings, remembering that she had been given the money to help publish her poetry and a painting that would always remind her of her wonderful grandmother. She doubted that she'd ever set foot on her grandmother's estate again until her aunt died, and knowing the stubborn woman like she did, she was certain old Aunt Beulah would hang on another thirty years just for spite. She was now even more determined to strike the bargain that would save her parents.

Frances spent the rest of the week talking to agents and sending out her poems to various publications. In between, she thought about Edwin. She was delighted to receive a letter from him, until she read it while sitting under a tree at her favorite park. He reported that he had lost the business deal and his father's health was rapidly declining. He recounted their special time together on the train and once again apologized for causing her to lose her inheritance. After thanking her for the lovely poem, he wished her a bright future and wrote that he was looking forward to reading her poetry in publications across America. His last sentence expressed his regrets that he did not have anything to offer her, or he would have already been at her door with flowers. There was no return address.

Feeling her emotions surge, an intense sadness took Frances by surprise. Until that moment she had not realized just how much she had hoped for more.

Edwin walked slowly in circles around the small city park. His thoughts centered on that fateful day. Bumping into Frances was perfectly planned, but losing the will was pure luck. Still, no amount of justifying his actions could stop the truth surrounding them. He regretted that he had foolishly agreed to aid the ruthless Aunt Beulah with all her lies. As chairman of the board, she had convinced him that by destroying the new will, she would remain the principal beneficiary and be able to save their failing company and Edwin's position. A raise would also be in order. He believed her claim that Frances, a spoiled niece, a silly poet, had seduced her grandmother during her fragile and final days, and stole what was rightfully Beulah's.

What a fool he had been.

With Beulah Wolski having the upper hand, especially now that she would be among the rich and famous, she made sure that Edwin would not have a leg to stand on. He was defamed in front of the Board and immediately discharged.

While the shame bore a hole in his spirit, Edwin wanted desperately to believe that if the will had not been lost, he would not have carried out the plan to steal it from Frances. How could he have, when he knew he was falling for the idealistic young wood nymph with the grand ideas and exaggerated eyes.

A smile crossed his face when he recalled Frances comically chasing down the last piece of paper and how he had rescued the little boy from falling onto the tracks. At least I did one good deed, he concluded. Then suddenly, he remembered that the young lad had been carrying one of the papers in his hand. Did he retrieve it from him? He recalled the scene: the mother's eyes, full of fear and tears of gratitude and how he was frantically trying to gather loose papers all around him, his heart beating loudly in his chest. There was no time to think, and when he stumbled over the old man, Edwin had lost sight of her.

"Oh, good Lord!" he blurted out. He wondered what the chances were of finding that family again and if the paper was still in their possession. It all seemed highly impractical, nearly impossible, but he would have to try. He owed it to Frances. He owed it to his family. His father's words sounded off loud and clear in his head. "Son, you have made a grave error. You will have to live with it forever, unless something good can come from it. I pray you will know when the time comes."

It was only a matter of hours when he found himself boarding the train back to Miami.

In a hopeless attempt to locate the mother and child on the train, he ended up in the lounge spewing the whole story to the bartender. "Poetic justice is what this is my friend, no pun intended," he lamented. "I'm just another knucklehead whistling Dixie." Pointing to his empty glass, he signaled for another drink.

"Sure, mister. But let's make this one your last. No reason to add to your misery."

"Of course, you are right. Make it the last one," Edwin agreed, not wanting to aid the impending depression either, but he was enjoying numbing himself to some degree. It was not in his nature to give up, but the pull was getting stronger. He recalled when Frances had pounded her tightened fist on the table, expressing her passion for family and her desire to help others. Watching her blush and her pupils enlarge reminded him of someone he used to be. How did he let himself get in such a bad way? Fear and desperation, the poor choices he had made, they were finally taking their toll on him.

A couple next to him were in a heated discussion. The woman was crying, and the man was holding her close to his chest. He ran his fingers through her hair and said, "Honey, I promise I will make it up to you."

Edwin remembered telling Frances the same. In one long gulp he finished the last drink. Stumbling to his room with renewed determination, he purposely marched down every aisle on the train looking once again for the woman and child that could change Frances' future, and if he played his cards right, possibly his own.

In the upper bunk, falling in and out of consciousness, Edwin finally gave into sleep. In a dream he imagined Frances as a wood nymph perched high in a tree, blowing kisses to him as he watched from below. When she put the flute to her lips, there was no sound. The scene quickly faded, and he appeared inside a beautiful mansion with children running all around him from room to room. Not an unusual dream except all of them wore thick glasses.

When the train pulled into the station, the platform was full of people. It was summer in Miami, and families were flocking to the bustling shorelines to soak up the warm sun, while the natives fled to get away from the crowds. Edwin was glad that he had only one small suitcase in tow as he squeezed past people from all walks of life, and when he waded through a group of men in turbans dragging crates of something indescribable, the repugnant odor made his eyes water and his stomach queasy. The after-effect from drinking the night before was still with him. He held his breath and charged through. Bracing himself against a wall, he broke out in a cold sweat and waited for the crowd to lessen.

No one in sight fit his recollection of the woman and child. He decided to check with the main office again. All he found was yet another brick wall. Running out of ideas, he decided to go for a long walk. He heard drum beating and continuous clapping. He turned the corner and was faced with a crowd of people gathered on each side of the street waving American flags. Slowly moving between them was a marching military band followed by a big float filled with streaming red, white, and blue ribbons. He had forgotten it was the 4th of July.

The crowd was giddy with excitement – sheer happiness shown on their faces. Children were waving madly, in one hand a lollypop or an ice cream cone; the younger ones begging to be lifted higher so they could see. Room was respectfully carved out for the elderly. Edwin took a moment to enjoy the scene.

Suddenly, the crowd came to a low hush, and directed by their parents, children stood at attention. Palms met hearts as the largest float of all carrying an American flag standing thirty feet tall stopped before them. A trumpeter positioned high on a pedestal blew the first notes to "America the Beautiful."

All around Edwin, folks began singing and the tears of love for their country could not be held back. Edwin fought back his own tears and took this opportunity to search for the woman and child. He moved methodically up and down the street, until every mother and child began to take on the faces of those he was searching for. Useless, he thought. Utterly useless! The singing stopped, and the drums began to rumble. Giving up, he walked away from all the commotion.

He was drawn to a billboard displaying the new movie release, *Moon Over Miami*. There she was, Betty Grable in blonde curls clutching the moon in a backless swimsuit. He closed his eyes and pictured the star with thick lens glasses.

Minutes later, he was seated mid-section in the theatre, the only seat available for the big debut.

The plot was about a woman who hoped to hook a rich man at a resort in Miami. It was all about lies, but in a nonsensical way, with outbursts of laughter from the audience, and in the end, a sigh of relief was heard when the truth prevailed. Typical, Edwin thought, yet throughout the movie he seriously questioned his own motives.

The lights raised and the moviegoers exited the cinema, leaving Edwin sitting alone tired of thinking. He slumped down in the comfy chair and fell asleep.

"So, do you always sleep in theatres?" a woman's voice asked from above.

Edwin thought he was dreaming again. He answered, "Yes, it's peaceful here."

"What are you running from?"

"Me, I think," he groaned.

"Why? Did you do something wrong?"

Edwin squirmed in his seat. "Yes, I took advantage of an innocent woman."

"How so?"

"I ruined her future."

"No one has the power to ruin another's future."

It was then that Edwin recognized the voice, and his eyes opened wide. He looked straight ahead at the empty screen and let out a jagged breath. Rubbing his hand through his hair, he threw his head back. A face gazed down at him from above. He jerked and bolted out of the chair.

"You…you, I don't understand…how…" He held on to the back of the seat behind him. The lovely, flirtatious woman on the train stood staring at him, a mischievous smile crossing her lips.

"Isn't this simply uncanny, running into each other like

this? I don't believe we've been properly introduced," she said, bending over and holding out her hand across the aisle.

Hesitantly, Edwin took her fingers in his.

"That's no way to shake a hand," she scolded him. "Here, try this." She pushed her hand in his and locked them together with a warm squeeze. "Women are not all that fragile, darling."

"Yes, um," he muttered, standing up straighter.

"Next, you'll be wondering why I'm here, or better yet, how did I know *you* were here. But before we begin that conversation, my name is Angela. And you are Edwin. So nice to see you, again."

"Well, Angela, I have never been more confused. Shall we talk about it over drinks?"

"That would be lovely. The Seven Seas restaurant is just a short walk from here."

"After you," Edwin said, waving his hand toward the exit. He had no idea what was happening, but he could not resist this intriguing woman a fourth time.

The restaurant's ceiling was an impressive two-stories high, and the walls were filled with expansive windows framed in colorful decorative wallpaper. Round tables were covered in two layers of white linen, in the middle sat delicate flowers in blue glass vases shaped like fish. They were led to a table under a towering palm tree. Edwin was suitably pleased. Angela took no apparent notice and kept her eyes on Edwin.

They ordered a drink and before Edwin could ask the first question, Angela said, "Questions are sometimes better left without answers. Don't you agree?"

"I'm not sure. I suppose it depends on the questions."

"What if I told you, I have the will?"

Edwin dropped his hands in his lap. Filled with uncertainty, he wasn't sure how to react. Who is this woman? How does she know about the will? The questions flew at him like bullets from a machine gun.

Angela kept her drink pressed against her chin and eyed him over the rim of the glass. He could see a slight smile rising on her lips. Edwin was sure that she was toying with him.

"Pick only one question, Edwin." Her smile slowly slipped away, and she raised a curious eyebrow. "I know too much and answering all the others is a waste of time."

Beads of sweat popped out on Edwin's forehead. This was not a tease. She was serious. He thought quickly. "Can I have the will, please? I would like to return it to the rightful owner." He stared directly into her eyes, no longer twinkling with sensuality, now, unblinking, and dark.

She threw back her head and laughed. "Excellent question, dear man. Now I have a question for you. Just who is the rightful owner? Because you are actually in quite a dilemma once you have the will in your possession."

"What do you mean? I know exactly who the will should go to."

"Do you now? You are currently feeling guilty and perhaps a bit infatuated with the poet. But once the will is in your hands, those feelings will naturally dissolve as you begin to doubt whether Miss Goody Two-shoes will want you in her life after she learns of your scheme. And to make matters worse, you collaborated with her aunt – the black sheep of the family. You do see that everyone gets hurt in this scenario, don't you?"

Edwin gulped. "I, I wasn't planning on telling Frances that part."

"Oh, I see. So, you'd give it to her willingly, knowing that there is no reward, no certainty you will gain anything from your heroic deed. You'd do this from the heart, when you're missing a clear opportunity that would assure you a bright future?"

"I don't understand. Explain." Edward took a big gulp of his drink in hopes to calm the shaking nerves that returned without warning.

"Think, Edwin. The only person that would be willing to reward you for that will would be Beulah Wolski. You could destroy her with that one document. I'm certain she would eagerly pay you a million dollars for it."

She wants to make a deal, he immediately surmised. The words stuck in his throat. He could barely breathe.

"While you're thinking about it, and please think sensibly, I'll tell you how it is I am a part of this charade."

Angela took the liberty of ordering them both another drink. Edwin sat quietly watching her laughing with the waiter. He felt a knot in his stomach.

"The will came into my hands when I watched you rescue that child, and by the way that was a remarkable feat. When the mother started to chase you down to give it to you, her husband bellowed for her, and she turned around and ran toward him instead. The poor flustered woman couldn't wait to put her child in the safety of his father's arms. That's when I took the opportunity to snatch it."

"Why didn't you give it to me, or for that matter to Frances?"

"That part I will leave to your imagination, Edwin."

"What then do *you* want from this, should I choose to deal with Beulah?"

"Oh, I think it's only fair that I get half of whatever you negotiate. With that said, you may wish to up the ante."

Edwin sat thinking. He couldn't believe this was happening. The simplest of questions rose before him. "Why don't *you* negotiate with Beulah? If you have the will, you don't need me at all."

"Oh, where is your sense of adventure?" she asked, clucking her tongue disappointedly. "But if you must know, I have sound reasons why I cannot and will not deal with the shrewd Beulah Wolski. You are the perfect candidate. I mean, surely you'd like the sweet taste of revenge."

Only a short snort came from Edwin as the thought rolled around in his brain. He recalled the scene as Beulah, in front of the entire Board, shamed him with lies he could not defend; crippled by that one truth. Rendering him help-less, his career destroyed, he had stormed out of the room.

He reached for his drink, eager to numb his brain. Before it touched his lips, he heard his mother's voice. He put the drink down and dropped his head in his hands. "I have made too many mistakes," he said. His mother's face evolved in the darkness behind his closed eyes. When he was a child and had denied a wrongdoing, his mother would have him sit in front of her and stretch his arms across the table, placing his palms flat, fingers pointing her direction. She would mimic him, her fingers touching his, only her palms were facing up. In the softest, mildly firm voice, she would say, "The truth will set you free. Give it away. You are at your strongest when you tell the truth." It was a powerful moment, and she was right, once the truth came out, Edwin felt weightless.

Sitting up straight, he placed his hands flat out on the table, his fingers facing Angela. She sat perfectly still and watched him curiously.

"I did a terrible thing. I must set myself free. I have nothing else to say, dear lady. As for you, do what you must. Fate will do the rest." Then he stood, placed several bills on the table for the drinks, and walked out of the restaurant.

Angela looked strangely amused.

Relieved, though bone weary, Edwin booked a room at the nearest hotel. He hoped for a good night's sleep to prepare him for what he knew he must do the next day.

~

Rising early, Edwin enjoyed a full breakfast in a small, cozy diner. Each bite felt like his last meal. It was not going to be easy telling Frances the truth, but he knew he had no choice. She needed to be warned of her aunt, and he needed to be relieved of the guilt. In a booth, he listened to the patrons, still excited from the festivities the night before. Outside the window, the streets were crowded. Everyone smiled brightly. Even Edwin found his smile. And all for the same reason. The taste of freedom.

"Excuse me, sir," a woman's voice was heard to his right. "I believe you're the man that saved my son from falling off the train platform."

Startled, Edwin thought he was hallucinating until the little boy popped up in front of him grinning from ear to ear. He ruffled the boy's hair and smiled up at his mother.

"Yes, I remember you."

"May we join you for a just a minute?" she asked.

"Yes, of course." He stood and motioned to the seat across from him. How uncanny, he said to himself.

"Isn't this uncanny," she said, "running into each other like this?" Edwin chuckled, having had the same thought, and then remembering Angela saying the exact same thing, he felt an odd sensation of déjà vu. He snapped out of it when the woman plunked down her exceptionally large purse on the table.

"I have something that belongs to you." She opened the wildly colored fabric bag and dug through its contents. "It looks especially important, and I had no idea Timmy had it until this morning. I'm afraid it's not in the best of shape. It served another purpose as you can see." She handed it to Edwin, apologizing for its condition.

Thinking she was handing him one of Frances' poems, he was nearly stupefied reading what was clearly the will. The document was covered with orange crayon scribbles and had been folded several times, but the signatures were legible and the message incontestable.

"Well, I confess, I did read it, and it seems to me that someone is going to have a very bright future," she admitted.

Edwin shook his head, utterly confused.

Standing at the door, waiting for his wife, her husband yelled, "Philomena, let's go. We'll miss our train!" She grabbed her son's hand and began scooting out of the booth.

"Philomena? That's my mother's name," Edwin said.

She giggled when her husband yelled again, apologizing for his cross behavior. "He does so fuss over me. We must take leave now."

"Thank you. Thank you very much."

"Oh, don't thank *me*. You can thank that beautiful red-headed woman from the train I just saw moments ago. She reminded me of the paper our Timmy rescued and sure enough it was right where she said it would be."

"In my pocket!" Timmy proudly boasted.

"Then she told me where you'd be this morning, and here you are, just as she said. I have no doubt that she's an angel. How else can we explain all of this?"

Dumbfounded, Edwin watched the husband pick up his son and wrap his arm around his wife. When they exited the diner, he gazed through the window at them parting a way through the crowd who politely stepped aside for the family passing through. That simple sentimental display tugged at his heart. He knew right then what was missing in his life.

Questioning any further, he decided, was not only futile, but tiring. He couldn't flag down a taxi fast enough, and before he reached his destination, he stopped at a florist and bought a dozen roses. When he arrived at Frances' flat, he pounded on the door like a child who had been locked out. No one was home. He slumped to the ground and sat on the step. Feeling depleted from all that had happened, he closed his eyes and wearily dropped his head to his knees. A sweet voice was heard from a distance. He looked up, thinking it was coming from the pine tree hovering overhead. "I'm losing my mind," he grumbled.

"Why, Mr. Dunworthy, what a wonderful surprise."

Edwin turned to see Frances slowly approaching him. She stopped short when she saw his worried face. He rose from the stoop, gave her an affectionate smile, and rushed toward her, leaving the flowers on the step. He held her tightly in his arms. She easily reciprocated, until her glasses slid down to the tip of her nose. He caught them before they fell to the ground. Through nervous laughter, she allowed him to place them back on her face. It was the perfect moment for a kiss. Instead, Edwin took a step back and reached inside his jacket. Without a word, he unfolded the will and held it in front of her.

Then, he told her everything. Well, almost everything.

HENRY'S ADVENTURE

In less than three hours everything was going to change for Henry as he drove down Hwy 281, away from the dryness of the crusty little town he was born in toward the bright lights of the "live music capital of the world," Austin, Texas. Between static-filled country songs and Tejano music, once every couple of miles a pop song would fade in and out, reminding him that he was getting closer to a new adventure.

It was spring, Henry's favorite season, when folks from all around grew excited about planting exotic flowers and green lawns on their land, hoping to take the focus off the thousands of ugly cedars that seemed to pop up overnight across the Texas hill country. This was also when Henry would shine, for it was known by all those who participated in the spring festivities that he was the finest banjo player this side of Gillespie County.

Playing banjo was second nature to Henry mostly because he started at the ripe age of six, and now at twenty-five, he had truly mastered the four-string instrument. The news was spreading fast that he should take that talent to the big city, and somebody took the liberty to make sure that he did. He'd be back home mixing fertilizer at old man Spencer's Feed Store if it hadn't been for the letter.

It was addressed to Mr. Henry P. Montgomery III in bold type with a P.O. Box return address, which made the recipient feel certain that it was of great importance. He placed it on top of the bedroom dresser to read later that evening after scrubbing dirt and cow manure from under his fingernails and finishing off the leftover pulled pork rib sandwich in the fridge and a sixteen-ounce can of Lone Star beer.

Washing the melamine plate three times, as his mother had taught him and then stepping out on the porch for an after-dinner smoke from his cherry tobacco-filled pipe was a nightly ritual for Henry. It wasn't always so while he was dating Ida Jean – she was what they call in the big city, "high maintenance." That girl kept Henry hopping to her every whim, until one day she went a little too far when she insisted that he give up the banjo because it took precious time from their togetherness. Painfully aware that Ida Jean was the last of the pretty single gals within thirty miles, he chose his banjo and a life of celibacy all alone with his bloodhound, Wilford Duke, named after his grandfather Wilford, and Duke, Jed's dog on the *Beverly Hillbillies* sitcom.

Watching the sky fill up with stars, Henry discarded the dottle from his pipe and went inside to fetch the letter he had patiently waited to read. He slid out of his boots, stretched diagonally across the bed, and propped himself up on his elbows under the soft golden lamplight.

The letter was an invitation to participate in a banjo playing contest at the Broken Spoke in Austin. Only one out of fifteen contestants would be chosen to perform a U.S. tour with one of the most prestigious country bands in the south.

Knowing his family would approve, Henry filled out the attached form and dropped it in the mailbox on the way to work the next morning. Practicing often, during lunch and before bedtime, he waited patiently, and without much hope, for that special day when by pure luck he would find himself heading east. What were the odds?

Well, the odds were pretty much in his favor, and that day did come. He was feeling mighty confident when he filled his gas tank, placed a dog bed in the back of his truck, and carried his prized banjo in the sturdy leather case to the front seat where he could keep a close eye on it.

In the country, a man could wear his Levi's for days, and as long as he changed his t-shirt underneath, he could wear his shirt just as long. So, Henry traveled light, except for the ninety-two-pound bloodhound that had replaced Ida Jean.

Approaching the big city, he stopped at a convenience store to get his bearings and buy one of those big fountain drinks he was so fond of back home. When he came back to his truck to make sure Wilford had enough water, he noticed a red car had parked him in. Thinking the patron would be out in a few minutes, he took the time to rub behind his dog's ears.

The longest five minutes crawled by, and Henry started to get agitated. He had timed this trip perfectly to arrive at the hotel just two hours before the contest began – giving him time to floss, practice, and shine his boots. He walked up to the big, plate-glass window and peered inside between the painted letters advertising Cold Beer. No one was in the store except for the cashier.

"Excuse me sir," he asked politely, "do you know who's driving that red car that's blocking my truck?"

"Thought I saw a pretty blonde get out of it earlier. Don't see her in the store though. Couldn't miss her, she was a sight for sore eyes," the cashier spoke, sliding his tongue between two missing front teeth.

Considering the time passing by Henry decided to scope out the car and see if he could find any evidence of the owner. He immediately noticed that there was no key in the ignition but lying on its side on the floor was a denim bag. Feeling intrusive, but anxious, he combed through it and found a small wallet with the owner's credentials. The cashier was right, she was a knockout, even on her driver's license. With not a trace of a phone number, he called a taxi, paid him extra to let the dog ride in the backseat, and instructed the driver to take him to the address on the license. If anything, maybe there was a family member who could move the car.

Arriving at their destination, the driver demanded more money when Henry asked him to wait. He handed him five dollars and ordered his dog to stay. Wilford disobeyed and jumped over the front seat right onto the cab driver and forced his way out of the only open window. At that point, the discombobulated driver – with a mouth full of dog hair and slobber on his shirt – drove off screeching his tires, leaving his passengers stranded.

Collecting his dog was not a problem, as Wilford had raced directly to the backyard of the house to relieve himself in private. While there, Henry noticed that the back door was open behind a closed screen door. He knocked on it several times. "Hello, hello," he shouted, but no one answered. He sat the girl's purse on a nearby lawn chair and when he turned to leave, Wilford raced past him and smashed right through the screen, ramming his head smackdab into a wall. Wobbly, but determined, he began to howl, that deep hound dog howl, like a wolf's bark at the moon, only much throatier.

Henry frantically entered the house and grabbed Wilford by the collar. That's when his dog made the strangest move and pulled his master down the hall toward one of the rooms at the end. Looking up at Henry with big, brown pleading eyes, he nudged him to go in. Henry slowly opened the door, inch by inch. Reluctantly, he stepped one foot into the dark room and felt the wall for the light switch. Finding it, he flipped it on and at the same time a body slammed into him, nearly knocking him over.

Wilford barged into the room and stood between Henry and a woman with duct tape on her mouth – her hands tied behind her, completely unfazed by his low-pitched growl.

"Why, you're the woman who owns the red car! You're Shelby, right?" Henry asked.

The blonde haired, wide-eyed female screamed from her trapped mouth and jumped up and down frantically trying to say something. Henry pushed his dog aside and stepped toward her to remove the duct tape. "If you'll be still, I'll take that off," he spoke firmly, but gently.

Henry felt for the end of the tape and gave her a look of warning just in time to yank only half of it off her lips.

"Oh, my *gawd* that hurts! Just untie me, I'll do the rest," she ordered, the words spewing from the side of her crooked mouth.

Not only were the woman's hands tied behind her back, she also had one ankle tied to the closet doorknob. It didn't take much effort to set her free – whoever tied these ropes had never been a boy scout.

"I don't know who you are, but thank you, thank you, and thank you!" the blonde squealed and kissed Henry hard on the mouth. Then she leaned in to hug Wilford, but when she spotted the drool dripping from his fat lip, she pulled back. Looking up wild-eyed at her liberator, she said, "It's very important that you take me somewhere, right now, and as fast as you can!"

"Well, uh," Henry stuttered, "I, I need to get somewhere fast myself…it's really important, too."

"Can you at least git me to my car?" She pleaded while picking duct tape residue off her lips.

"That's the reason why I'm here lady. You have me pinned in. I'll just call another taxi. By the way, who did this to you?" he suddenly realized to ask.

"Oh, don't worry about them, I know where they are, and they're not coming back here soon, that's for sure! I have another set of car keys – you git us a ride, and I'll meet you out front."

While Henry and Wilford sat outside waiting for the taxi, Shelby came running out of the house and threw the car keys at Henry's feet. "Move my car for me, please and leave the keys on top of the front wheel," she ordered and while running back inside, she yelled, "I don't have time to go with you. My neighbor's taking me. Thanks again for everything!" And then she slammed the door.

Baffled, Henry said to his dog, "Why, she never even asked us our names." He dismissed it all when the taxi arrived. Reading his watch, he realized there was no time to go to the hotel, but just enough time to fetch his truck and make it to the contest. As instructed, he left Shelby's keys on the top of the tire and rushed to the Broken Spoke.

He wouldn't have been nearly as late if he hadn't had to bribe the hard-headed, shifty-eyed lady at the door with a twenty-dollar bill to let his dog wait in the corner. Inside the musty old building, all the contestants were seated around a dance floor in a dimly lit room with a low ceiling and a small stage that could barely hold a four-piece band. Behind them sat the spectators. The announcer was fully into introducing the fourth contestant, "Ladies and gents, I'd like to introduce the cutest little banjo player on Austin's south side…hereee's Shelby Whistlestop!"

Henry looked up when he heard the name, and his jaw dropped watching the woman he just rescued carry her banjo to the stage. When she sat on the stool, the crowd went dead silent and waited. Shelby closed her eyes, took a deep, slow, and sultry breath and plucked the first chord. You could've heard a pin drop after that. Then without any warning, the player dropped her head and began strumming wildly a tune that could raise Earl Scruggs right from his grave. Henry thought she was simply amazing.

By the time Henry was called up to perform, he was exhausted after listening to so many banjo solos. But when he looked around the room and spotted Shelby sitting on a bar stool looking so pretty with a surprised look on her face, he closed his eyes and let his imagination soar. He pretended he was on his deck after a hard rain that left the air smelling like fresh dirt, with his dog curled up at his feet, and a new song floating over his head. It came that easy. When he completed his piece, the crowd jumped to their feet applauding.

After the fifteenth contestant, the announcer told everyone to grab a drink and sit back while the judges conferred. Shelby walked over to Henry and handed him a cold beer.

"I at least owe you a drink," she said, "and probably an explanation, too."

Henry took the beer and swallowed hard. It had been one heck of a day, and he was beat. Back home, he would have been watching the news and settling in for the night. He suppressed a yawn and said, "You play banjo like an angel. But how can you be so cool after what happened today?"

"Oh, that was nothin." She rolled her eyes. "My cousins did that to me. You see, my dad's a preacher, and he doesn't want me to win this contest because if I git a chance to play with a famous band, then he's afraid I'll git too big for my britches and become a star like Ruby Jane or one of the Quebe Sisters, so he sent Luther and Ed to stop me." She paused to take a sip. "Big dumb bruisers…heck, if it weren't for you, I wouldn't even be here."

She eyed Henry warily before she spoke again. "By the way, Henry, yer playing ain't too bad either."

The announcer stepped back onto the small stage and called for everyone's attention. "Folks, looks like we've got two winners, which means we'll have to have a face-off tomorrow to determine who the real winner will be. Those two fine banjo players are Shelby Whistlestop and Henry P. Montgomery." The audience roared and the two were shoved under the stage lights for everyone to view. Someone shouted out, "They make a cute couple!" Henry dropped his chin to his chest and waited until the clapping stopped before he'd face them again. Shelby took the liberty to take a couple of deep bows and one long and dramatic curtsy.

Later, out in the parking lot, Wilford was promised an extra bowl of kibble for being so patient and for not howling during the contest. It crossed Henry's mind that he hadn't checked into the hotel, and it was now close to ten o'clock. When he called, they had given his room away and there were no more vacancies due to the Gay Pride Festival being held all weekend long.

"Great, just great!" he yelled and kicked the tire on his truck, just when Shelby walked by.

"What's the matter?" she asked.

"Oh, just lost my hotel reservation, and the guy at the desk said there wasn't much chance of finding a room… something about a pride parade. Guess I'll join my dog here in the back of the truck tonight," he sighed.

"That's nonsense!" she blurted out and grabbed his arm. "I've got an extra room, and yer welcome to stay. How bout you take me to my car and follow me home?"

"It's hard to resist a smile like yours – especially from a girl who can play the banjo like you do. If it's really no trouble, I'll take you up on your offer."

Back at her place, Shelby gave Henry a cold can of Shiner Bock and insisted that he put his feet up and get comfy while she put clean sheets on the guest bed. When she returned, he had fallen asleep on the sofa. Lightweight, she thought to herself, as she sat opposite him devising a plan while she sipped what was left of his beer and eyeing Wilford, who slept lazily at his master's feet. The dog's a lightweight, too. And he snores! I'll be darned if I'll let this country bumpkin beat me tomorrow. I've been planning a lifetime for this moment. Ain't gonna happen! Just ain't!

Shelby walked in circles around the kitchen thinking about what to do next. Suddenly a plan began to form. She tiptoed to the living room and changed the time on the clock to read two hours later. Then she did the same on the alarm clock in the guest room. Leading Henry and Wilford to their bed, she told Henry not to worry, that she would make sure he got up in time for breakfast and a hot shower. Henry nodded incoherently while pulling off his boots, then loosening his big, silver belt buckle and tossing his wallet, keys and cell phone on the bedside table, he let out a long yawn and slid backwards on the bed where he promptly fell into a deep sleep. Wilford yawned, too, and dropped his big weary and bruised head on Henry's boots; neither of them noticing the sneaky banjo player slipping out the door with Henry's belongings.

When Shelby's cell phone alarm went off underneath her pillow the next morning, she sat up in bed trying to remember just exactly what she had schemed. She adjusted her eyes in the dark and very quietly turned on the lamp. The note she had written the night before lay on the dresser.

It read: Henry, I hope someday you will forgive me. I took your keys, your wallet and cell phone, which you can find at the Lost and Found in a building in downtown Austin that is shaped like nose hair clippers. By the time you get there, I will have won. I deserve this break. No time to share. Thank you again for yesterday and please help yourself to cereal and a blueberry muffin I left in the microwave. Thanks! Shelby.

To soften the blow, she added to the note: BTW I think you're cute.

Stealthily gathering her things, the bag full of Henry's possessions, along with her beloved banjo, she locked the front door behind her.

Hearing the car starting outside, Wilford woke up and nudged his sleeping master awake. Groggily, Henry read the note he found lying on the table where his personal belongings should have been, and then he read it again in disbelief. "What the heck does BTW mean?"

"Shelby, Shelby," her name stuck to the walls when he yelled it running down the narrow hallway with Wilford at his feet panting heavily. He stopped and looked from his watch to the clock that read two hours later. "Dad-gum it, Wilford. Why'd she do this? Look, at least she left me my banjo! Come on boy, let's start walking!"

He grabbed the muffin out of the microwave and searching the kitchen he spotted a jar of coins. He dumped them out onto the counter and selected as many quarters he could find and stuffed them in his jean pockets. "Golly, only about eight dollars…not even enough for a taxi!"

It'd been years since Henry hitched a ride and putting his thumb out while walking a main city street felt different than it did when he was younger walking along the open highways between small Texas towns – this time he felt humiliated and a little bit stupid. It wasn't long before a yellow Volkswagen, with pictures pasted all over the sides, slowed down next to him.

"Hey, honey," a large woman with big teeth leaned out of the passenger side window and cooed, "need a ride?"

"Well, yes, I do," Henry sputtered through the answer. "And so does my dog, here." He pointed behind him where Wilford was cowering, his nose crammed between Henry's thighs.

The very thin driver, who was wearing a low-cut, orange dress and a purple wig leaned over and said in a raucous voice, "We're heading downtown if that's where you need to be."

The husky passenger motioned for them to get in. Henry figured that they had to be harmless with cute Sesame Street figures pasted all over the car. Wilford must have thought differently, for he fervently resisted while being pushed and shoved into the back seat.

As they approached downtown, the traffic got heavier. They were moving at such a slow pace, Henry felt certain that he could walk there faster. Looking over the back seat, the front-seat passenger eyed Henry suspiciously. "Are you going downtown for the Gay Pride Parade?"

"Oh, no, don't want any part of that!" Henry raised his hands in a defensive gesture.

With that, the driver slammed her army boot on the

brake and turned around to glare at Henry. Resting her long hairy arm on the back of the seat, she snarled, "Get out of my car, you pervert!"

"What'd you say?" Henry looked utterly confused.

"You heard him," the husky passenger barked. "Get out and take your ugly dog with you!"

Henry's eyes darted back and forth at the strangers. Without waiting for an explanation, he secured his banjo, grabbed his dog by the collar and climbed out of the car, knocking the angry passenger into the dashboard as Wilford clumsily squeezed past.

The two of them dodged oncoming cars until they made it to the nearest sidewalk. "Whoa," he exclaimed, looking down at his dog burrowing his nose into Henry's thigh again. "Don't you let that bother you, boy. You are *not* ugly. Now, let's go!"

Sprinting toward the city, he came upon a large crowd of people marching down the street, barricaded by a line of policemen and one officer on a horse directing the traffic to a side road. Someone from behind shoved Henry into the bunch, and he found himself stuck in a moving session of bizarrely dressed people, all ranting, raving, shouting out their slogans.

There was such a commotion Henry didn't know who to ask for directions. So, he randomly chose a person wearing a clown outfit in red high heels. "Sir, I mean, ma'am, I mean, well, heck…do you know where there's a building downtown that looks like nose hair clippers?"

The clown responded, "Clippers?" Then he turned to his friend and shouted, "This guy wants to know where Clippers is."

"Oh sure, it's four blocks that way," he shouted back,

pointing with a long, green fingernail covered in tiny yellow bananas.

"Four blocks that way," repeated the clown.

Thanking them both, Henry forced his way through the lively group, sparing the pardons since he was certain they couldn't hear him anyway, and tried desperately to get to the other side of the four-lane street. Three men in black lingerie came up from behind and swept him off his feet, carrying him high above their shoulders. Wildford's howls could not be heard under their chanting, "Hetero, Hetero!"

Henry, now clutching his banjo to his chest, was passed from hand to hand in a crowd surfing fashion until finally Wilford slammed into their legs causing them to lose their balance and fall forward. When Henry hit the ground, Wilford grabbed him by the pant leg and started pulling him away. The others were left behind picking each other up and adjusting their costumes. Having stopped their flow, the group behind them became unruly and fighting broke out.

Back on his feet, Henry cried out, "Come on, Wilford!" as they pushed through flying arms and obscenities that even Henry had never heard before. They smashed through the angry mob and darted into an alleyway, just when the police arrived.

Frustrated, tired, hungry, and clearly confused, the two lost visitors walked to the next main street where they found a small pizza parlor. After buying two bottled waters that took half of his quarters, they sat on the curb while Henry quenched his thirst and poured water down the mouth of his very thirsty and loyal companion.

This has got to be a joke, he thought, and at the same time Wilford looked up in agreement. He smiled at the idea of his dog reading his mind and said aloud, "I'm sorry ole boy." Then he took his banjo out to strum a little ditty – a never-failing way to calm the old hound down.

Halfway through the song, a fashionably dressed man walked by and tossed a five-dollar bill into Henry's banjo case. Henry looked up quite surprised. "Well, I'll be..." Others dropped more bills and within minutes, he counted sixteen dollars. Stuffing the money in his pockets and the fifty-cent piece a little boy had timidly tossed in the mix, Henry felt a new wave of hope.

Seeing that poor Wilford was on his last legs, he flagged down a pedicab driven by a cute girl dressed in cut-off shorts and a frilly, white peasant blouse. Assured that she knew where to take them and thinking he just might meet the deadline for the contest, Henry settled back and spent most of the thirteen-block ride trying to read the tiny paragraph tattooed on the back of the girl's neck. As they came around the corner, she pointed to a bank building.

Straining to look up, Henry declared, "Wow, it does sort of look like nose hair clippers." He thanked the girl and gave her every dollar in his pocket.

Inside the building, a security guard stopped the two from approaching the information desk. "I'm sorry, no dogs allowed."

"But sir, I just need to get my belongings that were left in the Lost and Found," Henry earnestly explained.

"Dogs not allowed!" he repeated, taking Henry by the arm to lead him outside.

There was absolutely no way he felt comfortable leaving Wilford alone in a strange city after all they had been through. He spotted a woman at a flower kiosk not far from the front door of the building and after shooting the breeze with her, he gave her a brief explanation for his kind request to watch his dog for just a matter of minutes. She gladly agreed, pulled a milk-bone treat out of her apron and handed it to Wilford. She then suggested that the dog rest close behind her against the wall. At her gentle touch, Wilford obeyed and eyed his owner nervously as he disappeared through the glass doors.

Henry walked quickly past the security guard and waved at the man behind the customer service desk. "I've been told that you have several items of mine that were dropped off by Shelby Whistlestop. My name is Henry Montgomery…with a middle P."

"I do have thoth itemth, thir," the man spoke with a lisp. "But firtht I need thum ID." Then he stuck his hand out as if Henry would automatically present such a thing.

"You have my ID, sir, and that's what I'm here to get, along with my wallet, truck keys and cell phone."

"But thir," the man argued, "I don't know if you're the owner of the itemth without identificathion."

Exasperated, Henry took a deep breath and thought before he spoke again, this is becoming even more of a joke. "Sir," he was growing tired of that word, "How many Henry Montgomery's come up to your counter and ask for items that have been left for them?"

The employee looked thoughtfully at his notebook and said, "Well, none, but that ith not the point. I thtill need your ID," putting his hand out for the second time.

"You've got to be kidding!" Henry pounded on the counter and when he turned around, the security cop was standing just two feet behind him with his hands placed firmly on his hips.

"Sir!" There was that word again. "I think you should come with me," he ordered.

"But sir!" Henry raised his voice. "Is there not one person in this town with common sense?" Hearing his echo bounce from wall to wall in the three-story marble room, Henry dropped his head apologetically.

At the kiosk, the hair on Wilford's back stood at attention upon hearing his master's voice coming through the revolving door swirling past a short stout woman charging her way out the other side. With all his canine strength Wilford rammed into the moving glass wall, forcing the woman out onto the sidewalk, and entering the building so quickly, he slid across the slick polished floor like a bowling ball and knocked the security guard right off his feet.

The guard, not knowing what had hit him, excitably pulled his gun, and pointed it at the dazed dog sprawled out on the floor. The terrified employee behind the counter let out a high-pitched scream.

"Wait sir, wait SIR," Henry urged. "He was just looking out for me. He's just a good ole hound dog…gets a little excited, but he wouldn't hurt a flea."

Slowly and disappointingly putting his gun away, the guard asked the man and his dog to leave the premises. Crestfallen, Henry took Wilford by the collar and started to lead him out. "Where's your dog tags, boy?" he asked, looking around the floor to see where they had fallen.

"Right here," said a voice from across the room. "They fell off when he ran in." The pretty flower girl with the wholesome smile handed Henry the tags and another milk bone to the tail-wagging bloodhound. "I'm sorry I couldn't catch him in time. He's a lot of dog."

"That, he is." Henry started chuckling. He peered over her shoulder at the officer eyeing him warily, and snapped his mouth shut. "I've been asked to leave. They won't give me my stuff without proof of identification."

"Well?" the flower girl nodded and pointed to his hand.

"What?" Henry didn't understand, what she was alluding

to. The girl took the silver dog tags from his hand and jingled them in front of his face.

"Ohhh, I forgot all about this ID. Thank you very much," he said, lifting the petite girl in the air like a toddler. When he realized he was making a scene, he carefully put her down. She stepped up high on her toes and kissed him lightly on the cheek. Bashfully, his cheeks burning scarlet, Henry handed the dog tags to the man behind the counter, who was sniffing loudly and dabbing at a tear in the corner of his eye.

Both his name, address and phone number were on the ID, and that was enough to satisfy everyone. Minutes later, everything was accounted for and back in Henry's possession where they belonged.

"I'm in a big hurry, or I'd thank you properly," he said, giving the flower girl his best smile. "Think I could have your name and number and call you later?"

"Sure, I'd like that," she said and pulled a shiny yellow card from her pocket. With a twinkle in her eye, she gently placed it in his palm.

Outside, a taxi was flagged down and right before Henry jumped in, she stuffed a red rose in his shirt pocket.

As they drove off, he looked back at the girl standing there waving, a big grin on her face. He turned to his pal and said, "You know what boy, I think this trip may turn out right after all."

Wilford looked out the back window, placed his tired head on his human's shoulder and drooled.

Back in the comfort of his Ford pick-up, Henry drove again toward South Lamar Street. Just a few blocks away from the Broken Spoke, he pulled off the road, got out of the truck and looked meaningfully at his worn-out companion. "You know, they say it's not an adventure unless something goes wrong, and boy did it ever. I think I've got the good sense to know when we've had enough. What do you say we turn around and go home?" he asked his faithful friend, while pulling on his soft, drooping ears. "I think Shelby wants this prize more than I do."

Wilford howled with such gusto, Henry was sure, if the dog could, he would jump into his arms.

Heading west, away from the city that might have changed his life forever – and still could, he thought, while absentmindedly sniffing the rose that he pulled from his pocket – Henry spotted a bumper sticker on the car in front of him. It read: Keep Austin Weird.

As he passed the driver, waving enthusiastically he yelled, "You go right ahead and do that!" Then he turned up the music and let out a "Yippy-ki-yay!"

WAKE UP DOROTHY!

Scenes from my life are flashing before me from an old Bell and Howell Super 8 movie projector. Each one flutters by, colorless, a dull patina flattening the images, the camera moving slow, then fast, and then crazy-like as if the person behind the lens wanted to speed up their miserable life. I see my mother, her strained smile and narrowed reproachful eyes, her plump body bouncing around like a balloon being carried by a toddler, her finger wagging, always scolding. My boyfriend Landon is popping his head in and out of the picture frame, making sure he is seen, "What about *me?*" he cries, shaking his long dirty blonde hair wildly like a rock star as he plays air guitar. His fake grin is exposing his pale upper gums and his top lip is stuck to his braces. No, he's not a teenager…he's twenty-seven.

Now the camera jerks away and points to the sky and the bare trees and then it suddenly lands on its side filming a line of marching ants, a crashed bicycle wheel– the spokes going around and around – and just beyond that, there's me, running barefoot up a hill in my favorite green hippie dress, in the background an old employee punch-out clock is making that clunky clicking noise over and over again until the scene cracks and the film slowly begins to burn, and I hear a faint voice from faraway.

"Snap out of it, Dorothy!" my co-worker yells again in my ear, and I am jolted back to reality – me at work holding my empty stained coffee cup.

Drifting off like that is not unusual these days because I've been in a strange kind of sleep mode ever since I met Landon. And by the way, my name's not Dorothy, but because of my frequent visits to OZ, they call me that at work. Before Landon came along, I could see clearly, the rich color of butter, children playing in the park, pictures of Paris on my refrigerator, the things I bought with my own hard-earned money. But now, everything seems to be coated in a film of Vaseline, and it's really not his fault. Really.

Landon was special, and although I was the only one who thought so, I convinced myself that given the chance, this ordinary person would eventually meet his full potential all because of my unselfish love. Just watch! I have so much to give, he will blossom right before my eyes, and then everyone will see what I see that they don't see. And just wait until his braces come off!

I'm now working two jobs plus overtime to put this budding human being through college. Quitting school in his second year and wasting away four more years on odd jobs, surfing, and dimwitted girls, Landon confessed, with those flickering blue eyes, that he wanted to go back and get his degree. But at his age, without the means, how could he? And that thing about his attention deficit disorder really pushed my pity button. How lucky for him that I stepped into his miserable life and offered to pave, well, okay, pay the way, as he shamelessly agreed to let me work to the bone for him while he enriched his mind, learned to braid his own hair, and beefed up his pectoral muscles.

Of course, he moved in with me after the arrangement was made. I would pay the rent, the groceries, the utilities, the whole shebang and never mention it or make him feel bad about it. All he had to do was pass his classes in between going to the gym. A bargain for a man with such possibilities! And did I mention his muscles?

On my only night off, we went to parties, always at a student's place. I was embarrassed to hang out with these people nearly eight years younger than me, but Landon explained that they were taking the same classes and there was much for them to talk about since the subjects were fresh in their heads. I tried to fit in, but usually I was so tired from working nonstop, I found myself falling asleep in a chair or, if lucky enough, in the bedroom, if not already occupied by students having wild, random sex while high on their drug of choice.

Jealous, that's what he called me whenever I suggested that we go to a movie instead, or even stay home and have dinner together with music, a game of cards, or that crazy all-white puzzle my mother gave me along with her words of wisdom, "Figure this out, and maybe you'll figure out your life."

Jealous? Not a word I wanted to sully my list of praise-worthy traits, so from then on, I bowed out gracefully as he cheerily walked out the door with a twenty he had snatched from my purse, so he could at least buy some beer because no one should ever go to those parties empty handed. No way, man! Not cool!

The first year of this grueling routine nearly wiped me out, but I never protested once, nor did I tell him that the rent had gone up. Considerably. During that time, he managed to pass his classes, barely, and I managed to get a raise and more hours which allowed us to have a little extra cash for maybe a nice dinner out, or rather, pet bills; because one day while I was slaving away, waiting on tables at the local restaurant, he walked by the plate glass window with a puppy in his arms and waved the little guy's paws at me. The "Can I have him" look was plastered all over his face, and the puppy was as cute and irresistible as a puppy can be, especially in my love's arms. With everyone watching the scene from their tables, their eyes pleading along with Landon's, what else could I do but nod a yes and offer a cheesy smile, which I quickly dropped like a hot potato when turning away from view, knowing full well that having a pet would raise the rent and my blood pressure.

I don't think I ever hated an animal in my entire life, but this canine turned out to be a demon dog. Nothing was spared from Gilligan's razor-sharp teeth, and when he gnawed off the claws of the lion's paws on my grandmother's antique dresser, I cried for the longest, cross-legged on the floor, while the mutt yapped like crazy from behind the bathroom door where I heard him chewing and scratching on the door jamb as if it were coated in melted beef jerky. But even with mangled shoes, the strap of my only good purse wrapped in duct tape, the bristles of my hairbrush stuck between Gilligan's teeth, I would not let this dog from hell distract me from my goal. I will get Landon through school even if it kills me!

Only five more months, Landon reminded me after I threw myself face down on the living room floor and fell fast asleep, waking up in the middle of the night with dog hair stuck to my tongue. A mere hundred and fifty days and Landon will have his degree, and I know that, humbled with gratitude, he'll become the man of the house, get a fabulous job, pay the rent, and I can quit work, stay at home, wear muumuus, and take Gilligan for long walks while my boney white arms get a much-needed tan. But not until then will we finally clinch the deal with those three little unspoken one-syllable words, "I love you." We got drunk on cheap wine toasting to his graduation on my Saturday night off, and I was knocked out by nine o'clock while Landon left with his buddies to celebrate passing yet another semester.

Christmas, finally, a three-day weekend with nothing else to do but rig a small tree in the corner of the apartment and watch *Christmas Vacation* in front of my giant poster of a flaming fireplace while Landon went skiing with his brother. My gift. After all, someone had to stay home with the mutt. I'm pathetic, and I know it, so I offered to feed the neighbor's python for extra cash.

She's cute, petite, big-breasted for her size, and her hips couldn't hold up a pair of hip-huggers even with a belt. But she is smart and a great tutor, Landon claimed, and it was necessary that he have help with the final course of the year if he were to graduate. So, while I was at work, stocking Ranch Style beans, he was at home with Luna studying his little heart out. Landon soon reported that he felt adequately prepared for the final exams *all* because of *her*.

Someone at work asked me if I was depressed. I avoided that unsettling question and instead of my usual lunch in the back of the meat section where we could have all the six-day-old cold cuts we could eat, I walked right past the black plastic curtains and out the front door without removing my work apron. I didn't even punch out as regulations required.

I found myself sitting on a park bench reading the carved

initials and philosophical sayings etched in its old soft wood. Words like, "The end of the world was yesterday," and "Screw your teacher for an A," – stuff like that. I rubbed my fingers across the letters and imagined the young and care-free students who had all that leisurely time to sit there carving into the wood well enough for it to be legible. Never having experienced that life, I felt a sadness for myself and my stupidity, and my only goal, to lift Landon to a higher level as I sunk deeper into my ineptness.

Curious, I stood up and looked at the carvings where my bottom had been sitting and saw two letters I recognized – two large L's. I twisted my head around and positioned it just so to read the rest. Luna + Landon. It read just that, Luna + Landon. Hoping no one had seen me, I quickly sat down, looking cautiously around as if I had just found a wallet full of money. What are the odds that there is another Luna and another Landon besides the ones that are under my ass?

Have you ever been so tired that you were too tired to sleep? Tossing and turning was becoming a nightly routine, so naturally I moved to the sofa to allow Landon that precious REM sleep he claimed was necessary to keep him focused. Have you ever been so tired that you didn't notice you were fifteen pounds lighter than your usual weight? So tired that you didn't remember if you had brushed your teeth, filled the gas tank, shut the refrigerator door, took the clothes from the washer to the dryer? I was so tired I didn't even know I was tired. Now that's effing tired!

What's more, I was so weary, I thought that I had dreamed about the L+L names carved in the bench and let that potentially disastrous clue fly right out the window. But when I picked up one of Landon's school books and out dropped a note with a big 'L' in a swoopy loopy font surrounded by a heart, I could not deny that clue number two was more than a figment of my imagination. Matter of fact, that little note that promised more sex like the last time, thrust me into a whole new dimension. But by the time my only day off was right before me, and it just happened to be my twenty-ninth birthday, and poor Landon had to attend his great aunt's funeral, I was relieved that I wouldn't have to challenge him. I slept through the entire day in the same position until I woke up in the middle of the night to a dark empty apartment – a reminder of the denial I was in. "Happy Birthday to me."

I sat up in bed and had the same recurring vision of me riding my bicycle in my green hippie dress. Then suddenly I'm running barefoot up a path to nowhere. Before I get to the top, the scene fades to black and what is on the other side remains a mystery.

One day I decided to come home for lunch. I don't even remember driving, much less walking up the steps, but I became aware when I heard voices coming from the bathroom. I stood at the door and listened. I heard giggling, then a sudden hush, then a gasp for air and something like a bar of soap dropping to the shower floor with a thud, and then the sound of water hitting the wall in a constant rhythm with sighs or groans, or both, but whatever they were doing in there, I was certain that they weren't scrubbing down the shower together. I could have opened the door and caused a scene, but maybe I didn't want to see what I already saw in my own fuzzy imagination, which was probably not near as good as what I'd actually see.

I went to the refrigerator, took out a chicken leg from dinner two days back and ate it with a wilted salad I found behind a gallon of something green. I sat there eyeing the bathroom door until I heard the water turn off and them moving around, talking. I took my last bite, grabbed an apple next to two oranges coated in mold fuzz and turned to leave. Just when I did, Luna came out of the bathroom wrapped in a towel with my shower cap on her head. She stood and looked at me, and when I smiled at her, she dropped her surprised expression, but not the towel. I took a big crunchy symbolic bite out of the apple, and I left.

I'm guessing we had a quiet understanding between us because none of us ever spoke about that day. It just kind of got pulled into "The Suck Zone", like the other clues, landing some place where secrets and birthdays go to die.

The day of the final exams, I came home early with a serious headache and found Landon pacing the floor in worry. When I asked what was on his mind, he expressed his fear of not passing and what the consequences would mean. He looked nervous when he asked me where we stood if he had to take another year of classes. I didn't have an answer for him because I was frankly feeling too ill to think about the future and what it might hold, for mine was so bland it was not worth considering. And besides, deep down inside, I was in a bizarre way enjoying the unattractive, pitiful anguish on his usually smug face. Instead, I offered to help him study, but he decided that a beer with his buds is really what he needed, so I handed him my wallet, shoved the dog off the sofa, and curled up in my usual fetal position. Oddly enough, my headache went away shortly after I heard the door slam.

I awoke to the big day when I would come home late that evening to hear the verdict. For a moment I nursed a sense of pride that I did not renege on a promise. I truly went into this arrangement with Landon purely from the heart. He had a goal, and I didn't. Why not help this soul achieve his? La dee da, what a wonderful selfless act, and I fulfilled my part without complaints, excuses, or judgement. I'm a saint! Another chapter of my life would begin all based on Landon's success.

I knew when he didn't come home, that he had failed.

I blew out the candles burned down to less than an inch of their life, put the cake and the champagne in the refrigerator, and crawled into bed still wearing my long green hippie dress. It was my favorite – silky and backless with thin spaghetti straps. The full chiffon fabric felt like a fine sheet against my skin. I wrapped myself in it, and with the bed all to myself, and without a dog sniffing my feet, I slept like a baby for reasons I would figure out later.

The following morning, it took everything I had to call my mother and give her the news about Landon. I dealt briskly with the delusion that I could handle another year of supporting him. Her silence said it all. "I know what you're thinking, mom…I'm pitiful." I hung up before she could say, "I told you so."

My cruiser bicycle has been used as a clothes rack for much too long, so I removed all the scarves, socks, and panties from its metal protrusions, aired up the tires and took off for a nice long Saturday morning ride to nowhere in particular. Remaining in my green dress, I tied the flowing fabric between my legs. The campus was the last place I wanted to go, but somehow, I ended up there and in my bare feet.

The school grounds were empty; no sign of anyone, anywhere. I enjoyed zooming around the carless spaces, in and out of the 'reserved for teachers only' area and along the vacant sidewalk covered with thousands of black, fried gum glops carelessly spit out from the mouths of our future leaders. I could almost hear my tires screaming in delight as we flew down the hill toward the park where students studied, or smoked pot, or groped one another in between classes.

Wheeeee!

I rode through the thick woods, dodging tree limbs and squirrels, the sun racing with me through the shadows from the towering limbs overhead. I was beginning to feel and see the beauty around me – so much that I spotted a path leading to the top of a hill, like the one I've been imagining. I jumped off my bike and began running up it. When I got to the top, it hit me! I'm free! Free, at last! I stood there looking down at the new world below. It was then that I knew exactly what I was going to do next, and I felt wonderful, even ecstatic about my decision.

Back down the pathway and back on my bicycle I took off. Could it be that easy? Yes, yes, yes, I squealed with delight, and when I came out of the woods to the main street, I stepped on the breaks just in time to avoid colliding with a car zipping by right in front of me. What a close call! I could have been killed! I was spared. But why me? Is there another purpose in store for me?

My heart is pounding in my chest. My hands are shaking. My feet are on fire. I'm so fucking alive! Across the street I see Landon and Luna walking down the sidewalk, hand in hand, heads bent as if in a serious conversation, the devil dog lunging ahead of them on a taut leash. I yell, "Landon, Luna, Gilligan! I'm awake!"

Spotting me, they quickly let go of each other's hands and gave me a stiff wave. At least the dog was happy to see me as he broke loose and ran my direction. I stood up on the pedals and moved toward them, when suddenly a cargo van with a goofy looking goat painted on its side panel swerved to keep from running over Gilligan and hit me instead, head on. I was thrown like a beer bottle from the bike to the curb.

Everything went cerulean blue.

I don't know how long I was on my back looking up at the cloudless sky, completely motionless, not a feeling or awareness of my body at all. It was the most marvelous sleep state ever, and when Gilligan's rough tongue licked my nose clean, and Landon and Luna appeared above me, their faces distorted, their eyes full of guilt, and wait a second – when did Landon get his braces taken off? – I'm sure that I smiled before I closed my eyes and let the warm light lift me.

"Wake up, Dorothy!" someone whispered

While I was being rocked in the softest angel's wings, I said my very last words to Landon, loud and bold, as clear as day, words I had kept inside me for two whole years, words that I had practiced over and over just for him that were bursting to come out. Just three little one-syllable words. "The rent's due!"

I was asked, no, more like begged, to take my friend's grumpy, but exceptionally bright four-year-old boy with me to run errands. Seeing his crabby expression in the rearview mirror, I attempted to engage the unhappy little fellow. I hid the keys in my pocket and acting frustrated, I repeated over and  over, "What am I forgetting?" He sat amazingly stoic for a kid who just recently stopped wetting the bed. "Come on, Wynn, I bet you know," I teasingly coaxed him. Heaven knows why his dogged determination not to fall for an obviously silly game pushed me further. I turned around in my seat to stare him down and asked again, "What am I forgetting?" He looked directly into my eyes with the face of a staunch diplomat, a tiny, annoyed smirk lifting at the corner of his mouth, and he said with unflappable self-assurance, "YOUR DIGNITY!"

DIGGING FOR DIGNITY

T ootsie considered the first two years of his dog life an utter failure. Born a Scottish Terrier, a small, yet known as fast, alert, and playful breed of dog nicknamed "the diehard" by the Earl of Dumbarton was a hard act to follow.

Left behind by his siblings, he remained the runt of the litter until he was eventually passed on to his second owner. With nothing to do but sleep all day, he grew lazy with no goals or desires, except to mount the poodle two doors down if it wasn't too inconvenient or raining. A steak bone might get him off his duff to enter the kitchen when called. Even then, if it wasn't served on a clean dish, he'd rather not have it at all. He hated the name Tootsie and would have rather been called Ramsay. He loathed walks or a car ride with his owner, Victor and his boyfriend, Lance, who fought constantly in his presence. On the window seat of their apartment overlooking a busy street was where he spent most of his time sitting absentmindedly in a bright red plaid vest that was rarely removed, even during the summer. People walking by probably thought he was a stuffed animal. In a soft fluffy blanket wadded up in the bowels of the ostentatious grand piano that nobody played was where Tootsie wanted to die and preferably, sooner than later.

When Victor and Lance decided to split up, they sat down at the table and played a game of Monopoly, agreeing that the loser would get to keep Tootsie, and the winner would get the Scottie dog playing piece and the apartment. Lance lost the game, landing too many times on the *Go to Jail* space. Victor sent the two of them down the road with Lance rambling on and on how he had been cheated, while beating on the steering wheel, looking disdainfully at his unwanted pet prize, and violently shaking his head in disapproval, until he ran smack-dab into the back of a city bus.

That wreck was how Tootsie lost his front tooth and his second owner all in one night. He found himself, the very next day, in a pound with forty-three other yapping dogs that made him so nervous, he cowered in the corner and covered his eyes, not caring if he was rescued or not.

In the same town, Erma Dunstan had lost her husband, her dog, and her dignity, all in one month. Losing your husband at the age of eighty-two is a common thing. Losing your dog is another unfortunate fact of life. But, losing your dignity, well, that's just something no one should have to lose anytime, for any reason.

Before these losses, Erma had a sweet life with her husband Ted, and her pet dog, a cute Scottish Terrier who she named Roosevelt after the great late Franklin D. who owned Fala, a Scottie named after Murray the Outlaw of Falahill. (Thank you, Wikipedia!) Erma would never dream of putting clothing on her dog, believing that he should be unencumbered and free as a bird. She even refused to put tags or bells on Roosevelt's neck; winning her case when she asked Ted, "How would you like to hear clanking in your ears every time you moved?" After a diligent training course, her Scottie didn't even require a leash.

Erma faithfully attended church on Sundays, and on Tuesdays she rarely missed lady's poker night – storing a flask of whiskey inside her stocking and carrying a stack of freshly baked cookies that were just soft enough to chew without irritating the old gums of her card playing comrades. She was greatly admired and had been the sounding board for most of her geriatric friends who complained about their lazy, unimpassioned husbands, or the daughter-in-law that ruined a perfectly raised son. Many came to her for advice and answers that she didn't always have. But they could be darn sure that she would find them, one way or another.

Above anything else, gardens were Erma's passion. Some of her best thinking came to her while digging in fresh dirt, inhaling the mixture of mineral particles, water, air, organic matter and living organisms providing life to the roots of the beautiful plants she nurtured. She remembered digging in her father's garden, and the time she tasted her first bite of soil. Oh, how he laughed at the joy on his daughter's face. For years after, Erma wondered if a garden was growing inside her. It turned out there was – a most wonderful garden of love for Ted and her pal, Roosevelt.

Life with Ted had been a remarkable sixty years, but as the cards were dealt, Ted developed a brain tumor that, in Erma's opinion, plucked him much too soon from this world. With no children to turn to, she grew wearier each day without him. So weary, she abandoned her lovely gardens, while Roosevelt stayed helplessly nearby, rarely leaving her side.

One afternoon, during a walk through the park, Erma stopped to study the community garden that was in a terrible state of neglect. A sadness overwhelmed her when she saw numerous ant piles smothering what used to be a healthy cabbage leaf or carrot sprout. Wild vines trekked erratically over and around the wilted plants, squeezing what little life was left in them. A sudden dizziness forced Erma to seek out the nearest tree where she leaned, clutching her chest until she collapsed. Running in circles around her motionless body, Roosevelt whined fretfully, stopping only to lick her face. The brave Scottie ran to the nearest human and beckoned him to follow. A man who had been flying a remote-control airplane rushed to her aid. The ambulance was called, and Erma later found herself in a convalescent home, without a clue as to what happened to Roosevelt.

As she sat in a wheelchair on the grounds of Brightland Gardens, *Caring with a Servant's Heart*, Erma's memories flooded her thoughts. The physical therapy was working well, walking was easier, and her speech was getting better each day, but she found herself searching anxiously for a reason to live. With Ted gone and now Roosevelt living who knows where, she tried to imagine him happy with a family or the alternative, playing with Ted in Heaven, both patiently waiting for her to come home. But now and then it would strike her hard that he might be stuck in a cage or tied to a stake in a grassless backyard and hopefully not living with someone who throws shoes at him and forgets to feed him. The morbid thoughts became unbearable and sitting under that big tree, looking down at the silly flowered sack dress and pink house shoes she would have never worn at home, she discovered a reason for living – she would find her dog, restore her gardens and her dignity, if it was the last thing she did on earth.

A remarkable recovery, the doctor had reported at Erma's next visit, and he approved her request to leave the facility, as long as she followed strict guidelines. Erma pledged to cooperate, and two days later, one of the kinder nurses offered to drive her home.

"Oh, it's good to be here," she said to the front door when unlocking it. Entering the foyer, she sat her purse on the dusty entry table and timidly walked through her dark and lifeless home. An hour later, with the windows all opened and the light curtains flapping in the breeze, Erma set out an elaborate plan to find her dog.

Lost dog posters with a picture of Roosevelt and a hefty reward were sighted in places one would never expect to see them – above toilets in the men's restrooms at the local diners, at the dry cleaners and hair salons in between magazines, and at the bowling alley where they serve warm beer and greasy fries. Erma left no stone unturned and even went as far as leaving a poster at the sleazy X-rated movie store on a creepy street east of the city. Even perverts like dogs, she considered while taping the poster above the triple X-rated section. Now, all she could do was pray and wait.

John Shreveport, at thirty, still lived with his mother, locking himself up in his bedroom where he built model planes, trains, and automobiles until the wee hours of the morning and when finally, high on the glue, fell asleep to the shopping channel. When the pound keeper yanked Tootsie out of the cage and handed him to John – who was tight-lipped, but clearly pleased with his find – John took the dog straight home without even looking at his teeth, which was probably a good thing, since one was missing. And he didn't even bother to check out his paws or that other unmentionable part to determine his sex. Tootsie was promptly given another home and another name.

John had picked out the dog for his terminally ill mother. In her sensitive state, she confessed that she had always wanted a Scottish Terrier, but her militant and highly allergic husband would not allow it. Although John had not always been the perfect son, realizing that her days were numbered awakened something so powerful in him he wanted nothing more than to please her. So, when he found Tootsie at the pound, in his distinguished attire, he quickly renamed him Terrance, after his late father, and presented him to his mother as a final gift from an indebted son who was bound and determined to remain the one and only beneficiary in her will.

As Terrance's fate would have it, owner number three went to Heaven within a month of his arrival, and he nearly accompanied her. She had wrapped him up like a baby in a blanket, tightly tucking him under her arm. When she fell asleep to never wake up again, he was wedged between her rigid body and the wall. Kicking like crazy, he managed to chew his way through the blanket to a freedom he had never felt before. The awful experience had cured his death wish, and he now imagined himself having fun, running, chasing a ball, and maybe even chewing on steak bones right off the floor. He wanted to be loved, trusted, and yes, even trained.

During the preparations for the funeral and after, Terrance was forgotten by John, and the poor dog spent the next few weeks alone and depressed. It's not that he wasn't fed. John piled a week's worth of dry kibble in his bowl, filled a bucket full of water, and had a doggy door installed that took him outside to a ten by ten fenced-in space with not one tree to whiz on or one stick of lawn furniture to sink his teeth into. And a poop scoop? Nope, not even one.

With his newfound attitude, Terrance knew he could not exist like this. Escape was the only answer. And how? He would dig his way out! Naturally a "digger" at heart, the Scottie was originally bred to hunt and kill vermin on farms. It didn't take long before his muscular thighs remembered what they were made for. Terrance immersed himself into digging a hole big enough to let a nineteen-pound Terrier out and a family of possums in. That night he fell asleep exhausted and ready to find his dignity.

The next morning, Terrance ate his bowl of kibble down to the last morsel and waited until John ascended the stairs to his room full of projects before he escaped. Squeezing under the fence was not as easy as he thought it would be. Since he had eaten such large quantities, his stomach, now bloated, got in the way. With a mouthful of dirt and his vest soiled and torn, he gradually made it to the other side. Determined to choose his next new owner himself, he scanned the neighborhood, eyeing each home carefully as he marched down the sidewalk, his gait agile and coordinated. Exuding ruggedness and power, head and tail held high, he conveyed both assurance and control. Terrance had never felt more alive.

Erma still enjoyed drying her laundry on a clothesline that Ted had lovingly installed for her years earlier. The morning promised a cool breeze and a warm sun, so with clothespins piled on top of wet sheets, she set about the task of hanging them on the line.

Meanwhile, Terrance decided, after walking several miles, that he needed to relieve himself and proceeded to look for a backyard to do his business. Most of the homes were fenced in, so it took him awhile to find the perfect setting. When he spotted Erma's friendly place, surrounded by beautiful flowering bushes, he instinctively knew it was right and trotted around the back to find a nicely shaded area.

On the clothesline, the flat sheet flapped in the breeze. When Erma shook out the fitted sheet, she fumbled with its elastic edges and lost her grip. A gust of wind took it from her delicate fingers just when Terrance was approaching the yard, and it landed right on top of him. Trapped and in a panic – flashing back to the time he was suffocating in the blanket next to a corpse – he fought and tumbled with the sheet until he was completely wrapped up in it.

Erma stood back and watched the scene, thinking she had captured a big cat, or good heavens, not a possum, she hoped – those blind ugly creatures were not her favorite animal. Still, she knew she had to rescue the poor thing and valiantly attempted to do so. Grabbing one end of the sheet, she slowly unraveled the fabric. With a final tug, Terrance surrendered, stopped wiggling, and rolled out clumsily, landing on his back.

The minute she saw the little upside-down Scottie she let out a yell that is not often heard from sweet, elderly women of her fragile age. "I'll be damn! Is that you Roosevelt?"

Terrance rolled over, clearly stunned and a little wobbly, but capable of standing on all fours. Before he could shake off the experience, Erma snatched him up into her arms and snuggled him against her cheek. She smelled like cookies and her hands were so soft, Terrance buckled under her touch; his rapid heartbeat slowing down with each kiss. Before he knew it, Erma had him in the house on the kitchen countertop.

"My goodness, who has done this to you, Roosevelt?" she murmured, as she cut away the tattered and soiled vest and removed the dirt-caked rhinestone collar from his wiry, matted hair. She promptly filled the kitchen sink and gave him a warm bubble bath. The little terrier naturally thought he had gone to heaven after all.

The following days were wonderful, as Erma tended to her dog and her gardens, making up for the time they had lost together. Terrance, now Roosevelt, was happy to inherit a new, bolder, and more masculine name, although Ramsay was still at the top of the list. He felt himself walking taller and eager to please his new master. But when he didn't follow the routine that the real Roosevelt was trained to do, Erma began to doubt that he was her missing dog.

Reading together was once an intimate time well spent for Erma and Ted. They would sit on the sofa, feet up on an ottoman, books propped up on their bellies, elbows touching, and glasses of hibiscus tea at their fingertips. Even with Ted gone, she kept the routine alive. Her Roosevelt knew he was invited to sit between them where they could each take turns petting him in between chapters. But this dog sat idly on Ted's recliner and watched her read.

From across the room, Erma looked deeply into his almond shaped eyes. "You're not my Roosevelt, are you?" she questioned the Scottie in a soft and somber voice.

His eyes said it all, and she imagined the dog answering, "No, but I wish I were."

As glad as she was to have him in her lonely life, the old feeling of loss and the need to find her Scottie friend returned even stronger. She spent the rest of the day posting more signs.

Finally, a caller responded to her ads. The man sounded nervous and spoke softly, as if he didn't want to be heard by others nearby. Erma agreed to meet him and his wife at the park by her home. Excited, she left the Roosevelt imposter comfortably curled up on Ted's recliner.

As soon as she spotted a couple sitting on a park bench, she approached them cautiously. They were younger with pleasant faces. The man recognized Erma and spoke first, extending his hand. "I am so glad to see you looking so well."

Erma cocked her head. "Do I know you, sir?"

"Well, not really, but I know you. I was the one that called the ambulance when you fell ill here in the park," he explained, pointing to the tree where Erma had fallen. "Your little Scottie saved your life. He's quite a dog." Then the man turned and introduced his wife.

"Yes, he is," Erma agreed, shaking the woman's hand "Yes, I had a wonderful dog. Please tell me what you know about him."

The man looked down and then up. His wife put her arm around him, coaxing him to speak. "I brought your dog home with me after the ambulance took you away. When I learned that you were sent to a nursing home, we decided to keep him for you. Before we knew it, we grew attached to him. He's such a smart dog. But now that you're well, and I saw your posters," he stalled, "and in the oddest places," he cracked a smile and lifted his eyebrows toward Erma, "I realized that you desperately wanted your dog back. Only, I've been reluctant to call you because…well, I thought we could meet to discuss it further."

"Oh my," Erma's tone was mixed with concern and relief. "I'm so glad to learn that Roosevelt has been with a nice family. This is a bit of a pickle we're in, but the truth is," she paused to dab at the tears forming in her eyes, not wanting to dash their hopes, but unable to hold in the truth, "I miss him so terribly."

"We understand, we do," the wife spoke quickly trying to disguise her disappointment. Then she turned and went to the car, leaving her husband standing there with his head down, kicking the grass beneath his feet. A minute later she returned with Roosevelt in tow.

The second Roosevelt saw Erma, he tore after her and stopped just short of her feet, jumping up and down until she picked him up. A precious reunion that brought tears to everyone's eyes erased any doubt that the couple had done the right thing.

Refusing the reward, Erma urged them to at least join her for a cup of tea and a bite of cake. They did so willingly and followed her home.

Erma let Roosevelt be the first to enter, and he ran through the house like a child arriving home from the last day of school. He was overly excited, running past the sleeping lump on the chair three times before he stopped in his tracks and raised his nose to sniff the air.

Erma picked up the napping Scottie – once again without a name since the original owner would be clearly claiming it. She kissed the little pooch on the head and let Roosevelt smell him before she handed him to the man.

"Trade?" she lightly chuckled.

The wife looked eagerly at her husband, and they both said in unison, "You bet!"

"But are you sure?" the man asked with a look of doubt suppressing his growing smile.

"Oh yes, this particular breed is very territorial, as you will find out in time." Roosevelt stepped up and nudged Erma's leg with his nose. "Isn't that right, Roosevelt?"

Over tea, Erma gave the happy couple tips on how to live with a Scottie. As they sipped, they noticed with admiration the two dogs sitting separately, each intently regarding them seated at the kitchen table. "They make wonderful guard dogs, but they can be easily insulted. More importantly, they are most loyal."

With promises to meet each other at the park with their pets during the weekends, they ended their visit. When they were walking out to their car, Erma, standing at the front door with the real Roosevelt at her feet, remembered to ask, "By the way, what will you name your Scottie?"

"Ramsay," the husband yelled back, "my late grandfather's name."

"As it should be," Erma whispered, looking down at her canine friend. "Ramsey, eh? Would you prefer that name?"

Roosevelt snorted indignantly and marched back inside.

With one last soulful glance at Erma, Ramsay proudly held his head high with the dignity of a true Scotsman, as he sat erect and recharged in the back seat of his new family's car, eagerly awaiting his next adventure and hopefully his last home. If not, he would simply dig his way out.

THE P.P. WOMEN'S CLUB

To the best of my recollection, I was just sitting there, as usual, minding my own business, when suddenly everyone, even the dog, started screaming.

My boss had insisted that I join the P. P. Women's club where his sister held membership, even though she vehemently protested after meeting me for the first time. He had offered me the club opportunity because I was beginning to show signs of burn-out, slumping at my desk and not meeting my deadlines. He said I needed to be around positive women, and not wanting to lose his best employee, he forced the issue. So, there I was, in what they call a trial run; meaning that after four consecutive meetings, I could be voted out by the members if they found that I did not fit the criteria for "perfect poise." This was my third meeting, and I had a gut feeling that it would be my last.

"The party is to be casual," our leader said, stretching

out the word to make sure that everyone knew not to wear pearls or stockings. "Casual…you know, somewhere in between Capris and sundress. We'll be sitting out on the patio on my new outdoor furniture, so do wear something pretty for pictures."

Mylie walked purposely around each table and one by one handed the coveted invitations out to the fourteen ladies who had just spent the past hour listening to their favorite speaker talk about how to keep your man happy and your pocketbook full. Chart included. She hesitated when she got to me. And there I was, so excited to be invited, I don't even know why. I guess I really did want to be a part of the group – holding my hand out like a little kid, smiling ever so demurely.

"Um," Mylie mumbled, with pursed lips.

I gave her the look – the look that said, please let me be on the team. Why, I'll be the water girl if you do. I'll even wash your uniforms. Please! And when that didn't work, I blurted out, "I have a camera. I'll gladly take pictures."

Mylie stood up taller and inhaled, forcing a lop-sided smile with her thin lips as she reluctantly placed the invitation on the table in front of me, avoiding my outstretched and shaking hand altogether. "Well, we *will* need pictures," she declared.

Phew, that was a close one! Rubbing my fingers over the thick raised letters and taking my time to open the card with its glorious message announcing that I, yes me, Pammy Gail Pfeiffer is invited to a party. And not just any party, but a private affair at Mylie Finkerstrom's very own home. I have never had the privilege of being amongst the ladies of society outside our monthly meeting of the Perfect Poise Women's Club. It has always been held in this small hotel event room rented by Dr. Finkerstrom, who wanted to give his wife every opportunity to spread the word that she was married to the finest cosmetic surgeon in town and if referred by her, you could count on a substantial discount. Things were indeed looking up.

As the ladies filed out of the meeting, each beaming with their coveted invitations slid in between the pages of the "How to" guide, I stayed back and watched the room empty. I am always the last to leave at any event. Even as a child in school I waited patiently for everyone to exit, leaving me in the magic of whatever had taken place at the time. This is my way of absorbing life, remembering the interesting things that were said or noticed, so that later I could relive them when I felt lonely.

Almost giddy, I stopped in the ladies' room on the way out and being that it was unoccupied, I took the opportunity to look at myself in the mirror with the pink flowery covered wallpaper reflecting behind me, making me look softer somehow, and maybe even pretty. I removed my glasses with the stylish red frames and squinted to see the new me. I was a blur. A blotch. A smear on the mirror, describing me to a tee – a smudge on the face of life. I felt my spirit drop to my stomach where a glop of bile churned violently and like a geyser, it shot straight up to my tonsils. Here it comes, the self-loathing, the contempt for my being, the poor pitiful me syndrome…but wait! I have an invitation to a party! I slipped my glasses back on and held up the card to the mirror and smiled. This was going to be a great week!

The next few days I spent buried in my work. I am a technical writer and editor for small appliance manuals, and on the side, I have a blog where I share my private fantasies under a fake name – Rene Lu've. But there's no time for that nonsense now. Pleased to see that I was beginning to perk up, my boss left a huge stack of papers for me to edit, leaving me last minute shopping for an outfit for the party.

I never ask for help when I shop; heading straight to the clearance racks, seldom glancing at the merchandise priced too high for my budget. I refuse to be seduced by the retail market and as a result, I have quite a savings account. I drink cheap wine at home, dine on leftovers, purchase most of my clothes at consignment stores, (anything that comes near the pubic area, I refuse to buy used). I cut out coupons, save every plastic container and bag, reuse coffee grounds, and mop the floor with a big beach towel that I slide around with my feet to Buddy Holly music. I ride my old Schwinn bicycle everywhere, and because it is rusty and has stickers pasted on it from countries I've never been to, nobody tries to steal it, so I don't need a lock. I even cut my hair myself and use Vaseline to keep it spiked just the way I like it. I do, however, splurge on my prescription eyeglasses. I have every color, even Battery Charged Blue, which I mix and match with my daily wear.

I sometimes think I'm happy, except I don't have any friends, unless of course you want to call the neighbor's dog, Maggie, my friend. She comes over often, and I give her frozen beef bones that the butcher saves for me. She listens to fifties music with me, too, and occasionally runs beside me when I go for an evening bike ride. Sometimes I wish I had a friend like Maggie, or a boyfriend like her owner, Jeff. We have a lot in common. He's a writer, too, only he writes fiction and is published, with a long list of readers, and he's a member of the Horror Writers Association.

Sometimes I can see him writing from my kitchen window, if I prop myself up on the counter and strain my neck to look around the big Blue Texas Ranger shrub that has grown out of control since I planted it in my small backyard three years ago. He sits at a picnic table under a tree that shades him like an umbrella, and I can hear him reading out loud or laughing at something he wrote. Oh, he is a dreamboat and probably in his early thirties, about my age, which I think is a sign.

Last year I started making pumpkin pies for him. The first time I made one, he happened to be in the backyard writing. I pointed a table fan at the pie and sent the wonderful spices, nutmeg, cinnamon, and ginger out the window directly to his thin nostrils. Minutes later, I handed him a piece over the fence, and from that day on I have been baking him a pie at least once a month. Nearly two years of handing it over the fence, he hasn't once invited me into his home or on a date. I guess he's too busy writing because I have noticed that he's gotten heavier. That happened to me the first year I started my job, but when I realized that I had to buy new clothes to fit my new plump body, I quickly lost weight and have retained my posture perfect 121 pounds ever since.

The sundress that I found for the party at Ragalicious, the gently used resale shop, had a round stain right where my left nipple rested. But since the dress fit so well and was just long enough to cover my bony knees, I convinced the saleslady to drop another ten per cent off the price.

I tried like crazy to get the stain out, but when it wouldn't budge, and it got larger as I rubbed, I ended up gluing a flower applique over it, and it made sense to do the same on the other side to make it even. I stood in front of the mirror and admired the bright yellow dress with the sunflowers on each nipple and decided that it was quite lovely. But the longer I looked, the flowers seemed to grow bigger and bigger accentuating my breasts (boobies, for you heathens). Suddenly, the dress disappeared and only the sunflowers remained. I know just what it needs! Accessories! I found a pink belt that I usually wear on Easter Sunday. To complete the ensemble, I glued a sunflower on the tops of each of my brown sandals and one on my orange hair band. Pink lipstick and purple eye shadow applied, and I was ready to impress the PP women and their trendy leader.

Mylie's home was about a mile away in the swanky part of Perrytown where folks had torn down the old homes from the forties and rebuilt mini mansions in mostly Santa Fe style. I decided that instead of walking, I would ride my bike. Mylie had said that it was a garden party, so I put a bow around one of my potted pencil cactus plants and secured it in the wire basket sitting just above the fat, front wheel. It was one of my favorites, an Opuntia polyacantha that I had grown from a tiny little thing. I was sure that my host would be thrilled with the gift and its fragile pink flowers.

I grew anxious as I approached the street to Mylie's home. Thrusting my arm straight out to take a right turn, a lady in a convertible flew past me. The bumper clipped my front tire and sent me flying backwards where I hit my head on the curb, and the potted plant came flying from out of nowhere, crashing into my chin. The bike seemed to have a mind of its own and rolled the other direction.

"Ow!" I yelled, lying there long enough to realize what had happened; a dull ache developing from a potentially cracked skull. A little dazed, I sat up and located the bike, now on its side about ten feet away and the pot lay broken in pieces just inches from my knees. Where is the cactus? Twisting to look behind me, I saw it propped up on the curb. I gave myself a second to decompress and very carefully stood up. I studied my shoes, the flowers still attached, swiped the back of my dress, and looked down at my breasts, eyeing the drooping sunflowers moving up and down as I took in deep breaths, my heart pounding loudly in my ears. No blood anywhere, the bike uninjured, the camera safe inside my fanny pack, but the pot was a goner. Thinking efficiently, I shimmied out of the slip underneath my sundress and carefully, very carefully wrapped the injured plant, placed it in the basket, and looked both ways before proceeding to the party. I do not like to be late.

When I arrived, no one answered the front door. Then I remembered that it was a party by the pool. As I walked around to the backyard, I spotted the car that nearly killed me. The driver must be one of the invitees. I would find out who she is and tell her a thing or two. Or maybe not. I so wanted to be liked by all of them. I'm still not sure why.

I heard people laughing and Michael Bublé crooning from speakers mounted high on the patio cover. I stood still and observed the ladies from the women's club that I had known only by face, as they had not given me much thought at the meetings. It's true, I am shy, and it takes time for me to get to know someone, so I am kind of a voyeur. So, it was no surprise that none of them acknowledged my presence until Mylie approached me, her eyes darting from nipple to nipple as she studied the sunflowers. And without a salutation of any kind, she asked if I'd brought the camera.

I unzipped my fanny pack and held it out in front of her.

"What is on your chin?" she asked, with a look of repulsion mixed with a slight trace of concern on her heavily powdered face.

"What?" I said, sucking in my nose and crossing my eyes, looking down to see what she was talking about.

There were thin, what appeared to be, hairs sticking out

beyond the length of my nose, and my nose is pretty lengthy. (Mylie had twice reminded me that I could get a discount at her husband's clinic when I was ready to make that vital and necessary change.) I slowly reached up to touch the intruders and when I did, I let out a scream, dropping the cactus on the ground. "Oh! That hurts! What is it?" I felt my eyes widen in fear.

"Looks like you had a bout with a porcupine," one of the ladies said, as the rest of the party hurriedly gathered around to see.

Mylie grabbed me by the arm, "Come inside and look in the mirror." The ladies all filed in behind us, snickering and guessing aloud what had happened to me, as if I were deaf and unable to hear their snide remarks about my dress, too.

"Look!" Mylie ordered, shoving me in front of the big mirror that took up half of an entire wall. The ladies all squeezed in the guest bathroom and hovered over me, staring.

My mouth dropped open wide, and I could see the silverish black fillings in my molars, so I quickly shut it and explained, "I had a bicycle accident on the way here. The cactus I brought as a gift to you, Mylie, flew out of the basket and landed on my face. These are cactus needles, and now that I know what they are, they hurt like the dickens!"

"I bet so." Mylie turned to the lady standing next to her. "Steph, go get the tweezers out of my vanity drawer. And you," she grabbed my shoulders, "you, sit on the toilet and wait here. I'll be right back."

Then the questions came at me like a swarm of bees, and before I knew it, I had changed the story to suit the listeners. I told them that I had been accosted by a big, tattooed teenager on skates that tried to steal my bike, and the story blossomed from there.

"Oh, you poor thing," and "I hope you remember his face so you can report him." Sighs from all around filled the tiled bathroom, and when I tried to cover my big smile from all the attention I was getting, I pushed the stickers deeper into my chin. "Owwww!"

The ladies reared back and cleared a path for Mylie's daughter who entered dressed in a surgical mask, hospital gloves, and a large pair of tweezers held high in the air, followed by Mylie who closed the door behind her, after ordering the protesting ladies out to the hall.

"Don't worry," the daughter said when she saw the frightened look in my eyes. "I'm a med student. This will look great on my resume."

Mylie crouched on the floor, snapping more pictures of the inside of my nostrils than necessary.

Outside the ladies went about their socializing and paid no particular attention to the screaming coming from the guest bathroom. Only the family pet Pomeranian stayed close by, whining, and scratching at the door. When the task was completed, Mylie and her daughter took the sharp cactus spines outside to show to the ladies. I stared alarmingly at my face in the mirror and at the four Band-aids now on my chin. I looked like an idiot!

It took every ounce of courage I had left to go back to the party instead of sneaking out the front door. Fortunately, the ladies were engrossed in a game of Hearts and paid no attention to me. I scooped up a ladle of punch and poured it in one of the tall purple glasses with hand painted daisies. "Oh my, is this punch spiked?"

"Well, of course," Mylie said. "Wouldn't be a party without a little spikey-poo."

"Here, here," the ladies all held up their glasses and toasted.

I hesitated to take another drink, since I tend to get tipsy very quickly. A cheap drunk, I am told. So, I decided one glass would be quite enough.

Sitting there watching the ladies play cards made me feel odd. It reminded me of when I was little, and the girls all played with their Barbie dolls while I sat outside the circle and watched. My mother refused to buy me one. She said they were vulgar and anatomically incorrect. Instead, she bought me books. Lots and lots of books. Which is probably why I became an editor. I wish I had one in my hand right now.

"Don't forget to take pictures," Mylie said, pointing at the camera nearby.

"Of course." I promptly picked up the camera while the ladies fluffed their hair and posed with cards fanned out in their hands. I snapped a few and sat back down, wondering what to do next.

Appetizers were in bowls on a fabric-covered table. I scooped a teaspoon of guacamole on a chip and put the whole thing in my mouth. The dip was so spicy, my eyes began to water, and I nearly gagged, so I rushed over to the trash can and turned my back to the women, pretending to throw away a napkin as I carefully spit out the green mushy chip. Just then I noticed my slip in the trashcan, the blobby appetizer clinging to the soft material.

She threw my gift away! I wanted to reach in and claim my slip, the only one I owned and rescue the cactus at the same time, but I didn't have the courage. Instead, I moseyed over to a plate of cookies. I took two and walked out into the sun by the pool to savor them with my second glass of punch. The Pomeranian that had been whining outside the bathroom door came running at me and began nipping at my heels.

"Stop, stop!" I ordered, but it wouldn't listen to me, and its sharp teeth grazed my ankle. "Stop right now you little creep!" I yelled again and kicked at the crazed animal, sending it sliding across the tile and into the pool.

"My baby, oh my baby!" Mylie screamed, rushing toward me. "What have you done? She can't swim! My lord, she's sinking!"

The little critter was indeed sinking and sinking fast. Mylie screamed, "Save her, save her!" and pushed me into the pool, the contents in my hands flying into the air. The water was deeper than I thought, and it felt like I was nine feet under by the time I reached the dog. I grabbed her and swam back to the surface. Mylie was leaning over the edge, her arms outstretched. "Give me my baby. Give me my baby!"

And just as I was handing the soggy, little fur ball to her, it bit into the soft web of skin between my thumb and forefinger. "Owee!" I screamed, as blood began to spurt.

"You deserve that!" Mylie yelled. "You kicked my Poofy. Now get out of the pool before you bloody up the darn thing!"

The ladies were now huddled around Mylie and her precious canine, babbling like a bunch of old hens, and looking at me as if I was some kind of criminal.

I stood there soaked and dripping, holding up my hand as the blood drizzled down my arm.

"Napkins are over there," one of the ladies stiffly pointed. I picked up several and blotted my bloody hand and dried off my glasses. The chlorine started to sting my chin, and I felt like crying. I poured another glass of punch and sat down in a vinyl padded chair. I felt myself deflate along with the air escaping from the foamed cushion.

"Good Lord!" Mylie cried. "Don't sit on my new furniture in those wet clothes!"

"Oh, I'm sorry," I said, jumping up at her command and looking around for a seat without fabric. A small plastic step stool is where I sat squeezing out the water in my dress while I nursed my drink and my pride, keeping a close eye on the wicked little dog staring at me from its master's lap as the ladies continued their mindless card game.

The alcohol and the sun were beginning to warm me, and before I knew it, the wet underwear caught in my natal cleft (butt crack, for the uncouth) was no longer annoying me, nor was the whispering from the catty group of women who periodically glanced at me all at once. I looked down in my glass and saw an ugly brown cockroach stuck to the cherry at the bottom. Instead of getting upset, as any sober woman would do, I had a most brilliant idea.

Mylie was just finishing up her drink, when one of the ladies looked over at me and said, "You're close to the punch bowl, would you get me another drink?"

"Me, too," Mylie spoke up.

I smiled wide. "Of course." How perfect! How perfectly poised perfect!

"And put two cherries in mine," Mylie ordered.

I poured two fresh glasses of punch and filled my own, the roach kicking its tiny legs wildly as it reached the top. I plopped another cherry on top of its head, and it quickly sunk. I handed the glasses to the ladies, the extra cherry-filled one, the cockroach à la carte to Mylie. Standing back to watch what I thought was the cleverest thing I had ever done, and shall I say, the cruelest, (besides the time I put paste in Mary Peppers hair in kindergarten), I quickly picked up the camera and waited.

Mylie lifted her glass to the ladies and smiled into the

camera. "Cheers, my dears," she said, holding her perfectly poised pose, the ladies following suit.

Clinking glasses all around, Mylie took a sip. Then, just as I hoped, she absentmindedly put her mouth to the edge of the glass and fished out a cherry with her tongue, the roach clinging to it for dear life. Mylie liked sucking on cherries and rolling them around the inside of her cheeks before she bit into the tender skin and swallowed the nectar. Only this time, she noticed something different, and the bottom of her mouth dropped open, a look on her face I cannot describe, except to say she looked a little like Jeff Daniels in the movie *Dumb and Dumber.* One of the ladies abruptly pushed her chair back in horror and shouted, "You have a bug in your mouth!"

"Oh!" and "My God!" and "Good Lord!" the women eeked and shrieked and shoved their chairs back, one of them falling down right on her buttock while the others stood slapping at their clothes and shaking their heads wildly as if a swarm of roaches had descended on them. Mylie, who now was spitting violently onto the table, first the cherry and then the roach that sat lifeless on the queen of hearts, swung her head and vomited on the lady next to her, who in turn screamed and fell backwards on the woman who was at that moment getting up from her fall. Both toppled backwards, and like a line of dominoes, the ladies fell to the floor as they held onto each other trying to avoid the woman now covered in puke. Meanwhile, I kept my finger pressing up and down on the camera's shutter button, capturing everything as I promised I would do for the slideshow at the next P. P. Women's meeting.

"Time for me to go," I spoke softly, as the women cried and scooted away from each other on their elbows and bottoms, looking fearfully around for anything remotely resembling bugs or slime, while Mylie ran choking in disgust into the house to brush her tongue with peroxide. My suggestion, of course, and the last photo I would snap for the day.

I reached into the trashcan and collected my slip-covered cactus. Just as I was leaving, I noticed several brown June bugs, you know, those bugs that stick to your clothing and the window screens. I'm not freaked out by them, as I am by scorpions, so I picked up three of them and held them gently in my palm. I also spotted the spines from the cactus neatly sitting on a napkin. I snatched them up and slipped away without anyone noticing or caring that I had left.

Out front, the white convertible that was responsible for my prickly chin was blessed with three fat June beetles clutching the steering wheel and a handful of spines scattered on the driver's seat.

The bike ride home was a relief, and I felt something very new to me – the sweet taste of revenge. Or even more than that, I felt glad to be me. Glad that I didn't have friends like those ladies in the club. Glad that they didn't want me to be their friend. Glad that I had a bike instead of a car that knocks people off the road. Glad that my neighbor's dog likes me, and that my neighbor liked my pumpkin pies, even if he didn't like me. Glad that I had not spent all my hard-earned money on clothes and things that would not change me or make me a better woman or buy me friends like those kind in the PPW club. And finally, I was glad that it was my clever idea to insert a tiny screwdriver in the small appliance manual, even though the publisher could not appreciate my ingenuity.

As I approached my home, the sun resting on the top of the wooden fence, I parked my bike in front of Jeff's house, and with my new burst of pride, I bravely knocked on his door. I greeted him with an exuberant, "Hi!"

"Oh, hi Fanny," he said in return and looked down at my empty hands. "No pumpkin pie today?" he asked, his eyes blinking wildly in anticipation.

"It's Pammy," I said dryly. "No, not today. Instead, I would like to ask you something."

"Oh, OK. Too bad, though. I love your pies."

"I know. I know. But I would rather you love me. Or, I mean," I stuttered, certain that the alcohol had made me say that. "I would rather that you liked me…as a friend. And maybe, maybe you could let me read one of your books. You've never offered, much less offered me a drink, or a cup of coffee, or…"

"I'm busy writing," Jeff said sourly and shut the door.

I stood there for quite a while staring at that ugly black door, long enough to notice how badly it needed painting and long enough to realize that he hadn't even asked me about my bandaged chin or my wet dress.

Now, there comes a time in a person's life that requires change. Not a little change, but a great deal of change, and I felt as though that day at the party, I had changed dramatically. Things will never be the same, and I'm okay with that. Because now, instead of feeling down about myself, I am using that energy for something far more important.

The next morning, I awoke with an idea that made me realize that I was totally different. It was Sunday, and I decided that my pie-loving neighbor was right – it was time to bake for him. I put on an apron, my mother's hand-me-down, turned on the oven, then the radio and set out to make the best pumpkin pie ever.

While the pie cooled, I went out to my garden and dug up the dirt around my geraniums. This is where I usually find those plump grub worms that dig so happily in the rich soil. I counted about sixteen of them and put them in a bowl. Very carefully, I strategically placed them in the pie, pressing them down with the eraser end of a pencil, close to the thick crust. Then I very carefully smoothed a layer of whipped cream over the top. It is a fact that most people start eating at the small pointy end of the pie, saving the fat crusty end for the last. I was counting on Jeff being like most people.

I am not saying I'm happy about my new obsession with bugs. But it's not just anybody who can raise a roach farm, collect grub worms, or hatch fly larvae. I'm actually looking forward to showing the ladies of the PPW club the colony of a thousand freshly hatched and hungry flies that I will set free once the lights are out during the slide show.

They are being especially nice to me since I've been voted out and this is my last meeting. The grub worm brownies I baked smell divine, and the gold trimmed flypaper hats that I made for all fourteen of the members look so cute on them. How kind of them to amuse me.

To the best of my recollection, I was just standing there, as usual, minding my own business, when suddenly, everyone in the room started screaming.

Overnight you're thirteen and suddenly it's a time for a girl to experience the unhinged joy and agonizing angst of adolescence.

I wish I'd kept my Barbie dolls.

13

I'm thirteen now. This is it, 1966, the year everything changes. I know it, I feel it, and even though it's kind of scary, I'm excited.

This change I'm talking about all started just recently when I no longer had to share a room with my little sister. My parents had spent the entire summer converting the garage into a big master bedroom, right off the kitchen, convenient for dad to grab a beer and mother to mix a high ball. They weren't the quietest partiers, and there were times when I wanted to tell them to settle down. But I was a child who knew better than to interrupt adults for any reason other than the house was on fire or one of my siblings was in danger. I don't think children are like that anymore. I guess maybe, they're insecure or too selfish. I find myself pondering things like this, especially now that I have my own room. And especially now that I'm no longer a child.

In honor of my thirteenth my parents are allowing me to attend my first slumber party at the Peever's, who live just six blocks away. You could say I've earned this privilege. After all, I've been an excellent example of what a daughter should be and an understanding and helpful sibling.

When I told my mother about Miranda Peever and that she was called Randy, I failed to tell her that she was two years older and boy crazy. I did mention that she had only sisters, but I left out that one was glued by the hip to a boyfriend that looked like he had never washed his hair or feet, and the other sister quit school to work at the bowling alley. I guess she suspected something because she said, "Honey, remember, if you feel the least bit uncomfortable, you can come home, no matter what time it is, even if it's after midnight, I will come and get you. And, if the girls come up with some big ideas like leaving the house after the parents are asleep, please don't do it. All kinds of things can go wrong in the middle of the night, including getting arrested for being out underage. Life's too sweet to mess it up for something not worth it."

Well, this was quite a different lecture from the one I'd gotten before I turned thirteen. The tactic she used to scare me then was that the old man that walked the bayou snatched up kids and carried them away in a knapsack. For years I tried to imagine how he could stuff me in a bag that small. I was tall for my age, and I liked to eat. But this new warning did make some sense, so I made my promises, grabbed my overnight bag, and pranced off to a new adventure.

We live in a modest suburban neighborhood where everyone knows a little about everyone. Randy's house is in an older section on a street where I never ride my bike. It seems like people don't care much about their yards in this area. I felt a little nervous walking down it, but I was nervous anyway – my first sleepover and all.

Randy's family had just finished dinner when I arrived.

She had told me that I would be joining them, but I guess she forgot. When I looked at the sink full of dirty dishes and watched Randy put the last bit of dinner in the refrigerator, pans and all, I lost my appetite. I politely asked if I could help her clean. She responded with a gleeful, "Yes!"

"Dry or wash?" I asked.

"Both. I have to change clothes. Karl's coming over. Be right back," she announced, darting past me.

"Karl? Who's Karl?" I spent the entire dishwashing duty wondering who in the world was Karl.

Hurrying past the gross food droppings on the chairs and underneath the table, I walked out to the backyard. I calculated by the time on my new watch, a birthday gift from my dad, that I had been there nearly thirty whole minutes. Just when I began to wonder if I shouldn't have come, Randy appeared, all made up – bright pink lips, tight short-shorts and a blouse that showed her midriff. I didn't know what to say, so I said, "Nice lipstick. By the way, who's Karl?"

"I just met him this morning at the gas station. He's my sister's friend's brother. He didn't waste any time asking me out," she bragged, plopping down in the lawn chair. "He's really cute."

I looked sideways at my new friend who had lifted her legs up high on the back of the chair in front of her, revealing the soft, white pooch of her fanny as it sneaked out from her panties. I had never seen her outside of school, and that certainly was not the dress code. I turned my head and pretended not to notice, and it suddenly occurred to me that she hadn't thanked me for washing the dishes. "Oh, by the way, I left the clean dishes out. I didn't know where they went. I hope that's okay."

"Sure," she said flippantly while studying her red toenails.

"You know, I've never met your parents. Are they here?"

"No, they went to a party. We have the house to ourselves." Randy batted her eyes and grinned. I guess I looked a little surprised, because she said next, "You don't look so happy about that. What's the matter?"

"Oh, it's just that, well, my mom talked to yours and she was under the impression that your parents would be home tonight...you know, to supervise."

"Supervise? You're kidding? My sister will be home later, and she's like an adult. Don't worry. I didn't know you were a worry wort."

"Well, I'm not that worried." I twisted uncomfortably in my chair and cleared my throat. "Where are the other girls? You said you were having a slumber party."

Randy leaned over and reached out for the transistor radio on the little crooked, plastic table next to her. "No one else is coming. You're it!" She found one of the two good stations available and turned up the volume on the song "Wild Thing" by the Troggs. I guess we weren't going to talk anymore. There was no chance of that with the music blaring in our ears.

A dog nudged through the screen door and sat directly on my feet. "Hi there, big boy," I greeted him, reaching down to touch his thick coat of hair. I like dogs, and none were a stranger to me, but not all dogs like to be touched. This mutt obviously loved it, so I rubbed my hand up and down his back until I felt something very hard, like a small stone. I dug through his hair and looked closer.

"What's this?" I asked Randy.

"What?" she yelled over the music.

"On your dog," I said, separating the hair so that she could see the strange looking thing.

Randy leaned in and crunched her nose, her eyes tightly

squinting, as if she needed glasses. "Oh, that's just a tick. He's got them all over him."

I pulled my hand back quickly. "Ew, that's terrible. Is someone going to remove them?"

"Nah, he gets them all the time. You can't see them under the hair, so why bother. Besides, he's my dad's dog. He named him Itchy because he scratches so much."

The poor tick infested creature looked up at me with glazed and cheerless eyes as if he knew just what she had said. He stood up and nuzzled his nose underneath my hand. I felt really bad for him and bad for me, because now I didn't want to pet him, so I patted his head for as long as I could, finally relieved when Randy ran inside to answer the phone. I jumped up and quickly followed, not looking back at the mistreated animal; not wanting to see those sad eyes again.

"He'll be here in ten minutes!" Randy squealed. "How do I look?" She turned in circles on her toes.

"Well, your shorts are a little...I can see your..."

"Oh, be quiet, they are not," she protested. "I don't see how in the world you can wear those grandma shorts all the way down to your knees! But that's just fine with me. I don't want Karl looking at your legs anyway. Come on, let's wait in the front yard."

I looked down at my legs. My mother had always told me that I have lovely legs. Then I looked around the living room for the first time. The furniture was old and torn. The fabric was seriously faded, as if it had been sitting outside under the blazing Texas sun for years. The wood paneling reminded me of the walls in my uncle's travel trailer, and the carpet was the thickest shag I had ever walked on. It felt gummy beneath my tennis shoes. Kind of like I was trudging through peanut butter.

Right then, I wondered if I should make an excuse and go home. But my curiosity about this boy, Karl, got the best of me.

We sat on the grass under a small tree that barely shared enough shade with both of us. I looked at my arm in the sunlight and saw the blonde hairs sparkling in the light. I looked over at Randy's and her hair was reddish and a lot thicker, hovering over a garden of pink freckles. Then I looked at her legs and they were the same, except without the hair. She had shaved almost up to her crotch. I had not started shaving yet, thinking the hair was not unsightly enough to remove, and besides, the thought of that sharp blade on my skin made me cringe. Next to her clean, shaven legs, I realized that mine looked like a monkey's. I was surprised by the difference and quickly tucked them underneath me.

The warm breeze that I had felt earlier on my walk to Randy's house had now changed to a coolness that suddenly gave me goose bumps. "Brrr," I said, rubbing my arms. "I think that cold front just came in. Isn't it weird how that happens?"

Randy moaned and looked at me cock-eyed. "You're cold? Man, I'm hot all over just sitting here thinking about Karl. Is my lipstick still on? I keep licking my lips and forget it's there."

I looked over and studied Randy's pooched-out lips. "Yep, still pink, and so is your front tooth."

"What? Why didn't you tell me sooner? Oh man, and here he comes now. Quick, give me your sleeve."

"Why?"

"Just give it to me. I don't have anything to wipe my teeth on. See, bare arms."

"Oh, great," I groaned and bent over to loan her my

white cotton sleeve. When she was finished wiping, she left a long line of pink lipstick smudged into my new blouse. There was no time to complain because right then, a pale, canary yellow car, the hood nearly rusted through, rolled up alongside the curb and before the driver got out, he revved the engine and whistled out the window, "You girls are lookin' hot!"

Randy looked over at me questionably, as if she was trying to figure out if I looked hot or not. She shrugged and stood up, pulling at the back of her shorts that were now stuck in her crack. She quickly sat back down.

"I told you they were too short," I whispered too softly for her to hear.

From the back seat of the car, a head popped up. A sleepy-eyed boy that looked to be about ten years old stretched his neck out the window and opened his eyes wide at seeing two girls sitting on the grass. He ducked down when Randy yelled, "Hi there, dude!"

"Who's that?" I asked.

"Karl's little brother, Shred," she answered, sitting up taller and pointing her toes. "And here's Karl."

A lanky boy with a Mohawk haircut swaggered toward us. He had on a black t-shirt that had either been washed too many times or left wadded up on the rear deck of his Ford Fairlane. I looked over at Randy to see if she was going to stand up to greet him, but she remained where she sat, pushing her chest up higher and leaning back on her elbows, crossing her feet at the ankles, toes still pointed and smiling widely from ear to ear.

"Hey, Randy," the boy started the conversation, "who's your friend?"

"My neighbor."

"Neighbor got a name?" Karl asked, leaning his head to the side, the stiff hair moving with it.

"I'm Jenny," I answered before Randy could say something stupid. "Do you go to Patrick Henry? I don't think I've seen you there."

"Nah, I go to school on the east side...whenever I decide to go," he answered nonchalantly, and looking down he noticed Randy's bare feet. "Wow, you even got freckles on your toes. Cool!"

"And lots of other places, too," Randy cooed. "Why don't you sit down with us?"

While Karl turned around and around like a dog searching for the perfect spot to sleep, I looked over to see if his little brother was still in the car. "How about your brother?"

"Oh him, yeah well, he's probably asleep. That kid sleeps all the time."

"I saw him stick his head up when you parked the car. Maybe I should check on him." I stood up and walked slowly toward the car window to peek inside. The boy was lying on his back reading a Mad Magazine.

"Hi," I said softly, so as not to scare him.

He jerked, sat up quickly and threw the magazine on the floorboard. "Oh hi. I didn't see you standing there."

"I bet not. Those Mad magazines can get you really engrossed in them." I stood a little taller. Using the word *engrossed* made me feel sophisticated.

"Want to get out of the car and sit with us?"

"I guess so."

When I opened the door, a pile of clothes mixed with paper cups and tin cans fell out onto the curb. "Oh, I'm sorry," I exclaimed, leaning down to retrieve them. The boy's face turned bright red when I picked up a pair of white Fruit of the Loom briefs that looked to be his size. He snatched them from my hand, stuffed them under the seat and climbed out through the car window. I turned to see if everyone had been watching the whole scene, but they were gone. The screen door slammed shut as the boy followed them into the house.

It felt strange looking around at the empty neighborhood on a block where I knew no one. I felt sort of lost and then a sudden need to go home. I don't know why I didn't. It was as if this was some sort of initiation into my adolescence, and I had no choice but to see it through. I felt a small cramp at the base of my belly and remembered that I hadn't had dinner, nor was I offered any food. Thinking back at the remains left on the plates, the ketchup-stained table, and the gooey floor, I decided that it might be for the best. The sudden music blaring from inside the house startled me. Curiosity pushed me through the door.

Randy had brought the transistor radio inside and turned it up to high. In the corner sat Shred, his hands wrapped around his knees, staring up at the ceiling while next to him on the sofa, Karl and Randy sat sharing a can of beer.

"Want a sip?" Karl said, holding the can of Lone Star that I recognized was the brand my dad drank.

"No thanks," I shrugged, "not a beer fan myself."

"Oh, really," Randy said snidely, grabbing the beer from Karl's hand and taking a big gulp. "I bet Jenny's a white wine girl."

"No, I, uh, haven't acquired a taste for any kind of alcohol yet." Another big word rolled off my tongue, *acquired*, how sweet. Shred looked over at me, his eyes widened with what I thought was a newfound respect for my command of the language. "I mean, I'm only thirteen and well, it is illegal to drink at our age."

"Oh rats, you sound like a teacher. My parents let us drink, as long as we're inside the house. Come on, have a sip."

I knew what beer tasted like having sneaked a taste of my dad's. My brother and I both took the liberty to find out why my father loved the drink so much. Neither of us liked it, and while my brother quickly swallowed his gulp, I ran to the bathroom to spew mine into the toilet. But Randy was right, I did like the taste of my mother's wine, but it was red and sweet, nothing like the horse piss, my brother called it, that my dad guzzled in front of the TV while watching *Combat* – a series that showed the grim lives of a squad of American soldiers fighting the Germans in France. I had read that from the TV Guide.

I squinched up my nose and turned to Shred, "Hey, do you want to meet their dog, Itchy?"

Shred eagerly jumped up and followed me to the backyard. I heard Randy giggle and say "scaredy cat" under her breath.

As soon as we walked outside, the big mutt ran straight up to us, his tail wagging violently, threatening to knock down anything that got in its path. Shred fell to his knees and let the dog lick his face all over. Within seconds, the red crusted stain from a can of cherry cola was removed by the canine's long tongue.

"Yuck," I cringed. "Better get up before he takes your eyebrows off."

"Good boy, good boy." Shred skirted around the excited dog and plopped down in a lawn chair.

"You know, he's got awful ticks all over him underneath that pretty coat of hair. That's why he's called Itchy."

"Really?" Shred reached down and brushed the side of the dog's stomach, instantly locating several ticks. "Oh man, he sure does. He can get really sick from these things. Have you got a pair of tweezers and a box of matches?"

"What?"

"Yeah, I know how to get these suckers off. My grandpa showed me. He lives on a farm and ticks are everywhere out there. You light a fire on their butt and that makes them stop digging into the skin, and then you pull them out with tweezers. Sometimes they burst and blood pops out. It's kind of neat."

"Ew!" I stood back and squirmed at the thought of the ugly gray globs bursting blood everywhere. But even at thirteen I couldn't stop morbid curiosity. "I know Randy has tweezers because she said she plucks her eyebrows. Stay here, I'll be right back."

When I entered the living room, Randy and Karl were locked in each other's arms, their lips smashed together. I tiptoed past them and found the tweezers on the bathroom sink and a box of matches in a kitchen drawer. I armed Shred with the weapons and sat back far enough to keep from getting blood on my lipstick-stained blouse. Itchy stayed still and rested his chin on the concrete patio.

"OK, Dr. Shred, do your thing. But whatever you do, don't hand me the ticks after you pull them off. Here, put them in this ashtray."

"My name's Jason," he said without looking at me.

"Nice name, Dr. Jason."

"Alright Nurse Jenny, light up a match."

I grabbed the box of kitchen matches and lit one. "Someone's got to hold the hair back while I burn it, unless you want to burn it," Jason eyed me with a sly look as if he were giving me first dibs.

"Me?"

"Yeah, you. Do you think Randy in there is going to come out and help us? Girls like that don't even touch the toilet seat. Besides, look at Itchy staring up at you. I think we're his heroes."

"You've got a point. OK, here goes." I lit another match and carefully placed the flame on the backside of the tick. It squirmed a little and did exactly what Jason said it would do – it started backing out.

"Hold it there just a little longer. He's getting the message. Now, stand back, here comes the surgeon."

Jason wrapped the tweezers around the fat tick and pulled. "This one's stubborn," he said, pulling a little harder. Out came the tick, still intact, its legs frantically moving. "A chubby one, eh?" And just when I thought he was acting much older for his age, he held the tick just inches from my face.

"Get it away! Here, put it in this!" I shoved the ashtray full of cigarette butts in front of him. Itchy turned his head to look but kept the rest of his body very still. I think he knew what we were doing, and instead of running away, he took a deep breath through his nose and dropped his chin.

Nearly an hour later we had removed all the ticks we could find. I counted twenty-four of the ugly things and sat proudly back in the lawn chair, smiling at Jason while he watched Itchy run around in circles, obviously pleased to be free of the blood sucking creatures.

The sun was setting, and the backyard was slowly dimming. "I think we should go in now," I suggested.

"Yeah, maybe the lovebirds in there need a break," Jason said, covering his mouth to hide a laugh.

"I bet. But I need to put these tweezers back before Randy finds out what we used them for." I wiped the tips of the tweezers on a stiff beach towel stuffed under the lawn chair. Jason followed me through the back door.

The living room was so dark, I couldn't see where I was going. "Randy, are you in here?" I asked, feeling the wall for a light-switch.

"Uh yeah, I'm here," she answered, shuffling around on the sofa. I heard a zipper going up or down, whichever, it made me stand perfectly still and stop looking for a light. Then I heard giggling, and something got knocked off the coffee table causing more giggling. I could feel Jason standing stiffly behind me.

Suddenly a lamp light went on, and I covered my eyes for a second to adjust to the light, or to keep from seeing my friend's face in an awkward moment. The tweezers were in my hand, and I nearly poked my eye. "Oh!" I cried, realizing what I had done.

"What are you doing with my tweezers?" Randy demanded.

"I uh, well, me and Jason, we uh…," I stammered, not certain if I should tell her the truth.

"I dropped a dime in a crack on the cement and Jenny helped me get it out with them," Jason spoke up quickly, still hiding behind me.

Randy started to protest when the front door flew open, and her sister and boyfriend burst into the room.

"Look, just in time for the party. I see you started without us. Drink all the beer?" Kathy bellowed, pulling her boyfriend next to her. "And who are your little friends?"

"This is Karl. And that over there is Jenny and Shred," Randy casually pointed, indifferent to social graces as if she were pointing directions to the bathroom.

I froze when Kathy walked over to me and lifted my hair off my shoulder. "Pretty hair. I used to have long hair like that," she said, tossing it behind me and reaching up to feel her own hair, much shorter than her boyfriend's. "Yeah, I kind of whacked mine off, and this here red is not my real color. And your name is Shred?" She moved me aside with one hand. "You're cute."

"Jason... my name's Jason."

"Yeah, his name is Jason," I concurred.

"Nice to meet you, Shred. Jenny, are you spending the night?" she asked, her look not at all conveying a welcome.

"Well, yeah, but I can go home, too. My mother thought that your mom would be here supervising, and she probably would want..."

"Honey, I'm nineteen years old and capable of holding down the fort. Me and Bruce here are practically married, so we'd be like the parents. Right Bruce?"

"Uh sure, got anymore beer?" Bruce turned to ask Randy.

"Think you better go for a beer run," Randy answered. "Karl and I shared one, and I think there's only one left. Jenny, didn't your mom give you five dollars in case we went to the movies?"

"Yes, why?"

"Well, fork it over girl. Everyone has to pitch in for the beer."

All eyes were on me, and I suddenly felt like I was on the witness stand. "Oh, sure, uh..." I reached inside the pocket of my shorts and pulled out the nicely folded bill. Kathy yanked it from my hand and stuffed it in her bra. She grabbed Bruce by the sleeve and pulled him out the door.

"I guess we're going to the store?" I heard him say as the screen door closed behind them.

"No, *you* are," Kathy laughed and pushed him toward his truck.

"So," she began when entering the front door again, "let me grab the last of the beer and join you."

While Kathy rummaged through the refrigerator, I sat down on the floor, bracing my back against the wall. Jason plopped down next to me. I wondered if he, too, didn't want to sit on the ugly, vinyl recliner with the stuffing oozing out of it. Someone's butt cheeks had made a permanent indention in the seat cushion, and faded beer can rings splattered the tops of both arms.

The chair had been abused by someone angry enough to put out their lit cigarettes on the edge of the foot lift, barely held up by bent metal arms that once held that person's big and tired feet. No doubt it was Mr. Peever's chair and would remain his throne until his death, which by the likes of his picture on the wall, would be not too far off. I imagine thirty years of building roads and coming home every night to only females, not one son to carry his name, could probably wear a man down. Randy had told me that he was mean to everyone, and I was glad that he wasn't home sitting in his dying chair snarling at his life and the dog.

Kathy returned with a beer in one hand and a lit cigarette in the other. She plopped down in her father's recliner and kicked off her sandals. One landed on Jason's knee which he quickly removed, stuffing it under the coffee table where other missing shoes were buried.

"So, Jenny, is Shred your boyfriend?" Kathy lifted her chin high and blew smoke into the air. "You pick them kind of young, don't you think?"

Jason glanced at me and put his head down between his knees. I could see that he liked me and was feeling a little embarrassed by the question. I patted him on the arm and said, "Not this year. Maybe when he's older." I couldn't believe I said that, but there was something about Jason that made me want to be especially nice to him. I admired how he quickly went to task, removing the ticks from Itchy's pocked skin and how he wouldn't quit until he got them all. We worked well together, and he had a patience about him that most boys don't acquire until they've grown into men. I also liked that he told me his real name, much nicer than the name Shred.

Randy and Karl were back at flirting with each other and when Kathy turned the TV on to watch *Twilight Zone*, she also turned off the lamp. "This is better to watch with the lights out," she explained just as Bruce walked in carrying bags of six-packs to the kitchen. He promptly sat them on the counter, opened one and dashed back to the living room to watch Rod Serling's finest. Kicking off his shoes, he climbed over the back of the recliner and straddled Kathy from behind. "Oh, yeah," she muttered, backing her rear end into his groin. "Umm, yeah baby."

I turned my head to watch the TV, but as I did, I noticed that Jason was watching the couple's every move. He looked intrigued and disgusted at the same time, as Bruce shoved his hand down Kathy's low-cut blouse and fondled her breast. I pretended not to see and kept my head still, facing the screen. I couldn't help but sneak a peek at them when Kathy would start moaning. With the lights low, the silhouette of them kissing looked almost beautiful, and I felt my skin get flush all over; a thin layer of perspiration formed across my nose. The cramp I had earlier came back and took me by surprise. "Oh!" Something didn't feel right. I tried to focus on the show before me: A society of older people were undergoing operations to look beautiful again at the age of nineteen. It was a law and one woman refused to let them change her. She wanted to keep her own identity. It made me think about myself and how different I was from the girls sitting in this living room. I realized that I didn't belong here and neither did Jason. Everything had felt wrong from the very beginning.

I glanced at my watch, and it was after nine. My parents would be winding down about now, my mom in her pretty gown and my dad in his boxers and t-shirt. I wanted to go home, but at the same time I felt like I needed to stay. My first sleep-over had to turn out right, or I wouldn't get to go to another one for a long time. I excused myself to the restroom, welcoming the light in the hallway. I closed the door behind me and attempted to turn the lock. It moved ever so slightly and then sprung back to its original position. I tried several more times before I realized that it was busted. I had to go badly and pulled my shorts down, quickly lowering myself onto the toilet with the fuzzy yellow lid cover. When I looked down, I discovered a blotch of blood on my panties. "Oh no!" I squealed, hoping the others hadn't heard me. I had started my period and for the very first time. I panicked, looking around the bathroom for a box of sanitary napkins to suddenly appear. With four females in the house, there had to be some. I grabbed a wad of toilet paper and folded it several times to create my own pad. Just when I stood up to adjust it beneath my crotch, Kathy burst into the bathroom.

"Move over honey, the beer wants out!" she ordered.

I pressed my back to the wall and tugged at my shorts, while Kathy sat relaxed on the toilet, openly expressing signs of relief. "Oh man, did you start your period?"

"Well, yes, I did. It's my first time." I felt kind of weird standing so close to Kathy in the small bathroom, my hands stuffed down my shorts. "Do you happen to have any sanitary napkins?"

"Sure, look in the cabinet there." Kathy pointed with one

hand, wiping herself with the other. "Well, now you are officially a real woman. W. O. M. A. N!"

I located a big box of Kotex and opened it. The napkins were huge. I stared at one and held it up to the light. "This sure is big."

"Oh yeah, those are my mom's. She wears the jumbo size. I think I'm out of my size, so that will have to do. Know how to put it on, seeing this is your first time and all?"

"Yes, my mother showed me how. I think she knew this might be my year."

"Well, have at it," she said and moved toward the mirror. "Oh man, look at this...another hickey!" Kathy pulled the elastic gathering from the top of her peasant blouse and showed me a big, ugly bruise. "Bruce just loves to give me these things." Then she pulled out her left breast and showed me two more, one on each side of her nipple. "The guy just loves my titties. Can't blame him really, they *are* juicy."

I caught my reflection in the mirror – my mouth was gaping open, and I looked dumbfounded staring at Kathy's love bites. "Don't they hurt? I mean, they look like they do." I tried not to sound too disturbed.

"Not really, except this one," she said, digging deeper into her blouse. "He bit into my flesh with this one. I gave him a swift kick afterwards. Think he'll be a lot gentler with me from now on." Seeing the alarm on my face, Kathy elbowed me. "Don't worry. When you get your first, you'll love it! I've got a beer that needs tending to," she said, neglecting to flush the commode before heading out the door.

I stood there in silence and shook off the unpleasant feeling I had just experienced. I wished my mother was here to encourage me and make me feel better about the change in my body. The word WOMAN echoed throughout my head and suddenly I felt older. I placed the oversized napkin in my panties and pulled up my shorts. It felt really uncomfortable. I wondered if anyone would notice it, while trying to see myself in the mirror that was too high to get a good view. I must have stayed in the bathroom a long time because Randy opened the door and peeked in.

"Hey, are you going to stay in here all night long?" she practically yelled.

"Don't think so. I'm coming out now."

She rushed past me and went straight to the mirror. "What'd you think about Karl? Isn't he far out?"

"He seems nice enough. That haircut is a little strange, but..."

"He asked me to go steady. Can you believe it? Our first date, and he wants me to be his girl." Randy reached into her shorts and tugged at her underwear. "He said he likes girls that kiss on the first date. Now, where's my pink lipstick?"

Randy spotted the Kotex box and looked over at me. "Did you start your period?"

"Yeah...my first one."

"Oh man, what a bummer. And you're wearing white shorts. Oh, man! Bummer."

"Maybe I should go home now," I said.

"And miss all the fun? We have another hour before my parents get home. Why don't you practice kissing on Shred? I can tell he likes you."

"What?" I felt my face pucker. "He's only ten or eleven years old."

"Yeah, I know. I kissed my first boy at ten. If you get an early start, you'll be a pro like me by the time you're fifteen."

I didn't know what to say at that moment. Kissing Jason never occurred to me. I felt strange inside just thinking about having his lips on mine. Although lately I had noticed that when I watched couples kissing on television, I found myself trying to imagine how it would feel. And when the Beach Boys sang "In My Room" I would grab a pillow and hug it, pretending it was a boy while slowly dancing around my bed. I admit, watching Randy and Karl smooch stirred something inside me, too.

"Come on, I've got a pair of hot lips waiting for me." Randy grabbed my arm and walked me to the living room.

"Drum roll, people. Miss Jenny here got her period tonight. The room is now full of real women," Randy proclaimed loudly to everyone.

I jerked away from her grasp and ran through the kitchen to the backyard, imagining all eyes on the big protrusion sticking out of the back of my shorts. How could she embarrass me like that? Now everyone knew. Just when I sat down on the crooked bench swing, Itchy jumped up to get my attention. "I think you might be the only normal one in this house, boy."

After a while I settled down and looked up at the stars. It was a beautiful night and the air had cooled off even more. I finished a yawn just when Jason came through the back door.

"Hi," he said meekly, wrapping his hand around the swing chain. "Are you going to stay out here all night?"

"I was considering it," I said, rolling my eyes in the dark.

"Can I sit with you?"

"Sure, why not." Jason scooted his rear to the edge of the seat and landed awkwardly, causing the swing to shake violently. Itchy stepped back before it hit his head.

"Sorry. It's kind of dark out here," he explained.

"Yeah, I like it. Look up. The stars are brilliant tonight," I reported, thinking how much I like the word brilliant.

"That's the Big Dipper," he pointed, his finger just inches from my nose. "And over there is Mars. See how it blinks red?"

"You're right, it does."

"And if you look real hard, Jupiter might be shining brightly over there. And sometimes I can find Cassiopeia."

I leaned my head against the back of the swing and let my body drop down. "It's amazing, the stars, the moon, the whole idea of a universe. Amazing."

Jason leaned back and copied me, "Amazing," he whispered.

The sweet night air erased all the startling things I had experienced since coming to Randy's house. I felt warm sitting next to Jason and the idea of kissing him suddenly didn't seem so farfetched. I looked over at him, and at the same time his face turned toward mine. He smiled at me, and I smiled back. "Can I kiss you?" I asked, without moving a muscle.

"Sure," he replied dreamily and closed his eyes. In the dark, he looked older somehow, or at least I wanted to think he was. I slowly leaned in and gently pressed my lips against his. He didn't move, he just let his lips relax in mine. They were warm and tasted like bubble gum. I pressed a little harder and he responded by opening wider. We both let go at the same time.

I turned away and looked back up at the stars. Neither of us said a word, but I could sense him smiling, rubbing his tongue over his top lip. I bit my bottom lip and smiled, too.

"It's getting late. I bet your mother wants you home now," the sensible side of me spoke.

"I'll go see if I can pull Karl away from Randy."

"I'll come with you. You'll probably need my help." I

laughed at the idea of Jason pulling on his big brother while I tackled Randy.

The television flickered in the dark and we made as much noise as possible to alert them. Jason spoke first, his voice surprisingly deep and commanding, "Karl, dad said be home early, so let's get going."

Karl stood up, pulled his shirt down and reached over to turn on the lamp. "Hey, little brother. Thanks for watching the time. Guess we'd better go."

I looked around for Kathy and Bruce. Only their shoes remained in the room. Randy followed Karl out the door. Jason gave me a quick hug and whispered, "Thanks for the kiss."

His hug brought a faint blush to my cheeks. "Thank *you*," I replied.

While I waited for Randy in the living room, that now didn't look as ugly as it had earlier, I watched from the window at Karl driving away, Jason waving at me from the back seat.

With a loud sigh, Randy walked past me and said, "Well, I'm pooped. My other sister is out for the night, so you can sleep in her bed."

"OK," I said and dutifully followed her to a small room with twin beds crammed against the walls, a child-like vanity between them, and magazine cut-outs of models, movie stars, and bands filling every available wall space, including the ceiling.

Tucked under the blanket, I listened for sounds throughout the house. Except for Randy's light breathing, it was eerily quiet. I heard her parents come home and go directly to their bedroom, shutting the door behind them. I lay there for what seemed like hours listening for something soothing, besides my heartbeat in my ears. Everything felt wrong, the bed, the room, the night, the house. I didn't want to wake up to these strange people if I even slept at all. I wanted desperately to go home.

"Randy, Randy," I whispered. She didn't answer but rolled over and groaned. "I'm going home." I grabbed my overnight bag, slipped into my shoes, and tiptoed out the unlocked front door, being extra careful to not let the flimsy screen door slam behind me.

The moon was brighter now, and porch lights were turned off. I started walking toward home when suddenly from the corner of my eye an animal leaped out from nowhere and approached me. I stood perfectly still, trying to decide what to do next. I was frightened, but not enough to go back inside Randy's house. I'd rather face a wolf than go back in there. As the creature got closer, I was relieved to see that it was Itchy. "Hey boy, are you running away from home, too?"

Itchy bounded toward me and circled my legs, licking at my knees each time he came around. "You can come with me if you want, but not all the way to my house." I rubbed behind his ears where earlier Jason and I had removed three ticks.

I walked in the middle of the road, thinking it would be safer. Within seconds, bats began to swoop down around our heads. Swift and accurate they barely missed us. I took off in a run with Itchy by my side. The bats came even faster, and one grazed the top of my head. They stopped chasing me the minute I got to the edge of my driveway. I figured they quit because my mom had left the porch light on. I was glad that she had also left the front door unlocked. The second I opened it, everything was right. I glanced back and there on the doormat sat Itchy, staring up at me, his big brown eyes full of love.

"OK, you can spend the night. Just don't bark. I'll see you in the morning."

I was relieved when I crawled into my bed after changing into a much smaller sanitary napkin. Lying there near the moonlit window, I knew I was safe. Shortly after, my mother came to the door and peeped in.

"Hi, honey. Glad you're home. Do you want to talk about it or wait until the morning?"

"I'm fine, Mom, but guess what? I started my period."

"Well, that's wonderful. Are you feeling okay?"

"Yes, I am…now. But I'm starving. Can we have pancakes for breakfast?"

"Absolutely. Goodnight, sweetheart."

I couldn't see her face in the dark, but I knew she was smiling.

As soon as she closed the door behind her, I thought about all the firsts that had happened to me in just one evening: my period, my first kiss, a sleep-over, disgusting hickeys, murdering ticks, *Twilight Zone*, dive bomber bats, and some feelings I can't explain yet. Out of habit I rolled over to share some of it with my sister, forgetting that we now had separate rooms. I realized then that no matter how grown up I felt experiencing these new things – including lying right in the middle of a brand-new bed – I needed a familiar comfort.

So, I tiptoed down the hall to my old room. Finding my sister still sleeping on her side of the bed with the blanket tucked tightly between her legs, I gently slid onto my side and eased into the molded impression of my own body. The faint sound of my dad's metrical snoring rocked me to sleep.

BATHROOM MATERIAL

I came from a one-bathroom family, and there were seven of us! That room was our library, our escape, the most coveted hideout in the house. The following stories are crafted for those untimely leg tingling visits when the bathroom is truly all yours. This is your special time, why not enhance it!

And if that's not your thing, enjoy reading them at the dentist office, on an airplane, in a hammock, on the beach, while you're sleepwalking. There's nothing like sharing a good short story with yourself.

HUMBLE FUMBLE

'll tell you what's wrong with you, toots! It's your hormones! You're losing a handful a day. Next, it'll be your brain cells. Then your hair. No wait, your bladder…then your hair.

What you just heard is the other voice in my head – my other "older, arguably wiser" self. A meme of sorts. Picture it, 1985: Sophia Petrillo on the American sitcom, *The Golden Girls*. That's her. That's the voice that has been nagging me since I woke up a half century old, and I'm afraid she's here to stay as long as I remain in this crummy state of mind. Fifty! Baloney!

Lately, I've been laying low, hiding out from the world, curtains drawn, decaying in the privacy of my little condo, until I ended up with houseguests – two stylish gay men, both classical musicians who love to talk about dead composers like Bach and Tchaikovsky, names that sound like a bad cough. Another time, an invitation to dinner would have been a lovely gesture. But with a pathetic excuse, and a lot of prodding from Sophia, I declined.

I don't want to go. I don't do the third wheel thingy! It's against my reli-gion! Just tell them you have Covid!

The sophisticated couple that they were posed no argument with my feigned fatigue, and they politely asked that I meet them afterwards for a drink. I could at least do that after a nice nap. Right! The very second they were out the door, I stripped down to my undies and sank into the sofa in front of another re-run of *The Golden Girls.* Besides being two inches shy of six feet, Dorothy and I have a lot in common.

So, this is how I fumble my way through the weekend. Two episodes and two bowls of ice cream later, I'm feeling guilty and a little silly slouching on the cushions on another wasted Friday night surrendering to my age. But the idea of going out in the same old outfit is depressing, until I come across the cute skirt that I was forced to purchase for a blind date that cancelled the last minute. "Go ahead, buy it," the saleslady insisted. "It'll make you feel younger!" No such miracle, but after I add my favorite black patterned stockings, a low-cut blouse, and a pair of Spanx to hold in my paunch, the skirt actually makes me look slimmer. Not a bad thing, as long as I don't look from behind or turn sideways.

Feeling younger yet? Don't hold your breath. You look like a washed-up hooker. But you'll be fine, just stay in the shadows.

With time to kill and before Sophia – that shrunken critic with the roadmap to hell – changes my mind, I meet my friend Eddie at the local pub. I order wine, he orders whiskey, and he gives me just the right number of compli-ments, plus a free ticket to see Austin's best boomer band, *Reel Sheboygan.* Eddie reminds me that now I have a place to show off my stylish skirt and hot stockings, and a great excuse to avoid drinks with my two chatty, musician friends. I shamelessly agree and promptly give them a call. They had just finished dessert after a two-hour dining experience and now they want to hear some jazz. When they don't laugh after I explain that I'm not a fan of that genre and would rather have a hysterectomy, I ask them to pick me up after my show instead. A bit miffed, I hear one of them say in exasperation, "Is she menopausal or what?"

Don't pay any attention to him, he's just jealous because he doesn't have a uterus.

I ignore his remark *and* Sophia's and end the call quickly, afraid to lose my buzz, which I am told is the code word for courage.

Eddie's cheery mood turns gloomy, and he confesses that he wants to break up with his girlfriend. Like the good pal that I am, I let him get it all out of his system, and while I'm agreeing to everything he says, including all the things he doesn't like about her, the girlfriend surprisingly walks into the pub. Eddie's eyes widen as he looks back and forth from me to her, and I sense his vulnerability. I cower and whisper in his ear, "You're on your own, buddy." Gosh, I hate to leave him in a daze, and his pouty face is not helping matters, but I'm just not up for this, and the way she's eyeing me, I don't think she is either.

Run, before he starts crying!

Clutching my free ticket, I rush out to catch a taxi. The taxi arrives. The driver says he's from New Delhi, and he's had plenty to eat in this country. He began our conversation by telling me it's his birthday. "Happy birthday," I said with little glee. He looked at me like I was supposed to clap or something. Then in a small, pathetic voice he tells me how Uber has ruined his life, about the last customer who vomited in his cab, high gas prices, and now his credit card machine is on the blink. I'm feeling sorry for his plight and wondering how much I should tip him. The smallest bill I have is a fifty, and the ride cost twenty-one dollars, so I reluctantly hand it to him. He continues ranting and not giving me back the change. I let him talk to see how long he will play this game, and it occurs to me that this could go on all night, so I flatly remind him, "Sir, you owe me change." He mumbles something in his own language, that I can guess by the tone is some form of profanity. Then he starts singing some weird version of the happy birthday song. Off-key! I am now quite annoyed, and we're at a standstill, and he isn't budging.

Before Sophia makes me say something I'll regret, I decide to get out of the car and speak to him face to face. But as I do, I rip my good stockings on the torn vinyl seat. While I'm standing there fingering the snag, cursing under my breath, he takes off with screeching tires. "Wait! Wait!" My favorite scarf is on the seat of his cab. "Oh no!" And where's the ticket?

You've got to be kidding! I know your heart is in the right place, but it looks like your brain cells have gone to your butt!

I can't tell Eddie I lost the ticket. The concert is sold out, so another fifty bucks for a twenty-dollar ticket dished out to a slimy scalper gets me inside The Continental Club. It's stuffed to the seams, of course. Above the swarm of heads, I spot one of my colleagues who stands well over six feet awkwardly braced against the back wall. He tells me his friends deserted him to the front of the stage. I know he won't join them because he thinks he's Andre the giant, and he feels bad blocking the view of those behind him. I pity the poor fool, so the best I can do is buy him a drink.

I mosey up to the bar and pretend that I have the power to summon the bartender with my sparkling hoop earrings and dazzling new skirt, and when he shows up quickly from all the way down the opposite end, I am sure that I have bewitched him – until he snubs me and serves the guy next to me instead.

Come on, give me a break! I need a drink and now! Do you think it's easy living inside the head of a giraffe?

While I'm standing there waiting, and waiting, arguing with Sophia about how I ended up here, I notice in the audience a guy in a bright red, plaid shirt. He is even taller than my friend over there holding up the wall. He's apologizing to those behind him for being in their way, lowering his shoulders in shame. "This isn't right," I hear Sophia say, and I find myself charging toward him, determined to right the wrong. When I tug on his arm and he looks down at me with a wide innocent grin, I know I must save him.

"I just wanted to tell you that my parents raised boys as tall as you, and I'm no shortie myself, but they taught all of us to be proud of our beautiful height, so don't you worry about those folks behind you because they can always move, or they can stand there and admire your gorgeous physique. Never apologize for being a tall man or you'll end up spending your life alone, stuck against the wall like my body-guard over there." His big, Bambi eyes follow my pointed finger to my wall-hugger friend who responds with a befuddled look and a flimsy wave.

Bodyguard? He couldn't even guard a dead body. Stand up straight, Dorothy, you're slumping!

I feel a lot of eyes on me after that scene. After all, they think I have a bodyguard. Standing next to me is a Rod Stewart look-alike. Out of the blue, an old memory plays in my head. I was a teenager at a music venue where Rod Stewart was playing with Jeff Beck. I had no idea who these musicians were, but the audience sure did like them. When Rod pulled me up on the stage and sang a song to me, I thought I was the cat's meow until everyone started ogling me. I looked down and saw that the black light overhead was revealing my bra underneath my white blouse. My hair was down to my waist back then, so I quickly pulled it all toward the front to hide my precious gems. Little did I know at the time that I should've been getting Rod and Jeff's autograph instead of worrying if a room full of complete strangers figured out that I had boobies!

And speaking of boobies, the memory faded when a funny looking short woman with huge torpedo breasts tugs at my skirt. I could hardly take my eyes off her spiked orange hair. On each tip hung a dangling bell that jingled on cue when she proudly announced, "I'm from New York! My name is Jingle Belle."

"Welcome to Austin!" I say, thinking she'll fit right in with the rest of our weirdos. "What brings you to our fair city?"

"Not sure," she shrugged. "I just kind of wandered down here." And even though the music had started, she continued rambling on and on about her misfortune, like my disgruntled taxi driver, and with each emphatic shake of her head, the bells got louder.

I think there's a connection between her brain and mincemeat pie.

Annoyed, I pull her over to the tall Texan in plaid, who is now glued to the wall next to my tall coworker, and I exuberantly introduce her as if she were a long-lost pal. "Hey, Tex, meet New York!"

I left her standing there straining her skinny neck between the two towering skyscrapers, while I pushed through the crowd closer to the band and as far away from the jingling bells as I could.

Geesh, little Jingle Belle with the big knockers over there gets two men, and you can't even get one?

You can't help but boogie to this band's music, but because we were all smashed together, shoulder-to-shoulder, I find myself jumping up and down in one spot with my arms glued to my side – just think River Dancing in a dill pickle jar. A couple of songs later, I'm aware of how ridiculous I look, so I move to the back of the crowd and wait for my friends to pick me up, while the run in my stocking travels further south. It's then that I realize my purse is missing.

The purse was ugly anyway. I thought you were carrying a dead squirrel that had been run over by a tractor! Twice!

It was useless searching through jostling arms and stomping feet and Sophia laughing in my head. Frantically, I beg the doorman to stop the band and have everyone in the room look for it.

"Fat chance," he says, so I promise him a couple of drinks if he finds it.

He looked like he had bitten into something rotten when he answered, "Uh, no thank you, ma'am."

Ma'am, oh great! You turn fifty and now you're a ma'am! What did I do to deserve this?

On the drive home, sulking in the back seat while pretending to laugh at my friend's silly viola jokes, I am feeling crummy about losing my purse, my favorite lipstick, an expensive tube of mascara, credit cards, driver's license, a corkscrew (yes, you heard me – a woman must always be prepared), and the ticket my friend gave me.

Don't forget your cell phone was in that ugly purse, too!
And what about your diaphragm? Oh wait, you haven't needed that for years. Besides, you couldn't get it past the cobwebs. Ha, ha, ha!

Oh lord, and my cell phone! Even the Reel Sheboygan band isn't worth that kind of loss. What a lousy day! I should have stayed home.

That night I went to bed feeling old, discombobulated, and disappointed in myself and mankind and really hoping it wasn't the little, spike-haired female from New York that snatched my purse.

Well, you know what they say…

"Go to your room, Sophia! I need my sleep!"

You sure do! Have you seen those bags under your eyes lately? You look like Mel Brooks!

～

The next morning, staring up at the ceiling, I carefully recapped the rotten day before. But above it all, the lost purse was still foremost in my mind.

The sun was rising outside my window. I rose from my bed to take a peek. A light rain was falling through the early morning sun rays, and I caught a pale hint of rainbow appearing beyond the trees. It was so magical, even Sophia was inspired.

Hey, what's wrong with you? You, who visualizes whirled peas. Surely you can visualize something as simple as someone returning your purse.

"You're right, Sophia." I close my eyes and imagine a woman picking it up and feeling very bad for the person who lost it, and although she couldn't resist keeping the expensive mascara, she turned the rest over to the police. It was easy to conjure that up, and I felt a lot better than I did feeling disenchanted about the whole human race.

Yeah, that's the ticket, pussycat. Now, see if you can dig deeper. You barely touched the surface.

As I watched the rainbow intensify, something much more important occurred to me. How could I be so self-centered? How could I desert my distraught friend for a band? And what about my two kind visitors who I so carelessly neglected? I didn't even buy my colleague that drink I promised. And what's the big deal about turning fifty? FIFTY! Hmmm, I wonder who's wearing my favorite scarf now?

Stay on track, you can do this. You're smarter than you look. To hell with the purse, I say! Repeat after me!

Yes, to hell with the purse! After I cancelled my credit cards – I may be optimistic, but I'm certainly not stupid – I spent the morning consoling Eddie, and over a big hearty lunch including homemade brownies, I apologized to my guests and promised to attend a classical concert with them that evening. I even invited my tall coworker. He couldn't make it. He was going to a basketball game with the big guy in red plaid. That sure did turn out well. Maybe I'm on a roll!

Feeling hopeful, just before we left for the concert, I took a chance and called The Continental Club to see if they had found my purse. The doorman answered and said it had been turned in with contents intact, including the mascara. "No kidding! Who found it?" I just had to know.

"A strange looking woman with big, uh, with uh…bells on her head," he stammered through the answer, and I certainly know why. He added, "She said you're a celebrity and have a bodyguard."

Ha! Ha! Jingle Belle is a saint! Elated! Euphoric! Jubilant! My faith in humanity is restored! And the funny thing is, the doorman suggested that he could deliver the purse himself. I guess he wanted that drink after all!

Oh, please…then why did he ask, "How much is the reward?"

I'll pretend I didn't hear that. You know, I'm usually the first to say that there are more good people in this world than bad. Today, I am so glad I'm beginning to think clearly again.

Submissively, I put my new and improved self in the hands of my two musical friends as we sit erect and perfectly still honoring Mozart and Haydn on the hard wooden pews of a beautiful church surrounded by heavenly, stained-glass windows. I was enjoying the most inappropriate thoughts about the gorgeous, silvery haired conductor in those black, sexy tails when I'm rudely interrupted by a loud sneeze. Across the aisle, I spot the perpetrator with a scarf wrapped around her neck that looks exactly like mine. My scarf is handmade, a one of-a-kind. I want it back!

The woman lets out another thunderous sneeze, and the man next to her caringly drapes the scarf over her shoulders. She caresses it with love and looks at him as if he hung the moon. It was a tender moment until I recognized him. It's my crazy taxi driver! When he saw me, his mouth popped wide open. He pleaded with his drooping eyes to let him keep the scarf. Remembering that I was in a church, I dropped my scowl and mouthed, "Happy birthday."

At that very moment, the second movement ended with a long stream of tinkling bells. Thrown off track, I jerk and look around the room for Jingle Belle. That's when I'm struck with an epiphany. Without yesterday's bizarre fumbles, today would have been just another plain old ordinary day cowering from life watching reruns of *The Golden Girls*. Everything suddenly made sense, and it was downright funny. I've been such an idiot!

I wouldn't say that. A nincompoop maybe, buffoon perhaps, knucklehead comes to mind…hold on, it's coming…pudding-head – that's it, you've been a pudding-head!

Sophia's right! I am a pudding-head! I started chuckling. I mean really chuckling. When my friends looked over at me aghast with stiff horrified faces, and the man behind me growls, I burst out laughing. I tried to muffle the laughter, but it gushed right out of me. There was no stopping it! I can't remember the last time I had a belly laugh. It felt so good, I yelled out, "I'm FIFTY!"

The conductor turned my direction. Instead of a stern look, he gave me the cutest smile. "Congratulations," he says. Giggles and titters were heard from the audience. I stopped laughing and found myself dreamily smiling back. Am I reading him right? Was that wink for me? Oh my god, I'm in love!

I wouldn't mind glancing over at the night table and seeing his teeth next to mine. Oh, baby!

"Sophia, will you *please* shut up!" Gees, please tell me I didn't say that out loud.

Oh, blow it out your ditty bag! I know when I'm not wanted. You're on your own now, kiddo. I'm leaving! Don't try to stop me.

Don't worry, I've got this! Goodbye, Sophia. I'll see you later when I turn sixty.

And the world heaves a collective sigh of relief.

THE TRUTH GAME

Georgia fumbled in the dark and answered the phone groggily, picking up after the sixth ring, knowing that if she didn't answer, he'd simply redial. "Hello," she sighed.

"Hi. I'm sorry to wake you. It's just that, well, things come back to me after midnight, and I remember them clearer in the dark, so I'm calling to tell you another secret."

Georgia rolled over and switched on the lamp. "It's OK. We agreed to tell each other everything when the truth hits the hardest. But unlike you, I think clearer in the light, so I turned on the lamp."

"That's good. Are you ready?"

"Oh, Wayne, I hate it when you start with that question. I'm never ready. Just start or call back tomorrow."

"I can't wait. I have to tell it while it's fresh, and frankly, while I have the nerve. Remember that party at our next-door neighbor's house? It was Phil's birthday, and you brought a Bundt cake, and I wore that cute red bowtie you gave me for Christmas, and it was the day you got your hair permed, and the curls were so tight you said you looked like Will Ferrell. Remember that?"

Georgia rolled over and bunched a pillow between her knees. "I hated my hair. That crazy hairdresser left the solution on too long. I told him my hair would curl fast. But did he listen?"

"Well, I thought you looked cute. It was a nice change. But anyway, it was late, and you said let's go home, and I told you I'd be right behind you after I finished the game of pool I was playing with John's wife. Funny, I can't even remember her name."

"Vinnie. Her name was Vinnie. Like *My Cousin Vinny*. Gosh, that was our first year married, right?"

"Something like that. Now…you promise not to be upset and hang up. That's our deal, to listen like mature adults." Wayne shifted the phone to the other ear and held his breath.

"Stop holding your breath. I'm not going to yell or interrupt you. I know I did that the first few times we started sharing these secrets, but I'm better at it now, and you are, too. Come on Wayne, please…give me a break. It's nearly three AM!"

"I'm sorry. OK, so after you left, and I lost the pool game, Vinnie challenged me to another one and, of course, handed me another glass of Scotch. Oh wait…I stand corrected. I poured myself another glass. No one offered it or forced me. I poured my own." Wayne let out a long sigh, pleased with his honesty. "So, we were halfway through the game when Vinnie's friend Faye came in pretty frickin' wasted and in a frisky mood. Every time I bent over to shoot a ball, she would come up behind me and grab my ass. After about the third time, I turned around and told her to stop. Well, I didn't really order her to stop. I kind of kiddingly grabbed her hand and placed it firmly on my crotch. At first, I thought it would shock her, but it got her so excited, she shoved me against the pool table and threw her body on top of mine. I looked over at Vinnie and she was standing there smiling, unbuttoning her blouse, and licking her lips. Before I knew it, I was on my back in the middle of the pool table with both women all over me. I, well, I think the rest is pretty much understood."

There was always a long pause after each of them told a secret. In the beginning they had agreed that it should take someone a few minutes to digest truths, especially those that hurt. Wayne held his breath again and waited.

Georgia could hear her heart beating faster and an uncomfortable ache growing between her legs. She and Wayne had been divorced nearly a year and the thought of him being ravaged by two women would have at one time sent her into a rage. But now, since they began this crazy truth game, they had uncovered so many hidden lies between them – lies about money, the moments of pretense, the flirtations, lying by omission – they knew they were gradually adding up the reasons that led to the inevitable divorce.

"Well, maybe," Georgia slowly began, "maybe understood by *you*. You got as far as both women were all over me. Would you care to elaborate? Truths are only understood when they're complete. Leave out the facts and you only have half-truths. Right?"

Wayne groaned, "You sure you want it all? It was kind of like exploratory surgery."

Georgia switched off the lamp, hugged the pillow tighter and whispered, "Well, your story might be the closest thing to phone sex I've ever had. Go on, give it to me, baby."

And Wayne told her everything, leaving nothing to her imagination.

Saturday came, and Georgia took her bike down to the park where she and Wayne had first met. She rode lazily around the pond where they had fed the ducks and shared a chicken salad sandwich. She stopped at the spot where they talked until the sun set, and a final promise to meet the next day was made. She placed her bike on its side and sat cross-legged at the water's edge. Deep in thought, she was startled by a hand touching her shoulder.

"Oh, Wayne! You scared me!" Georgia turned to get up.

"Don't get up. Can I join you?"

"Well, sure. I haven't been here all that long. Have you?"

"Long enough to watch you twirl your hair about fifty times," he chuckled and sat down next to her. "I've always known you to do that when you're preoccupied. What were you thinking about?"

"Funny you should ask." Georgia turned her face away and looked far beyond the water. "I was thinking of something that happened at our wedding. Something I never shared with you. Something I'm thinking now that I shouldn't share with you."

"If it had anything to do with me, we agreed to tell those secrets as they come to our attention. I think after divulging my pool table experience, you don't have a thing to worry about. I'm all ears, honey. Spill your guts."

"Remember my old boyfriend, Gary?"

"How could I forget him? You said he was your first sexual experience. What about him?"

"What I didn't tell you was how crazy in love I was with him. I know we were in college, and everyone was having sex with each other and trying to be cool about our recklessness. The parties were endless. I don't know how I got through the first year. Gary was a senior. Sophisticated. Going to be a doctor and the perfect catch for any girl who wanted a solid future. I wanted him. I wanted him bad. I know I told you that we broke up, but I didn't tell you why."

Wayne noticed the tears forming in Georgia's eyes. He reached for her hand and patted it. "Go on."

"I got pregnant…with his baby," choking on the words, she began to cry. "He said the timing was bad and gave me the name of a doctor. He told me to take care of it, but I couldn't. I couldn't believe he thought that was the right thing to do. I was devastated. I broke up with him. And the baby, well, seems I wasn't pregnant after all. I had some strange overactive thyroid. But still, I couldn't get over…"

Wayne pulled Georgia into his arms and waited until she stopped crying. "He was at our wedding," he said flatly.

She looked up at her ex-husband, and he saw the hesitation in her eyes. "And?" he prodded.

"He came to tell me that he was sorry. Three years later he decided to tell me he was sorry, and at my own wedding!" Georgia pulled away from Wayne, picked up a stone and threw it into the water. "But that's not all he said, Wayne. He confessed his love for me, wanted to get married, have kids, and he asked me to go away with him, right then and there. Leave you standing at the altar and move to London where he would practice medicine. A girl's dream come true, and here I was being proposed to at my own wedding!"

"Well, you didn't go. I can vouch for that."

"But I wanted to go. I wanted to go so badly my heart hurt. Remember we had to delay the wedding for nearly an hour because I was so sick?" Georgia glanced at Wayne, surprised to see how solemn his mood had become. "I'm sorry to tell you this, but I actually got in the car with him and just when we were backing out, your mother walked up to the window and asked me where I was going. She had the most dreadful look on her face. She knew what I was doing. She opened the car door, took me by the hand and led me back inside."

"My mother…hmmm. She's never said a word." Wayne rested his head in his hands and covered his face. An agonizing minute passed before he spoke again, and this time his voice was raised. "Well, I guess you could say I'm second best. Is that what you're trying to tell me now? That you *settled* for me. The guy with a business degree working for a mediocre company when you could've had a doctor."

"You promised. You promised we wouldn't judge. And why does this have to be all about you anyway? I gave up a man that wanted to have children and married a man that tells me a year later that he doesn't want children. Please don't forget that! I could've already had a child by now."

When Wayne wouldn't look at her, Georgia quickly rose, straddled her bike, and rode away, leaving him slumped over, sitting at the edge of the pond.

The weekend couldn't end fast enough for the alienated former couple, each welcoming their regular routines. Georgia tried not to think about how she had ended the meeting with Wayne, and she wondered if he could possibly top her last confession. But maybe there were no more secrets to tell, and this crazy game of truth could finally come to an end. Each day he didn't call, she began to feel her normal self. She was relieved when her friends from college came into town for a get-together. They planned a dinner party for the following Friday.

The wine went down as fast as it did while in school, only

it was a finer wine, and the preppy sorority girls were having a great time in Georgia's living room sharing the past and gossiping about the unfortunate girls outside their sisterhood.

When an unexpected knock at the door broke up the conversation, Georgia braced herself against the wall and said, "Shhhh. Maybe whoever it is will go away."

More knocking, louder and faster. "Did anyone order pizza?" Georgia shrugged and opened the door. Standing in the hall with a champagne bottle in one hand and a stuffed bunny rabbit in the other, stood Wayne. Georgia quickly shut the door.

"Nope, not the pizza man," she reported to the group, their faces suddenly stone-sober.

Wayne stuck his head into the room. "Hi ladies, remember me?"

The women looked at Georgia bewildered, hoping she would guide them on how to respond.

Georgia, relieved to see Wayne in a cheerful mood after the scene at the park, but not particularly happy to see him, faked a half-hearted greeting, "Girls, you all know Wayne, my ex?"

The women, also relieved to see Georgia's acceptance, all responded gaily.

"I have come bearing gifts." Wayne handed the champagne to Georgia. "And the bunny rabbit, well, this is the little guy I gave you for our first Easter. Found it in a box and thought you should have it." Wayne thrust the bunny out for all to see. "There's a funny story about this little furball. But first, let's have some bubbly!" Wayne snatched the bottle from Georgia's hands and went directly to the kitchen.

Everyone's eyes met Georgia's. "Who wants champagne?" she asked with a weak smile.

Another round of drinks with everyone continuing to

share stories, Wayne listening patiently finally stood up and said, "I have an announcement to make."

Giggles were heard amid the tipsy women, all ears eager to hear from the only man in the room, and a very cute one, at that.

"Well," Wayne started, "Georgia and I have been sharing deep, dark secrets of things we did and never told each other. We figured it would be therapeutic and take some of the sting out of the divorce. After all, we're only human." He raised a toast to Georgia and drank the remains of the beer he had been waving about. "I think we told them all, because I have been racking my brain and can't think of anything else to share, except…"

"Wait a second," Georgia interrupted. "These secrets are between you and me, no one else, especially not my girl-friends."

"Ahh, but this one concerns almost everyone in the room. Know why?"

"Why?" they all chorused eagerly.

"Because I happen to know that most of you ladies in this room wants me."

The women blushed and lowered their heads, laughing behind their drinks. Georgia scanned the room warily. Not one set of eyes looked her direction.

"I don't understand what you're getting at, Wayne. Don't tell me you've had affairs with everyone in this room!" Georgia looked horrified at her ex-husband.

Wayne, with his chin high in the air, his thick eyebrows furled, and a cocky grin spreading across his unblemished face said boastfully, "No, but they wanted to."

The women looked reproachfully at each other and finally at Georgia. "Is this true?" She scanned each guilty face.

"For me it is," the buxom blonde friend said, "but you were separated at the time."

"Same here," two others spoke up.

"Not me, I've never considered the guy," the only married one in the bunch said unabashedly, "my husband would kill me."

Georgia eyed the silent friend looking down at her spiked heels. "And, what about you, Cassie?"

"I confess, I confess," she threw up her hands. "I've always wanted Wayne. Ever since high school. There I said it. I'm sorry Georgia, you were engaged to Wayne when I came on to him. I'm very, very sorry. Nothing happened, nothing at all, right Wayne?" Cassie asked with pleading eyes.

Wayne answered quickly, "Nothing, nothing at all."

Insincere hugs and light pecks on the cheeks ended the party sooner than expected. "Got to get home to pay the babysitter," Cassie said, the first one hurrying toward the door.

"Here, give her this." Georgia snatched the stuffed animal from the coffee table. "Two-year-old's love bunnies, and I bet she'll appreciate it more than I will."

Cassie stuffed the bunny in her bag and darted out in such a hurry she left her bright yellow scarf behind. The other guests gathered their things, each avoiding contact with Wayne while filing out the door.

"Well, this has been one heck of an evening," Georgia grunted. "I doubt we'll get together again anytime soon. Why did you do this in front of all my friends, Wayne? Why couldn't you just tell me while we were in true confessions sitting at a restaurant or somewhere else?"

"I don't know, I guess it just seemed like the most honest thing to do. Now you know who your friends really are."

Georgia walked over to the sofa and picked up the ugly yellow scarf. Tiny feathers loosened when she shook it and floated to the floor. She gently tied the scarf around Wayne's neck and whispered in his ear, "Speaking of honesty, any more you want to share with me about my so-called friends?"

Wayne stepped back. Georgia moved with him, tightening the scarf around his throat. "Say it. Say it, Wayne. Say what you really came here to say."

Their eyes bore holes into each other.

"Tell me why you didn't want children with me. Say it now," she demanded, pulling tighter on the scarf.

"OK, OK." Wayne removed her hands and backed away. "Because I already have a child. Cassie's child is mine."

Resignedly, Georgia clasped her forehead, groaned, and shook her head. She released a pent-up breath, walked over to the door, and opened it. Wayne dragged his feet across the threshold, his hands stuffed in his pant pockets, the scarf, like a loose noose still hanging around his neck. He turned to look at his ex-wife.

They stood motionless, scrutinizing each other, as though complete strangers – a blank, guiltless, unapologetic stare between them. A mute appeal for an ending. Only Georgia found the right words to say before closing the door on the past. "Game over."

ICE CREAM MAN

The street was quiet, save the low grinding sound from the lawnmower being pushed by old Mrs. White who had recently lost three of her toes to the bladed monster. I sat quietly on the front lawn observing her, along with other neighbors who were peering behind venetian blinds or lifting back the curtains that protected their small living rooms from the blasting Texas sun; all of us morbidly waiting to see if she'd lose more toes. Mr. Pepperton drove slowly into his driveway, shaking his head in confusion upon seeing the spry old gal at it again. I guess no one could argue with a lady nearly six feet tall whose late husband was a retired boxer. But after the accident, everyone on the block traded their old lawnmowers in – those built without blade covers – for shiny, new 1963 models with large, grass-catching bags. Everyone, that is, except fearless, Mrs. White.

I'm what they call "an old soul," my mother tells me. Don't let my young age fool you. I'm a decade old, but I've been here before, and I sense it. I began to realize that I was wise beyond my years when I chose books over Barbie dolls and Chess over Checkers. I avoided conflicts with my siblings and when they'd start to argue over the silliest things, I had the good sense to go outside, preferring to listen to the birds and the neighbors chatting on their porches, and if I caught it in time, the deep low whistle from a train passing through our small town. I had sought peace at the ripe age of seven.

I enjoy history, which my grandmother said is rare for girls, and I like hiding under the kitchen table listening to my mother and her lady friends talk in Pig Latin, which when I finally figured it out, I decided maybe I shouldn't be there eavesdropping on such adult matters and moved on to the living room to read the National Geographic on the floor while my dad and my uncle discussed politics. Their intense conversations fascinate me and sometimes I feel like I could voice my opinion if only I knew the right words.

The older I get, the more I like being by myself and that's why today I'm sitting on the grass under our big shade tree writing on my Big Chief tablet watching my blue ball-point pen glide effortlessly across the thick, grainy paper.

Because I was this "old soul", I was fortunate enough – some might call it unfortunate – to witness isolated events firsthand that others only heard about through the grapevine. Like, when Mrs. White lost her toes: I was sitting on the curb, tightening my metal roller skates when it happened. She was turning the lawnmower around, and I looked up after hearing her curse for the first time and was startled that the saintly old gal knew such a word. Right after she yelled the obscenity, the lawnmower looked as if it had taken it personally and jumped in the air, deliberately dropping down on her foot. Blood spurted all over the freshly cut green grass and Mrs. White flew backwards and landed flat out on the lawn. The strangest thing was, she didn't scream or say another word. I'm guessing that that one bad word pretty much covered how she felt.

By the time I had reached her – falling down twice because I had tightened my left skate too much – her eyes were shut and three of her toes were gone. Standing there kind of frozen-like, and I'm not certain for how long, I didn't know what to do next – turn off the lawnmower, try to wake up Mrs. White, take off my skates, or go fetch my mother. So, I did all those things, and in that order.

Pulling my mother out the door, we saw nearly half the neighborhood running from their homes to the scene. Someone said that the doctor might be able to sew the toes back on, but nobody volunteered to look for them. While we waited for the ambulance, I searched the yard for the severed digits and realizing that they might be hidden, curiosity got the best of me. I carefully leaned the lawnmower on its side and there they were – two bloody toes with chipped, pink toenail polish on each one. My mother gasped and made me cover them back up with the lawnmower. Certain that three toes had been chopped off, I made it my job to find the lost one.

Mrs. White's dog, Radar, was sitting nearby licking the grass as he always did after he'd eaten a toad or a snail. It occurred to me that he might be sitting on the missing toe, so I went over to move him. As soon as I reached him, I saw that he wasn't licking the grass at all. He was actually licking Mrs. White's pinky toe. Before I could tell my mother, Radar grabbed the toe between his teeth and took off running. I chased him down, having had no idea that a Dachshund could run that fast. When I finally cornered him at the edge of the cliff that meets the bayou, he dropped the toe and slid down on his tummy waiting for his scolding. His beady, brown eyes looked up at me as if he knew he was in trouble.

Well, I don't know about you, but I have never picked up anything that strange in my life, except for a dead bird that was found on our back porch and my shoes that my brother vomited on when he had the flu. And even then, I wore my mom's latex gloves. I reached down and drew my hand back in disgust. I must've done that about three more times before I finally got the courage to pick it up between two fingers and with my eyes mostly closed.

The walk back to the scene of the accident seemed like it lasted forever. When my mother saw me coming, holding the shriveled-up thing as far from my body as possible, she tilted the lawnmower on its side and instructed me to place it gently back on the grass. I'll never forget the pride in her smile after I carefully placed the toe next to the other two. I felt like I had just won the National Spelling Bee.

Weeks later, rumor had it that Mrs. White had two toes sewed back on, but the pinky had teeth marks all around it and would probably look worse than having no toe at all. I wonder if toes can really be sewn back on, since even now I don't have the guts to look at her feet again and find out for myself.

As I sat there remembering that unforgettable scene, I heard the music from the ice cream truck several blocks over. It had been a long time since the ice cream man visited our street. I felt in my pocket for the fifty-cent piece my dad had given me for helping him pull weeds. I tried to focus on the Dreamsicle I knew I could buy, but the closer the music got, the more uncomfortable I felt. "Somewhere Over the Rainbow" will never remind me of the *Wizard of Oz* again and here it was, louder than ever, blasting like a horn as it echoed through the trees.

There's a reason why my palms start to sweat, and my breathing gets shallow whenever I hear that tune. I'm starting to feel like I'm wrapped up in a burlap sack, and I'm trying to get out of it by thinking about the rich, creamy ice cream I will soon be enjoying. But it's no use. The memory is in my head and won't go away.

Last year, when I had just barely turned nine years old, a new girl moved three houses down. Her name was Elizabeth Ann and even though she was only six, she was an "old soul" like me. She enunciated every syllable and never removed the *g* from *ing* at the end of words like Texans love to do. I think she was from somewhere up in the New England area that is so rich with history. She came alone with her mother to live with her grandmother, and I learned while we were pushing each other on the swing set that her father and mother were divorced. I hadn't heard that word spoken before by a kid and had to ask my mother just what it meant, and of course, how it was spelled. My mother looked sad when she explained it to me and told me to be extra nice to Elizabeth Ann because she wasn't lucky like me to have two parents. And then she quickly loosened the wrinkle in her brow and added, "parents that love you very much," and kissed me on the cheek. She also reminded me that my new playmate was far away from home and probably missed her friends and family a great deal; another reason why I took extra steps to be kind to her. I did notice cheerlessness about her when she was drawing a picture of her house that she said was right by the ocean. The same kind of sadness appeared on my uncle's face when he talked about his first wife, the only woman he would ever truly love.

I found myself knocking at her door often that spring until the first week of summer came and she was gone. She didn't move back up north, like I tried to pretend she did when the real reason came back to haunt me. What really happened, I am trying to erase from my memory, but that "Over the Rainbow" song, especially blaring from the brightly, colored ice cream truck, was bringing it back, and I couldn't help retracing every detail.

Everyone knew the rules about waiting for the ice cream truck to come to a complete stop before running as fast as you can to be the first in line. I always waited until everyone got theirs first, trying to make the experience last longer. If he ran out of my favorite, I would just have an excuse to try something different.

Elizabeth Ann stood at the end of her driveway with her little hands clasped behind her, just staring straight ahead. I thought she was waiting for the truck to come to her, so I yelled at her to come over with us, explaining that he doesn't stop at every house like the mailman does. She put her little hands out, palms up and shrugged. I was to understand that she didn't have any money. So, I told her to tell the driver to wait, and I would run inside and get some change for her. I knew my mom would never let a kid go without an ice cream. I ran fast, thinking that if I missed this truck, he wouldn't be back until the following Saturday, and my mother wouldn't even think of letting me run to the next block where he would stop again.

Naturally, my mom was pleased to pay for it and handed

me a crisp one-dollar bill that looked like it had just been ironed. I ran out trying to calculate the change that the ice cream man would be giving me back, to be sure that he didn't make a mistake with his math. The screen door slammed behind me, and I heard my dad yell, "Don't slam the darn door!" I yelled back, "I won't!" But, of course, that sounded silly because I already did.

Elizabeth Ann was still standing at the edge of her driveway when she spotted me coming out of my house. She had a wide grin on her pretty face, and I could see her big teeth sparkle in the sun. She held on to her red dress with both hands, as if it would run ahead of her if she let go. The thick, long curls of her shiny, brown hair bounced on her shoulders. I was happy to see how excited she was and was certain that this was her lucky day because they probably didn't have ice cream trucks up north, being it got so cold there.

Children were standing back away from the truck, the girls carefully unwrapping their popsicles, while the boys had theirs already half eaten after ripping the paper off and dropping it on the grass. Three-year-old, Denny was eating right through the wrapper, while his mother tried to pull it from his hands. The driver clanged the bell, which was the signal that he was moving on to the next stop. I panicked and ran faster, yelling over the music, "Wait, wait!"

The ice cream man rolled forward and distracted by my yelling, he stretched his neck out the window and waved at me. At the same time, Elizabeth Ann ran in front of him and was struck in the head by the silver bumper just as he put on his brakes. Her little body was pinned underneath the front end of the truck; her leg crushed by the tire. When I got to her, her hands were still clasped onto her dress and her eyes were shut. The blood oozing from her head matched the red bow clipped on the side of her hair. Before I knew it, I was being dragged away, and the screaming I heard that was so loud and awful was not only mine, but Elizabeth Ann's mother as she ran frantically toward her lifeless daughter.

And now, a year later, I'm sitting here waiting for the ice cream man to come again. My thoughts remain with Elizabeth Ann and how much I miss her. We were friends for a short time, and some of her face is beginning to fade from my memory, but the feeling I'm having now is not. I sense someone watching me, and I look around and see my mother standing nearby with her hands in her apron pockets. She is smiling at me, and I want to run to her and tell her how I feel, but I feel like I'm glued to the grass. The "old soul" in me is a little scared. She must have known, because she walked up behind me and handed me two quarters and said, "I'll have a Dreamsicle, too." When I stood up, I felt the imaginary burlap sack drop to my feet, and I was able to take a deep breath.

The ice cream truck parked two houses away from where it usually stopped, and I felt a sense of relief that it didn't park where the accident had happened. I think my mother felt the same, because she also took a deep breath before she signaled for me to go to the truck. When I got there, I backed off and waited to be last, as usual.

I slowly walked up to the window and looked up at the ice cream man. He recognized me and gave me a kind of crooked smile, and I noticed that his old, wrinkled eyes were filling with tears. I bit my quivering bottom lip to fight back my own and asked for two Dreamsicles. He handed me three. Somehow, I knew who the third one was for, and as I reached out to collect them, he patted my hand lightly with his icy fingertips and said, "I'm so sorry."

Balancing on the edge of the cement curb, I looked straight into his sad eyes and said something that had been stuck in my throat ever since that awful day. "I'm so sorry, too."

POP!

---

*P*arked in the driveway, the car's motor still running, the old man ran into the house scream-ing, "Psycho, it's a psycho!" He slung his body around the tall artificial Ficus tree and barely missed knocking over the big orange ceramic pumpkin that his wife had molded and left sitting there three Thanksgivings in a row. When he reached the guest bathroom it was locked. He banged on the door like a wild man until the occupant yelled, "Oh for heaven's sakes, go to the other one, you old coot!" Clutching the rear of his pants tightly, he hurried down the hall lifting his legs up high like the leader of a marching band, only faster and lacking grace.

Twenty minutes later, Ralph was awakened by a knock on the bathroom door. "Are you asleep on the john again?" Martha asked.

"Uh, well, no. Why, how long have I been in here?" he said groggily, leaning toward the door, no feeling in his right leg.

"Long enough, long enough." And Ralph knew she was

shaking her head and clucking her tongue and probably rolling her eyes as she passed by the mirror unable to stop herself from talking to her reflection. He'd seen her do that before when she was thinking about something someone did that made her unhappy.

"Are you coming out, or do I need to call the fire department?" Martha asked, pressing her ear against the door listening to her husband mumbling to himself, as he often did when he was frustrated.

"Yes, I'm coming out, only I need some more toilet paper, please."

"And why is it Ralphie that you can't go to public restrooms like everyone else on this planet? I thought by now you'd get over that silly problem. How long did you hold yourself this time?"

"Martha, just get me some toilet paper, please."

"Well, it's a darn good thing my brother works for that paper company in Garland, or we'd be broke with the amount of tissue you use. Hold on, I'll bring you a couple of rolls." Martha went to the pantry to see what was left in stock. As she stood admiring the abundance of neatly stacked rolls, the phone rang.

"Yello!" she always answered, and every time she did, Ralph would wince.

"Yello!" she said again, this time much louder. "Oh, hi Lou! I couldn't hear you. You must be on that stupid cell phone again."

Martha opened the refrigerator door to get a can of diet soda, her favorite drink that she had savored every day for the past twenty years. "Can you hear me now?" she yelled in between glugs. "You need a ride where? Excuse me, I have to do something ... hold on now, this will just take a second."

She held the phone to her chest and let out a long and throaty burp.

Pleased with herself, she took another big swallow of the fizzy soda and waited for her second burp to follow. "OK, now what is it you were saying? Take you to the hospital? You think you broke an egg?" Martha croaked out a laugh.

"NO!" the caller yelled.

"Oh, you think you broke your *leg*?"

At the other end of the phone, Martha's sister, beginning to unravel, repeated herself as loudly as she could in between the static and the burps. "Put that darn can of pop down and come get me now!"

"Oh, OK, Lou," Martha lowered her voice to almost a whimper. "Don't have a cow, I'm on my way!"

Forgetting all about the toilet paper run for Ralph, she grabbed her purse and ran out the door. When she saw that Ralph's car engine was still running and parked behind hers, she jumped in it and screeched out of the driveway.

"Crazy old fool!" she said right before she downed the bottom half of the soda and burped all the way to her sister's home. By the time she got there, the paramedics were rolling Lou out the front door and into an ambulance.

"Good gravy!" Martha exclaimed, clutching the gurney. "Did you have to call 911? I made it in record flat!"

"I had already called them before I called you. I had no idea they'd get here as soon as they did. You *are* going to follow me to the hospital, aren't you?" She looked up at her older sister with pleading eyes, the way she always had when they were children – like when she was persuading Martha to play the part of Roy Rogers while she took the role of Dale Evans.

"Well, of course. I'll be right behind you," Martha sighed, never being able to resist her little sister's demands.

At the hospital, it seemed like half the town was in the emergency room. Martha knew most of the folks there and took a little time chatting with all of them, while Lou waited behind a flimsy curtain to get x-rays.

An hour passed before they finally decided that the leg wasn't broken, but badly sprained. Not long afterwards, the two women were in Ralph's car, heading back to Lou's place.

"It's so hot in here," Lou complained. "Turn on the A/C."

"Can't, it's broken. Ralph says he loves the fresh air, so he won't fix it. Just roll down your window. It's only 102 out there. I think we'll be alright."

"We have a twenty-minute drive!" Lou bellowed.

"I'll put on some country music. That'll help."

Halfway there, Martha spotted a big hamburger on a billboard. "I'm starving. All that talking in the waiting room made me hungry. How about you, Lou?"

Lou had fallen asleep, her head resting awkwardly against the car door. Hearing her snore beginning to escalate, Martha decided to let her be and pulled into the drive-thru of Bag-a-Burger. Out of respect for her sleeping companion, she hung her head out the door and whispered her order into the microphone.

"Two burgers, two fries and two Diet Cokes."

To Martha, there is nothing like the smell of freshly fried potatoes. After the first one, she dug out handfuls and by the time she got out of the parking lot, she had eaten half the bag. Checking to make sure that Lou was still asleep, she poured a nice portion of Lou's package of fries into her own. She could already hear her sister complaining about skimpy servings and greedy corporations. And then she'd ramble on about how the world had changed for the worst, while Martha would guiltily nod in agreement. She hoped to avoid that scene and drove extra slow toward Lou's house, driving deliberately around the speed bumps in the suburban neighborhood where she lived.

Just a mile before they arrived, Lou woke up. "Smells good in here. What are you eating?"

Martha held out the bag and handed it to her groggy passenger.

"Oh good, burgers and fries. Thanks!" Lou smiled wide and dug into the bag. "Would you look at this?" she said with a scowl, holding the half-filled bag of fries out in front of her face. "This is a disgrace!"

Averting her eyes, Martha didn't see the next speed bump and rolled over it without slowing down. The impact caused the ladies to bounce in the air and at the same time a loud pop that sounded like a blown-out tire shattered the inside of the car.

"Oh, good gravy, what was that!" she yelled, braking so fast, she nearly flung Lou into the windshield.

"Oh dear!" Lou cried, straightening up, her hand cupped on the back of her head. "Something hit me!"

"What in God's name is in your hair?" Martha screamed, pointing at what looked like the inside of Lou's head coming out of her skull.

Lou felt the gooey substance in her hand and instantly panicked, "My brains are falling out!"

Martha's eyes nearly popped out of the sockets, and her mouth opened so wide she could hear her jaws crack in her ears. "You've been shot!"

Lou was afraid to move her hand, imagining her brains leaking out all over the car. "Drive you fool, get me back to the hospital, and hurry before you get shot next!"

Martha's eyes darted from one side of the street to the other looking for the perpetrator. "Hold on to your head!

We're going to fly over these speed bumps! Here we go!" A sudden flashback appeared before her – she was driving a jeep across rough terrain, her military buddies yelling at the top of their lungs like young warriors. "Yippeeee!" she howled after they hit the next bump going fifty miles per hour.

When they hit the third speed bump, another loud pop exploded in the car, and a gooey substance grazed Martha's shoulder and hit the windshield.

"Oh no!" Martha shrieked. "I've been shot, too!" She pressed on the gas pedal and flew out of the subdivision onto the main highway. The two women screamed all the way to the emergency room entrance, and while Martha jumped out of the car yelling for help, Lou pounded relentlessly on the horn. Within seconds, they were thrown into wheelchairs and rushed inside.

Three nurses and two doctors crowded the room, ready to go to work on the elderly gals. They had to pry Martha's old, but strong, military fingers from her shoulder as she barked, "I'm OK, it's my sister that's losing her brains!"

Lou had already fainted and was lying lifelessly in the next bed, her hand still clutching a wad of hair, while in the palm of the other hand were pieces of crumbled up French fries. One of the nurses quickly wiped the gooey substance dripping from Lou's head and kept it safely in a towel. She skillfully cut away at the short, silver curls to reach the scalp. "There's no sign of a wound of any kind," she reported to the doctor. "Maybe a small, red spot from some kind of impact, but certainly no bullet wound."

"Then what in the world is that stuff on her head?" he asked, expecting the nurse to quickly identify it, as if she were an intern being graded on her answer.

The nurse passed her hands under the light to observe it

on her gloves. The second nurse leaned over and eyed it, her thick eyebrows in a deep crease. "If I didn't know better," she paused, holding in a chuckle, "that looks like dough."

"Dough?" the doctors said in unison.

"Yep," the stocky nurse said. "I make biscuits and gravy every Sunday morning and that's exactly what it looks like to me."

The staff leaned forward and stared at the glop the nurse was now rolling between her fingers.

"Check them out for further, uh, injuries," one of the doctors said and turned to go to the next patient.

The others followed him and left the amused nurse behind to handle the rest. "So, what do you think of that diagnosis?" she asked Martha.

"Well, that sounds about like something my sister would do. She always was a prankster," she answered quickly, feeling a bit of embarrassment coming on.

"Your sister is knocked out cold in the next bed," the nurse reported. "If she's a prankster, looks like she fell for her own prank."

"Hmmm, well, then there's a madman out there shooting dough at old ladies. Guess that's better than a paintball."

Within the hour, they were back in the wheelchairs being escorted out of the hospital directly to their car. After arranging Lou's leg in the front seat, the orderly looked over at the back seat. "You ladies have a mess in here," he reported, sniffing loudly.

"I know," Lou said, "Our brains are probably everywhere."

"No ma'am. It looks like it got so hot in here that a couple cans of biscuits burst wide open. And I don't think you should open that six-pack of beer. If it's shook up and with this heat, well, unless you want the car to smell more like beer than biscuits, you ought to throw it away."

"So, that was it! Ralph must've gone grocery shopping… oh my gosh, Ralph! I forgot all about him!" Martha pounded the accelerator and sped out of the hospital parking lot, leaving the concerned and confused orderly scratching his head. The nurse next to him was clutching her crotch, doubled over in uncontrollable laughter.

Driving once again toward Lou's home, Martha leaned over the back seat and grabbed the six-pack and plopped it next to her sister. "That guy's nuts if he thinks I'm going to throw away a perfectly good six-pack! Heck, when I was in the army, we drank hot beer that we hid underneath tarps that rode for bumpy miles after miles in the heat. So what we lost a third of it when we opened it. So what?"

"My nerves are shattered, and I've got a bald spot on my head and a good for nothing leg. I've got to have one right now," Lou whined. She held the can out the window and pulled the aluminum ring. The beer spewed. She put the can to her lips to catch the rest. "Not bad, not bad at all," she grinned and offered a taste to the driver.

"No, just hand me my own," Martha insisted. "I don't share like I use to, ever since you got that fever blister. You know those are really contagious, don't you?"

"Yeah, I found out the hard way. I got mine from old man Trip. We went to the movies and naturally he just had to have a goodnight kiss. I mean, gosh, he bought me dinner and two Pina Coladas on top of paying for the movie. I thought it was just another one of his moles. It didn't look much different than the others. But three weeks later, here it came. The doctor said that they come and go like the wind. But I don't think I have one now."

Martha leaned over to grab a beer from Lou's lap, who

was contemplating her lips in the mirror on the visor. When she popped it open, the beer squirted from the tiny hole like a yard sprinkler. Martha swerved and barely missed a man on a bicycle. The sun sparked off his silver helmet and hit her smack dab in the eye, causing her to be temporarily blinded, spilling the beer, and ending up in the next lane where fortunately the car alongside her had sped up just in time to avoid an accident.

"Good gravy, Martha!" Lou yelled. "Think you can drive better than that? And please go slow over those speed bumps. I'd like to keep my dentures where they belong!"

By the time they made it to Lou's home, they were finishing up the last can of beer and quite frazzled. Martha helped her injured sibling maneuver over the lumpy stone patio and into her living room, where she propped up Lou's leg on two sofa cushions. While watching a round of "The Price is Right," they both fell promptly asleep.

Back at Martha's home, a weak and raspy wail could be heard coming from the bathroom.

THE UMBRELLA

It was early eve, and I was excited about wearing my new dress to the restaurant where I'd meet my friends and receive dozens of compliments with oohs and aahs. To find such a fabulous garment on the clearance rack was rare. While I was making my way to the cashier, it began raining outside. I spotted a beautiful umbrella held by a faceless mannequin dressed in a slick, stylish black raincoat. Not an ordinary umbrella, it was made from the finest Italian fabric, wood and brass, a jeweled bee with crystal eyes resting delicately on the curve of its handle. A thing of beauty not meant for rain. I imagined Mary Poppins carrying it as she glided down the streets of Paris on a sunny afternoon. I had longed for this kind of umbrella since I was a young girl, and I believed that one day I would own many such valuable things. Then I looked at the price tag and nearly choked. I could make three car payments with the cost of this splendid handmade beauty. I felt my body sag along with my smile. The fine dress draped over my arm would surely make me feel better.

The cashier was delighted when I told her about my amazing find at a huge reduction. I knew something was wrong when her smile dropped while reading the tag. It seemed the dress was not supposed to be on sale. I glumly watched her place it back on the appropriate rack next to all the others priced too high for my budget. I left the store discouraged and empty-handed.

Outside the rain had picked up, and I was without a raincoat or an umbrella. I recalled a little store at the end of the mall that carried everything practical. Hurrying through the shoppers, I scolded myself remembering how many times I had left umbrellas in public places. Always without one when it rained, I sighed and begrudgingly bought another one; a cheap, purple, basically ugly umbrella. I thought of the exquisite bee umbrella I would never own. My somber mood intensified.

I stepped outside and stood under the roof that sheltered the patrons. Raising the umbrella, I rushed to my car. From there I would call my friends and make an excuse not to join them for dinner. I could not tell them the truth, that I was feeling sorry for myself. A pathetic case of the "poor pitiful me" would not sit well with this group.

On the way home, I rounded the corner and came upon a wreck. Cars were jammed tight with no way out, and four police cars barred the way. Fortunately, I was stopped at a side road, which I quickly took to escape the mess. The small, dark lane was filled with potholes. An occasional dim porch light revealed shabby front doors on the run-down structures separated by narrow alleyways. I could barely see ahead through the heavy rain. I wove in and out around old rusty cars taking up most of the road. Garages were a luxury these residents could not afford. I turned on my high beams, which only made it worse.

Steadily moving forward at a slow ten miles per hour, I spotted a lone figure walking ahead. I assumed it was a woman; long scraggly hair was dripping wet over her stooped shoulders. I stopped the car and watched as she plodded along, struggling to keep her soaked jacket closed against the wind.

When I slowly drove past her, I saw her face from the rearview mirror. I wished I hadn't looked because now she was real – a sad and weary lined face squinting into the downpour.

I backed up and stopped next to her. She kept walking. I rolled the window down and tried to speak to her. She would not acknowledge me. Seeing her hunched over back moving at a snail's pace, I felt so deeply sad for this person.

I put the car in park and lowered the lights. I snatched up the umbrella and dashed out into the rain. Then I opened it and handed it to her. She took it, smiled at me, and continued down the road.

I stood paralyzed in the headlights watching her slowly disappear into the night; the ugly purple umbrella serving its purpose well. Lifting my face to the sky, I let the hard rain wash away my tears.

Wet and bedraggled, I walked into the little store at the end of the mall. I bought five umbrellas: red, green, yellow, orange and a lonely polka-dot. On my way out, I took one last look at the magnificent bee umbrella. Through a new pair of eyes, I saw it differently.

~

At the restaurant, surprised by my sudden appearance and to see me in such a disheveled state, my friends welcomed me with care and concern. I apologized for being late and for making up an excuse not to come. Leaving out nothing, I told them what I had experienced, genuinely from my heart. They were teary-eyed with childlike acceptance when I handed them each an umbrella, asking that they, too, open their eyes.

GOOFY GRIN

"**G**ood God Almighty! Did you read the morning headlines today?" she yelled across the room to her husband who was surfing through channels while sipping a warm beer he'd left just minutes before on the backyard deck and had forgotten all about when he put away the tools after hanging the American flag on a post next to the bird feeder that hit his head twice while he was driving screws through the thick wood.

"Not yet," he grunted between slurps, not wanting to waste the rest of the beer, but hoping to get it drunk before it got even warmer – like the top of his bald head did when he stood out in the sun for more than five minutes.

"It's a shame, a real shame," she said, shaking her head and clucking her tongue as she often did when scolding her grandchildren for toppling over a plant full of fresh dirt or writing on the bathroom wall with new crayons.

Her husband sat idly by and continued switching channels, hoping she'd forget the topic and move on to cleaning the kitchen after the hearty breakfast that left the heavy scent of pork sausage links cooked in honey lingering throughout their home. He imagined the burnt honey and egg remains now dry and stuck to the plates and how he'd hear her scrubbing them and complaining under her breath, while he sat guiltily in his overstuffed recliner pretending to multitask – the sports section in one hand, remote control in the other, a bag of chips nestled between his thighs.

Flattening out the newspaper, she read aloud the article. "The woman described the perpetrator as a man in his late fifties with dark, thick, curly hair down to his shoulders." Mumbling through the boring parts, she skimmed down and read on. "He didn't hurt me, he just stood in front of me, gave me a big grin and then opened his coat to reveal himself. When asked what was beneath the coat, she replied, he was naked, stark naked! And listen to this," the wife demanded. "This is the best part! When asked what happened next, the victim said, well, I started laughing. I couldn't help myself. You had to be there. The goofy grin on this man, his sagging pot belly, legs spread apart, that horrible plastic wig and well, let's just say…he wasn't all that happy to see me."

The wife then began laughing so hard, she couldn't continue reading and almost lost control of the bar stool as she swung around to see if her husband was enjoying the article as much as she was.

"Fred, Fred, where'd you go? This is too darn funny!"

Fred stood on the toilet seat and reached above the overhead cabinet, nervously feeling around for an object he had placed their earlier – the perfect hiding spot where his older brother said he used to keep his girly magazines. Finding it, he pulled it down and shook the dust from one side of the shiny, synthetic hairpiece. Making sure the bathroom door was locked, he turned to the mirror, slipped the rug over his profusely sweating head and smiled wide. *Just what the heck does she mean? I don't have a goofy grin!*

At that moment, his wife stood outside the bathroom door and continued laughing while reading the article. "He wasn't all that happy to see me. Matter of fact, I was laughing so hard, the man pulled his coat back together, turned around and ran away. But the funniest part is," the wife could barely contain herself, snorting snot from her nose, "when he got a block away, he leaned over, yanked the coat over his back and mooned me."

"Are you listening, Fred?" She rapped on the door with her knuckles. "Isn't this hysterical?" Fred quickly pulled the hairpiece from his crown and stepped back onto the edge of the toilet seat, reaching for the top of the cabinet. In his haste, he lost his balance and his foot slipped into the toilet. Falling sideways, he hit his head on the towel rack and found himself wedged between the wall and the throne; the thick, curly black wig clutched between his fat oily fingers.

Upon hearing the loud thud, the wife used the emergency key to unlock the door and burst her way into the bathroom. Finding her husband lumped over in the cramped space, groggy and moaning, his foot soaking in the commode, she yelled, "Good God Almighty, what happened?"

With a contorted expression, his eyes rolling back in his head, he muttered, "I do *not* have a goofy grin."

And then he passed out.

JUST STOP

———

The drive to the hill country was just short of an hour but seemed so much longer. Her passenger, an out-of-town guest she had been asked to entertain, was of utmost importance, and she felt small in his presence. An educated man, well beyond her high school diploma, a master in his field, his mind was full of facts and figures and philosophy, while insignificant thought bubbles bounced around in her head; a constant reminder of her failures and who she was no longer and will never be again.

Since he was worldly and accomplished, she knew this man would respond carelessly to a woman without clout, money, or beauty. She was like a servant that he grumbled at while drunk in the kitchen after all the guests had left the party. How could she possibly ignore his credentials, his status, his manicured fingernails.

"I hear you remarried," she said. "Congratulations." Curiosity drove her to ask, "How long were you married to your first wife?"

She felt his eyes on her as she focused beyond the steering wheel at the long and winding road ahead.

"Twenty-four years," he answered, with not even a blink.

"Wow. How do you get over something like that?"

She wondered if he would squander his words when given the opportunity to talk about a topic so personal. 'Don't cast your pearls before swine,' rang in her ear.

"Quite simple," he responded without hesitating, surprising the driver. "I just stopped grieving. I was told that it takes about two years to get over divorce. Much too long, in my opinion. It took me far less than that."

"I'm *still* grieving," she confessed, relieved to have something to share. "And it's been nearly three years since my divorce. But I'm tired of being miserable and ready to move on."

"How do you propose to do that?"

"I have it all figured out. One of these days, I'm going to ask my ex-husband to meet me in an open space, maybe a field, where we can stand before nature and God and apologize and forgive each other so that I, well, *we* can get on with our lives. We can say those things we couldn't say because we were too angry or too depleted. We can...." Her words trailed off, realizing that the scheme she had been planning for months now sounded ridiculous having said it out loud and to someone like him.

"Sounds like a scene in a B-rated romance movie," he said, maintaining a perfectly deadpan face.

He might as well have stamped "mediocre" on her forehead. She wished a deer would run across their path and startle them toward another topic.

"You know," she began, "Texas has an overpopulated deer..."

"You do know," he cleared his throat, "it's easier than

you think to let go of the past and move forward. Just stop making excuses. Like quitting smoking. Just stop. It's that simple."

There was no way she could argue with that. It was too logical, and who can argue with logic?

She felt herself shrinking and increasingly aware of the ugliness surrounding them. The dreadfully long drought had stripped the countryside of its color. Barren, she thought, like me. Even flashing by at seventy miles an hour, it remained what it was – dead. There was nothing of beauty to draw on, not even a sunset, and she felt embarrassed for taking him away from the vibrant city where at least there was plenty of pleasing architecture to behold.

"It's beautiful out here," he said, as if he could sense her growing agitation.

"It *was* beautiful before the drought caused all the fires." The derisive remark left her mouth dry.

As he gazed out the window in a silent reverie, she wondered if he saw something that she refused to see.

"With an end, comes a new beginning," he whispered.

Approaching the quaint town of Marble Falls where they were to meet her friend for lunch, she let out a deep sigh, grateful for something lovely to look at – the crystal blue lake. Grateful to hear another voice besides his and her own and the critical inner voice in her head.

Outside on the restaurant's deck, her friend chose a burger and fries, and he selected catfish. She was surprised that he would eat a valueless bottom feeder, and she looked at him differently. She saw this as an opportunity to show some restraint, perhaps outclass her guest, so she settled for a lifeless salad. Fortunately, all had agreed on wine.

The dialogue was lazy, and her friend introduced new topics with ease. The wine slowly went to work drowning out their mindless bantering. She heard them as a distant droning sound from a trombone stuffed with a toilet plunger, "wah wa wa wah wa wa."

On their second glass of wine, the conversation took a sharp turn when her friend openly complained about her miserable lonely life, her diabetes, and the fifty extra pounds impossible to shed. With everyone's attention, all napkins except hers placed back on the table, she confessed that she had been contemplating ending her life. If she had not said it as if she were reading the menu, jaws would have dropped.

In a smooth and somewhat feminine move, the guest crossed his legs, clasped his hands, and looked directly at her. His shiny leather shoe glistened in the sun. He spoke in a monotone voice. "You do know you could just stop eating like that. You may find that you don't want to die. Just stop."

"Just stop…hmmm. Well, who can argue with those two words?" she said nonchalantly, as she bit deeper into the burger. "Who can argue with logic?"

The ride back to the city went a lot faster, with very few words, and no more excuses.

ACKNOWLEDGEMENTS

In the writing business there's always someone to thank because we seldom do anything worthwhile completely alone. I am inspired by everyone who reads my stories, mentions, or shares my books, questions, suggests, and even those who look at me like I'm crazy.

Writing can be a lonely world unless you have fellow author friends to share with: Don Tassone, your wisdom and kindness has been instrumental in helping me grow as a writer. Evelyn M. Turner's encouragement is priceless. Sharing with Monika R. Martyn is a plus. Nothing short of amazing, Ron Carlson answered my emails. That small act of thoughtfulness from "a master of the short story" touched me deeply.

It is Rob Radmer who paved the way for me to begin my writing career with his love for the word and the ability to shed his professional skin long enough to get creatively nutty with me as I developed my style. I will always be grateful for your precious time and energy and the big push.

A mighty thank you to my brother, Marshall Rea who is not only my mentor but also a very fine writer. And beside every great man is a great woman. Thank you, Jeanie.

There are folks out there who I share a glass of wine with on occasion who say the sweetest things that spur me on: Suzie and Jens Busch, Wendy Savage, Simone and Chris Guidry, Mary Fitzpatrick, and my beautiful daughters

Vanessa and Charlotte. Patricia Lebo, you are an angel whispering in my ear. The warmest hugs to Jill Baker.

Thanks to the lovely and talented Nicolette Mallow who arranged my first full-length interview.

Kelsey Huse, violist, and avid reader, thank you for your beta reader skills. Your love for books is awesome!

I continue to thank my sisters Melody and Bonnie and my brothers Bill and Corky for the fondest of childhood memories that still spark my imagination. And as always, I appreciate my precious family for allowing me to make a fool of myself in the best way I know how.

I have a special place in my heart for indie authors. Your courage to self-publish, self-promote, trust your instincts, and share with other writers has given me wings.

Thank you to all those I mentioned in my first and second book. You know who you are.

ABOUT THE AUTHOR

Overly positive, over the hill, and over time, Libby Belle has fulfilled a dream she has nurtured since her seventh-grade teacher suggested that she would do well as a writer. Six children later and all grown up, the time had come when she would either fish or cut bait – if that saying is too outdated, try this one: S#*! or get off the pot!

And so, she did.

In November 2020, she cut her teeth on her first collection of short stories, *The Juicy Parts and other quirky stories*

followed by *A Woman Always Knows* and now *Humble Fumble*.
In the oven for 2022 is *Happy Hour Fools*.
If you think that's it for this writer, think again!

LibbyBelle.com

facebook.com/LibbyBelleStories

Other Books by Libby Belle